Wild Acclaim for Brian M. Wiprud's

STUFFED
A Seattle Times Bestseller

"A dizzying and sometimes dangerous romp across multiple state lines . . . Wiprud's imagination runs wild here, and he skillfully brings the reader along as the plot moves more and more out into left field. His protagonist's frequent and eccentric musings about everything from the joy of cheap moose heads to the pain of parking signs add to the lighthearted tone." —*Publishers Weekly*

"Wiprud establishes himself as a rising star in the comic mystery category. . . . For all its eccentricities, *Stuffed* is imbued with a sense of realism that makes this offbeat mystery all the more pleasurable. . . . Wiprud's skill at creating believable characters and realistic scenes, no matter how weird, makes *Stuffed* shine."
—*Florida Sun-Sentinel*

"*Stuffed* marks the long-awaited (especially by readers and reviewers who like their humorous mysteries clever and artful rather than just zany or wisecracking) return of crime-solving New York taxidermist Garth Carson, whose debut in 2002's *Pipsqueak* was a cause for much pleasure."
—*Chicago Tribune*

PIPSQUEAK

*Winner of the Lefty Award for
Most Humorous Crime Novel;
Barry Award Nominee;
Named One of the Best of 2002
by* January Magazine

for odd minutiae are fairly unique. Admirers of Donald Westlake and Elmore Leonard, especially, though, will find much here to enjoy. Wiprud is definitely a writer to watch."
—*Mystery Ink*

"Imagine, if you will, Dashiell Hammett's *The Maltese Falcon*—with the protagonist in search of a missing icon that people are willing to kill for—as conceived by Robin Williams. . . . *Pipsqueak* has a feel and pacing that is reminiscent of some of Donald Westlake's more inventive and humorous mysteries, but with a comic sensibility all its own. By the time I finally finished reading *Pipsqueak*, my face hurt from the constant grinning."
—ReviewingtheEvidence.com

"First get past the cover. Then the title. Now I dare you to get past the funniest book this year. A dead squirrel, a taxidermist and a crazy mystery that keeps you turning the pages and laughing out loud."
—*BookCrazy Radio*

"Zany [and] outrageous . . . This novel is highly recommended for readers who like quirky capers, or who simply remember sitting in front of TV cartoons for hours, never understanding the concept of the Off button."
—*January Magazine*, Best of 2002

CROOKED

BRIAN M. WIPRUD

A Dell Book

CROOKED
A Dell Book / August 2006

Published by Bantam Dell
A Division of Random House, Inc.
New York, New York

This is a work of fiction. Names, characters, places, and incidents
either are the product of the author's imagination or are used
fictitiously. Any resemblance to actual persons, living or dead,
events, or locales is entirely coincidental.

Dell is a registered trademark of Random House, Inc., and the
colophon is a trademark of Random House, Inc.

ISBN-13: 978-0-440-24312-0
ISBN-10: 0-440-24312-2

Printed in the United States of America
Published simultaneously in Canada

www.bantamdell.com

OPM 10 9 8 7 6 5 4 3 2 1

For my sister Rebecca, with love

"The prudence of the best heads is often defeated by tenderness of the best hearts."

—HENRY FIELDING

CROOKED

Chapter 1

Nicholas stepped under the awning and into the full bare-bulb glow of a Chinatown fish stand.

Behind him, Asian shoppers flooded the sidewalk, a turbid human river wielding pink plastic bags laden with pea pods, bok choy, mung beans, and squid. The evening air was filled with relentless rain, buzzing neon signs, exhaust grit, and the sour vowels of vendors bickering with their customers. Cars and semis crept by on Canal Street; traffic was jammed toward the Manhattan Bridge in one direction, toward the Holland Tunnel in the other.

Nicholas zeroed in on the fish shop proprietor, a blind old man with a wispy beard, skullcap, and pernicious smile who waved his cane through the air with the determination and panache of a maestro before his choral group. Even blind, the shopkeeper knew the locale and price of each variety of fish. He priced and protected the wares with his baton, while his harried assistant was relegated to making the actual exchanges of money for scaly food. A pair of crones double-teamed the geezer, singing their demands and gesturing with fists at a tin bucket full of writhing hornpout. The conductor barked a price at the chorus, only to be flanked by the staccato of two other women yowling and pointing to the sea robins and spiny urchins. The piscatorial patriarch swung his baton, thwacked the bucket to which they pointed, and barked a price. Upstarts in this glee club would not be tolerated.

Late that afternoon, Nicholas had been on the phone with a man who called himself "Dr. Bagby," a guy with a hot painting and a penchant for a noisy part of town. The background clamor was familiar— the honking, the cane smacking the metal buckets, the yammering. Two hours and seven cab rides later, Nicholas's search had brought him to this Canal Street fish stand. He'd finally pegged the specific market din not because he spent any appreciable time shopping in Chinatown but because of Figlio's, a Foley Square lounge around the corner. Courthouse-types watered there, and Nicholas had often had occasion to buttonhole young ADAs at Figlio's for information. He'd stood many times in front of the fish stand to hail a cab.

February bowled a wet ball of wind under the fish stand's awning, and Nicholas turned away from the tin bucket ensemble, water beading on his glasses and close-cropped hair. He waded back through the pedestrian current to a phone booth on the corner, where he found fugacious refuge from the tide of pink bags and two-dollar umbrellas.

Dr. Bagby hadn't called from a cell phone. Background noises are always strangely garbled in digital signals. No, this had been clear—a landline, but on the street.

Nicholas targeted a vendor close to the phone booth. Her shop comprised a huge golfer's umbrella, a Coleman lantern, and a peach crate, all assembled on the threshold of a defunct savings-and-loan building. Huddled beneath the umbrella, the Asian dwarf woman buzzed away with a hobby tool, fashioning netsuke from chunk plastic. The finished products hung by threads from the spokes of her umbrella. It was as if a tornado had lifted a yurt from a Mongolian bazaar and dropped it in downtown Manhattan.

Nicholas stepped forward and poked at a carving of a peanut, which twirled in the light of the lantern. "How much for this one?"

Magnifying goggles made the dwarf woman's eyes appear the size of fried eggs. Her tool buzzed to a stop.

"That special. Twenty buck." The giant eyes vanished as they reconsidered the masterpiece at hand. The tool buzzed, puffs of plastic dust pluming from where she crouched.

"Here." Nicholas held out a twenty, which undulated to the rhythm of grocery bags whacking him in the shins. The tool stopped buzzing, and the woman's egg eyes reappeared. She sniffed, looked at the twenty, wiped her gloved hand on the top of her greasy woolen cap, and snatched the bill.

"Tank you. En-joy." Nicholas turned up the collar of his tweed overcoat as wind battered the dwarf's umbrella overhead. He admired the twenty-dollar peanut between thumb and forefinger.

"I'd like to buy something else." Nicholas held out another twenty. "I want to buy what you know about a man who made a call from that phone booth. That phone booth there. Did you see a man? He coughed. He's sick."

She scratched her head in thought, wiping her nose with the back of her glove.

"Man? Sick man?"

"Yes. Sick." Nicholas demonstrated, coughing and holding an imaginary receiver to his head and pointing at the booth.

Her face sprouted a smile as wide as she was tall.

"I see. Sick man. I see all time. I see come, go, all time. Sick man. Twenty buck." She put out a hand, but Nicholas held the bill out of reach. The damp winter gusts looked like they might just blow it away.

"Where does he live?"

The building was a prewar four story. Spanish American War, that is, and every year seemed to weigh heavily upon its frame. Nicholas stood in the foyer dripping water, wiping the rain from his glasses, razzing the damp from his bristly hair, and re-flipping the small curl that formed at his widow's peak. He'd long since abandoned umbrellas, preferring to tough it out in an overcoat. He'd spent considerable time in the tropics, where one got used to being wet, and being caught in the rain was welcome relief from the heat. As his mentor in those days had been fond of saying, "Humans are already waterproof." Pretty absurd considering that the mentor in question drowned.

In the vestibule, ancient shellac was beaded on the chipped woodwork like yellow sweat. A low-watt bulb illuminated an amber tulip sconce and little else. The mailboxes were all unlabeled, flanked by ancient buzzer buttons. Nicholas wanted to arrive unannounced, so he tried the door's rusty knob. The oak door creaked, but it wouldn't budge. He put his face up to the murky glass and attempted to peer beyond the shredded lace curtain.

The door opened suddenly.

"Yahj!!" gasped a Chinese gent in a porkpie hat. A carpetbag fell from his grasp as he staggered back in alarm, hand raised defensively.

"It's OK...It's OK..." Nicholas took the opportunity to step past the door. He picked up the carpetbag and held it out to Porkpie.

Porkpie recovered quickly and snatched the bag back. His shock was replaced with indignation, and he wagged a threatening finger, scolding Nicholas in Cantonese. Nicholas shooed him out into the foyer with reassuring gestures, then turned to the building's interior.

The staircase was a rickety bit of architecture with a distinctly German Expressionist flair. The whole shebang looked as though it might spiral in on itself like a collapsing cup. Nicholas ascended quickly, each step voicing a creaky complaint. At each landing a dim sconce barely lit the way. Scents of sesame oil and soy grew stronger the higher he went. At the top landing, next to a sconce, stood a door made conspicuous by the lack of a Confucian icon thumbtacked over the apartment number. Nicholas put an ear to the door. Just the gentle slurping of steam heat came from within. He turned the knob and the latch clicked open.

Squinting into the apartment's gloom, Nicholas had a view along a crooked hallway that terminated in an island of light at the kitchen. A man was slumped at a table with a towel over his head. Wisps of steam snaked from under the towel. He was dressed in a worn terry bathrobe and grimy slippers. Dr. Bagby sleeping? Next to him, leaning against the stove, was a large, square, flat wooden crate— one that might hold, say, a painting. Somewhere a radiator valve hissed like a cobra ready to strike.

Nicholas slid quietly in and pushed the door closed. It was roasting hot in the apartment, and he loosened his overcoat. It didn't help that he was wearing a tweed suit. He pulled the neatly folded handkerchief from his top pocket and mopped the back of his neck while he did a quick survey of his surroundings. The place was stacked with old newspapers and magazines like some kind of recycling center. Bagby was evidently one of those freaks who couldn't throw away reading material of any kind. Furniture must be in there somewhere, along with legions of roaches. Chinatown was rife with roaches. Nicholas expected the place to smell musty, of decay. But instead it smelled of menthol.

His eyes latched back onto Bagby. He took a few steps in that direction and the floor squeaked a loud warning—but the man at the kitchen table didn't stir. Nicholas approached more swiftly and discerned that the man was more than asleep. Circling behind Dr. Bagby, he found a hypodermic needle jabbed into the base of Bagby's skull, just above a large bruise. Clubbed and stuck.

Nicholas circled to the side and lifted the towel. The corpse fit the dwarf's description of the man from the pay phone: a heavyset man, dark curly hair, eyebrows pierced by small silver rings. He might once have been swarthy, but his complexion now was waxy. Eyes open, dilated, dead. His cheek was smooshed against a croup kettle, and droplets of condensed steam clung to his beard stubble.

Raising one of Bagby's pant legs, Nicholas noted that the ankle over the white sock was just turning purplish—blood pooling in his legs. With the back of his hand, Nicholas felt a warm, hairy leg. Bagby had been kaput for a half hour or less.

The table was strewn with nasal sprays, cold formulas, used tissues, and lozenges, some of which had been knocked to the checkered tile floor. "Doctor Bagby's Croup Elixir" read one bottle; the source of the man's alias was one of the cold formulas.

Nicholas backed away from the table, self-consciously rubbing his hands on his coat. Time to start watching where he left his fingerprints. With his handkerchief, Nicholas tilted the crate toward him for a look-see. He lifted out the familiar gilt frame and saw the ragged ends of the blue canvass where the Moolman had been cut away. Sloppy, but quick. The 24" × 36" painting *Trampoline Nude, 1972*, had been lifted from a private collection in Westchester six weeks earlier by a man posing as an exterminator. Nicholas let the frame drop back into the crate with a thud.

"Super," he snorted.

Had Chinatown been first on his dance card, Nicholas would probably have had the canvass in hand, and Bagby would still be suffering from his head cold. Someone else had got to him first. Sorry son of a bitch.

A door slammed at street level. Heavy footsteps on the stair. The squelch of a police radio echoing from a few floors below.

Nicholas didn't have to think about his next move. He operated on instinct and turned to the kitchen window. Flipping the catch on the security gate with a forearm, he opened the grimy window with his palms and crawled out onto the fire escape. Flower pots and a mop tripped him in the dark. He grabbed the railing to keep from cartwheeling down the metal steps and into a long hospital stay, then sidled deftly down each flight toward the building's backyard. He kept his weight mostly on the railing—the steps on these rusty old fire escapes sometimes snapped unexpectedly.

He jumped from the fire escape to the ground below just as a cop appeared in Bagby's kitchen window, yammering into a radio. The backyard wasn't some grassy nirvana of sprinklers, lawn gnomes, and azaleas. It resembled a small prison yard: a patch of buckled concrete surrounded by a wall topped with razor wire. Nicholas skirted the wall, out of view, his footsteps crunching lightly on the faint glitter of broken beer bottles and cigarette butts. He stole around the corner, into a blind alley that stabbed between two buildings. At the far end was a basement walk-down. It was locked, but a few shoves of his shoulder and the moldering jamb gave way like stale bread. A wave of sewage reek flushed from the dark.

Nicholas paused, confronted by the unexplored cavern. Street light spilled into the rank basement through a coal grate at the far end of the long, black space. A grim beacon. He sensed he wasn't alone, and the scuttling claws of rats on concrete confirmed it. By the sound of them, he gauged that they were welterweights compared to the wharf-bruisers down near the Brooklyn Bridge where he lived. And certainly they were neither as fleet of paw as the Upper West Side rail yard design, nor as insouciant as the Tompkins Square model. Even as the bear was friend to Grizzly Adams, the rat was a pal of

Nicholas Palihnic. He took a shine to their independent nature, their tenacity, their gritty lifestyle. But he knew enough to respect the domain of the cellar rat. Generally slow, midsize, and shy, they also had a tendency to be defensive, if not openly hostile, on their home turf. Nicholas recalled the story of a man trapped in a Chicago basement who'd been reduced to a paraplegic before he was rescued. Nibbled around the edges like a saltine.

But Nicholas's years in gritty third-world slums had taught him not to fear places that were merely dark, squalid, or rat infested. Worldly battle scars that broke some men had armored Nicholas for a new lease on life. Disillusionment and subsequent hard lessons about human nature warped idealists into cynics, and Nicholas into a practical solipsist. Whatever New York could dish out, Nicholas had decided to bottle and turn into a buck. So a stroll through Ratville or shortcuts through subway tunnels were little more to him than a Park Avenue jaunt. It was hard on his tweed suits, but he had a lot of them.

He beelined for the coal grate at the far end of the blackness. He managed to avoid stepping on any rats, though one brushed his leg, perhaps a coy test of his resolve.

As he drew near, he could see cracks of light from sidewalk cellar doors to the right of the coal chute, and the steps leading up to them. His ears rang with the clicking of palm-sized roaches scattering as he climbed the steps. A padlock sealed the cellar doors.

Nicholas spied the shadow of another stairway hunkering mid-basement, as well as the dark forms of rats trundling from his path as he headed for it. He heard a roach flying toward his head and batted it away. Having once tangled with giant bird-eating Colombian spiders, roaches were nothing to him now.

Dull amber light spread from under a door at the top of the stairs. Reasoning that this door probably opened to the building's lobby, under the Fritz Lang staircase, Nicholas listened intently. All he could hear was creaking, several floors above.

A quick study of the door revealed that it was secured with an eyehook latch on the other side. A credit card easily flipped it. Nicholas slid the door open and scanned the empty hallway. He grinned.

Composing himself, he exited the cellar with a whistle on his lips, a song in his heart, and a roach on his lapel. He jettisoned the latter, maintained the former.

Emerging onto the stoop from the vestibule, Nicholas was confronted by a cop leaning on her patrol car. Clearly one had gone upstairs, while his partner kept an eye out downstairs. At least it had stopped raining.

Ditching any sign of alarm, Nicholas whistled tunelessly and smiled.

"Evening, Officer."

She watched him plod down the steps and turn toward the flow of pink plastic shopping bags on Canal Street.

"Sir . . ."

He kept whistling and walking as if he didn't hear. Just an ordinary gent out for a stroll.

"Sir. Hey, you. Mister, stop."

Behind him a snap snapped and leather flapped—the unmistakable sound of her holster at the ready. Damn. It was the cue that he had to turn. When the gun leaves the holster, a cop stops listening and starts cuffing. No talking your way out then.

Nicholas glanced back, did a double take, and then turned around, flashing his most charming smile—his patented "Who, me?" move.

"Yes, Officer?"

She approached, her hips' sway made huge and ducklike by the citation binder, flashlight, handcuffs, and radio stuffed in her trousers.

"Where you comin' from?" She sniffed, chewing hard on her gum, looking him up and down. The dark eyes under the brim of her hat settled on his face. His smile wasn't returned. But she put a hand to check her hair just the same.

"Me?" He let slip a sly grin, as though she were approaching him in a bar.

"Yeah." She considered him sidelong, eyes guarded. "You."

Sometimes Nicholas overestimated his charms. She'd seen his moves before, and whether from some discotheque lothario or street hustler, she knew his sly grin was a con.

It was the beginning of a long night that would turn into a longer day.

Chapter 2

Beatrice Belarus paced before the gargantuan windows of her new palatial SoHo loft like a captain on a quarterdeck, her energetic crew working feverishly around her. Painters rolled eggshell latex on one wall, tapers sanded plaster on another, and electricians drilled anchors into the ceiling for track lighting. Beatrice had a finger in one ear and a flip phone clamped over the other. She ducked beneath scaffolding from which two men carefully filled the outlined letters "B. Belarus. Gallery. Representation" onto the glass.

Her man in Hong Kong finally picked up.

"Tin Oo, I've been *trying* to reach you all morning. Shut up. Did I ask what time of day it was there? Did I say whether I cared? Listen to me, Tin Oo. I'm only going to say this once. You're dismissed."

Beatrice brushed some Sheetrock dust from her

lapel and smiled down at the throngs across Broadway flushing in and out of Bean & LeMocca Gourmet. She listened a moment.

"Tell me why I didn't just throw this phone right out the window. I should have. I don't need people like you, people who care more about food or sleep or dying mothers than about dealing. There are plenty of people, Tin Oo, who want only one thing in this world and will do anything for it."

Beatrice's obsidian eyes went soft, and her voice turned to a melodic whisper.

"I don't need agents who know art. I need agents who know money." Her thumb disconnected Tin Oo. She stood serenely and waited for his inevitable callback. Her phone chirped and Beatrice disconnected the ex-associate with another wave of her thumb. Her index finger pecked a long series of numbers buttons.

"It's BB. Give me Irwin." The sun had topped the east side of Broadway, dimmed by remnants of the previous night's rain clouds. The morning glow illuminated Beatrice's reflection on the glass as she took a quick inventory of her whipcord suit, cashmere turtleneck, and designer crocodile shoes. Turning a profile, she checked the pitch of her shiny black ponytail, fancying her severe sex appeal.

"Irwin, do you like money? I said: *Do you like money?* Good. I'm going to give you some. Yes, give you. If you really like money, then this is your day, because for doing very little you're going to make a lot more than you make most months in that 'gallery' of yours...I'm talking about you being my man in Hong Kong...Tin Oo? He's dead...Dead from a lack of avarice. You see, I have some very important jazz rattling and he was out of touch. Now, Irwin, you do have a phone with you at all times? Very good response, Irwin, I like that, very good. Now here's what's going to happen. Get dressed, go to your shop. I'm going to fax you a contract and you'll sign it and you'll messenger it to my Hong Kong attorney—his name and number will be on the cover sheet. He's probably home asleep, but you'll find his address in the book. I'll call ahead. He'll fax me a copy of the signed agreement, tell me we're square. Are you getting all this? Next, I want you to look up Casper Rautford, and...Yes, C. S. Rautford. Give him a ring...Irwin, Casper told me personally to call him day or night. Just tell his people you represent me and he'll get out of bed to talk to you. Tell him we have a Moolman he's interested in, and to be ready to wire two point five million to Chase Manhattan Bank, BRT 021001022, account number 00163052, my name, the day after tomorrow. Meanwhile I'll have a courier on the"—Beatrice held up her Fendi watch—"damn, it'll have to be the afternoon flight—to hook up with the Lufthansa red-eye. Arrange to meet and personally transport the messenger and the jazz up the hill to Casper. In other words, the item will be in his hot little hands the day after tomorrow.

"Before you give the jazz to Casper, remove the protective print...Yes, a protective print...Why?

I'll tell you why, Irwin. Because this is a very valuable painting and I don't want it ripped off, that's why. Besides, I always ship with the original canvass protected, as an added measure...Look, Irwin, the people at customs are going to screw this deal up with their red tape if they know it's a Moolman... Yes, they might even think it's that one, the stolen one, so let's just play it cool and get you your twenty-five thousand dollars, OK?"

BB bit her lip nervously, then sighed away her anxieties.

"OK, you still with me here, Irwin? Good. So, when he's satisfied with the painting, witness the wire transaction, personally of course, write down the confirmation number, and call me immediately from Casper's. I'll check with Chase. When I confirm it here, leave him the painting and take the messenger back to the airport. At that point the messenger will hand you a certified check for twenty-five thousand dollars. You got all that, Irwin?"

Beatrice listened impatiently.

"Irwin, Casper will like the painting. No, he doesn't need to know what painting...Neither do you. Tick tock, Irwin, the clock is running." Beatrice's thumb squashed the connection.

"'Scuse, p'ease." One of the little Ecuadorian window painters smiled apologetically, as though hoping he might escape a flogging. Beatrice edged back from the window so he could put some newspaper on the floor where a drip had already fallen.

Beatrice switched ears, plugging a finger in one,

clasping the cell phone to the other. She punched a button without looking and wandered back to the window, crocodile-clad toes tapping the edge of the newspaper.

"Karen, reserve a flight and priority cargo for Olbeter, an afternoon flight to Hong Kong. Get a limo on its way to the Empire State Building and have it wait at the Fifth Avenue entrance for Olbeter. Get a certified check for twenty-five thousand dollars..."

Beatrice flushed.

"OK, Karen, OK. Then get on the horn and liquidate the International Funds—break the bank, transfer all funds to the Chase Account and get the twenty-five-thousand-dollar check in my hand at the downtown studio by twelve thirty, even if you have to put your life's savings into it... Look, I don't want to hear that, Karen. It's a leveraged buyout, sweetie. We're running up the Jolly Roger. Just do it. Now." Beatrice's thumb squashed the end button, her finger pecking out another number. As she waited for the call to go through, she stared blankly down at the pages of that morning's *Daily News* spread out on the floor. Her black eyes focused, and she crouched to tear off the corner of the tabloid. Color bloomed on her cheeks.

"Olbeter, drop everything, grab your passport: you're headed to Hong Kong this afternoon. A car will be waiting at the Fifth Avenue entrance. Swing by here, pick up the jazz, and be on your way. You'll get the usual seven thou when you return, in cash...

Yes, that's right . . . Wait, Olbeter: you know a fellow named Nicholas Palihnic? Yes, I thought the name sounded familiar. Hmm, well, a bit in the paper says he murdered someone last night. You happen to know what he was working on?"

Chapter 3

The two detectives told Nicholas he was going up the river. They had him cold, carrying a rubber hose. Looked like he'd thwacked Bagby, then injected him—zinc phosphide, a rodenticide. Rat poison. Fingerprints taken from the underside of the fire escape railing matched Nicholas's.

"You're history, Palihnic," the hatchet-faced one said.

"So why'd you do it?" the roly-poly one said.

Nicholas didn't make a peep.

The wimpy public defender arrived and sagely confided, "It doesn't look good."

Nicholas turned to the attending ADA and said, "Get this guy outta here. I want a real lawyer." He asked for his wallet, from whence he produced a card for Mr. Patel, an attorney he'd met a while back at an FBI hangout called Pig & Thistle over on

Greenwich. That's when Hatchet Face and Roly-Poly had him moved from the precinct over to the holding cell at the Centre Street courthouse for arraignment.

Around ten the next morning Patel showed up, a portly badger-eyed Pakistani who claimed to know all the angles. They talked, got the story "re-phrased," and then went in with the ADA for more Q&A.

Nicholas told his tale. He'd tracked a guy interested in brokering the return of a stolen Moolman, a guy who called himself Dr. Bagby, to the building on Mott Street. The door was opened for Nicholas by a neighbor, and he went upstairs. From Bagby's voice on the phone, Nicholas had guessed he wasn't Asian, and therefore assumed the apartment with no Confucian icon was the one he wanted. The door was unlocked. The man seemed recently dead. The painting, clearly, was gone. What with the window open, Nicholas figured maybe the murderer and the painting escaped out that way. So he went out after him. The next thing Nicholas knew, a cop outside was arresting him. End of story.

That afternoon there was an arraignment, in the middle of which Thules "Slick" Fick, celebrity mob lawyer, barged in, conferred with Patel, and Patel bowed out. Fick suddenly became Nicholas's mouthpiece, a tall, pin-striped, silver-haired champion of the legal joust. With aplomb, Fick posited that the charges against Nicholas were entirely circumstantial and unfounded. The unnerved ADA

dismissed this, but then one of Fick's paralegals
rushed in with an advance transcription of the medical examiner's preliminary autopsy report. A classic
Slick Fick bit of magic—it was anyone's guess how
he'd gotten it so fast. The gist was that there was no
way Dr. Bagby had been hit with a rubber hose. The
weapon was hard, perhaps wood, and probably
cylindrical. Whatever it was, it was engraved with a
symbol that left an indentation on Bagby's neck—
what appeared to be a small crown or a *W*. Not only
that, but photocopies of photographs taken at the
scene and evidence inventories showed no such object in the apartment. And none had been found on
Nicholas's person.

The ADA complained that the weapon might
have been discarded when Nicholas fled.

Fick countered with Nicholas's rap sheet—blank.
No priors. A model citizen, an insurance investigator, not even a carry permit, no outstanding parking
tickets.

"Your Honor," Fick continued, a sparkle in his
eye, "I ask that my client be released so that the actual culprit might not escape."

The judge asked whether the District Attorney's
Office had any other compelling evidence against
the accused. The ADA stammered something about
flight risk as he flipped through the medical examiner's notes.

Magic. Before Nicholas could ask Fick who sent
him, the ADA pulled Nicholas aside and gave him
some crap about not leaving town. Court officers

guided Nicholas to a desk where he picked up his things, signed for them, and zoom—a veritable bum's rush out the front door.

All of this on his thirty-ninth birthday. Nicholas wasn't sentimental about such things. Hadn't gotten a card or gift on his birthday in ... well, couldn't remember when. Took pride in being isolated. What fool said no man is an island? Just a matter of not letting any tourist land and spoil the place.

When he approached Centre Street, he found a limousine waiting. Just like at the airport, a driver held up a card that read "Palihnic."

Grit from the gutter mixed with the wind and pricked the side of Nicholas's head.

"You Palihnic?" The driver gestured at his sign with mild annoyance. A burly Greek, he was the type Nicholas expected to see serving gyro platters at a diner.

"In the flesh." Nicholas climbed in the backseat. The door was slammed. They took off up Centre, toward Canal.

He leaned forward and rapped on the Plexiglas partition with a knuckle.

"You know who sent you?"

"I got a call, I got the name Palihnic, now I got you." The driver shrugged.

Nicholas slumped back against the seat. The limo continued uptown, taking him to parts unknown. Well, whoever it was that had orchestrated the rescue mission, Nicholas figured his savior was owed some of his time.

Gravy's Tavern, just off Gramercy Park, was the destination, and the Greek driver summarily dumped him there.

"We're here. Get out."

None too soon. It had been a long, mostly sleepless twenty-four hours. Nicholas figured his gizzard was due a little single malt. Maybe something expensive. Not a birthday present to himself, but a reward. He'd toughed out a bad situation.

He ran a hand across his stubble and pushed through the swinging doors. Gravy's was an old New York pub, lots of cut-glass partitions, dark wood booths, and bartenders in ties. Another one of those barrooms claiming to be the oldest in Manhattan, where such-and-so wrote such-and-such with both feet in the bag. Each of these bars had bragging rights because some genius drank himself to death in their hallowed gin mill.

It was past five, and the after-work patrons had already begun to flock around troughs of free chicken wings on the bar.

Nicholas squeezed behind two women who were talking as fast as they gobbled the wings. He had a finger raised and a request on his lips, but the bartender spoke first.

"You Palihnic?" She had both the requisite white shirt/black tie and a long blond braid.

"What makes you think so?" After his encounter with the police officer, he was hesitant to proffer his sly grin, but he did it out of reflex anyway.

The bartender returned the smile and shrugged.

"Said you'd be in a tweed suit, thin tie, and maybe glasses." Her blue eyes flashed playfully. "Said you had Pee-wee Herman hair."

"Uh huh." Nicholas's eyes narrowed. There was only one person who liked to make that crack about his hair. "Where is she?"

"Upstairs, door at the end, says 'Tammany Hall.'" The bartender pointed around to the back of the bar. "Said you should come on up."

"Not without a Macallan. You have the twenty-five year?"

She put a hand on her hip. "Twenty bucks a glass."

"On the rocks with a twist."

Twenty on the bar and drink in hand, Nicholas made his way up the stairs to Tammany Hall.

He found a paneled room with a big round table centered under an ornate skylight. A woman sat alone at the far side, shuffling a well-used deck of cards. Nicholas knew her from way back. She currently headed Trident Mutual's investigative unit.

"Nicasia, how the hell did you manage Fick? And from you—the woman who no longer returns my calls."

"Your ass now belongs to me." Nicasia looked like she might just cut the deck for his soul, her dark, sarcastic eyes fixed on the cards. "Sit."

"Treating me like dirt seems to please you." Nicholas made a point of not taking a chair. "Me, the guy that saved your life."

He'd met Nicasia Grieg in the Peace Corps.

Nicholas flipped through his mental photo album: Nicasia falling into a raging jungle river. Nicholas pulling a Tarzan, jumping in. The long hike back to the village. Making love to her under the mosquito netting. Her olive skin. Nicholas stealing a boat, then going AWOL: Averting Women, Obsession, and Love. It was only years later when he was already back in the States that he ran into her doing insurance investigation work, too. Only she worked with Trident Mutual, and had since moved up in the ranks.

"Nicholas, that card you keep playing is from the bottom of the deck." She flipped over a joker and tossed it at him. He caught it. "I've paid you back tenfold on that debt just by setting you up with your first reputable job in New York, though why I even did that after the way you bailed on me..."

Had they been in love? Nicholas didn't think so, but knew by her bitterness that she—at the very least—felt he'd stolen her heart. Yet at the same time he imagined she still admired his cool intensity and brash confidence. Not that she'd ever admit as much. Between them in a professional capacity it was all about brinkmanship filling the gap where friendship and feeling might have been.

"Bottom line, Nicholas? I can't trust you, and can't afford to associate with you. You have a shady reputation."

"Is my shady reputation really that expensive, considering I get results?" Nicholas waved the joker in the air.

"In terms of my credibility, yes. Your fiascoes make me and Trident Mutual look bad." She shot him an icy grin and sipped her seltzer like it was vodka.

"Have you forgotten the eighty thou I saved you guys? All the big ones I brought in for you? Are we forgetting?" He tossed the card onto the table like he was angry. He wasn't. "That was just last year about this time too."

"Oh yeah, the Louis XVI 'Liberace' Commode," Nicasia said flatly, slapping out cards in a game of solitaire. "Except the damages to the aircraft far exceeded the recovery cost."

"The pilot panicked." Nicholas produced wire-rimmed glasses from an inside pocket. Clear glass lenses. A tool: he just used them to look either innocent or authoritative.

"Nicholas, the pilot *panicked* when you knocked him cold with your sap while he was in the act of barreling the plane down the runway. I'm sorry, I should say *off the runway and into the bay*."

"We didn't go into the bay. Just along the pier a bit."

"The tail ended up in Jamaica Bay." She slapped down a card and glared at him. "They couldn't use a crane from shore to lift it out, so they had to bring in a very expensive barge. We've been tangled in litigation with the Port Authority and Avionic Leasing ever since."

"The commode was undamaged. And have you forgotten Barney? I hooked you up with Barney, didn't I? He made you look terrific at Trident."

Nicholas reflected on what a gold mine Barney Swires had turned out to be. Another in a long line of thieves that Nicholas had exposed. What had begun as simple investigative work had turned into a job as middleman, brokering the return of stolen art. The insurance companies didn't make back any money sending people to prison. Paying the burglar was a lot cheaper than paying lawyers. And of course, Nicholas got his vig as "broker." But Barney was not your garden-variety burglar. Nicholas liked his unrepentant nature, so he'd set him up working for Trident as a consultant on how to thwart burglars. But he'd had no idea Barney and Nicasia would hit it off romantically. He was tickled pink they had. Could wedding bells be far off? One more thing Nicasia owed him.

Nicasia flushed as her hands steadily laid out the cards like they were somebody else's. And yet her chin trembled almost imperceptibly.

"Nicasia?"

He considered the ruddy veil to her face. Eyes wet and fixed on the cards. Jaw flexing.

"Nicasia?" He took off his glasses and sat across from her. "Is Barney OK?"

"They say he's dead."

"Dead? Who said he's dead?"

"Newcastle."

"Newcastle Warranty?" Everybody in the business knew Newcastle. A huge shipping insurer. "Barney go down in a boat?"

"Crocodiles. Costa Rica." She sniffed deeply and

held back tears. "They...they hired him to find an angle on some boat thefts. Felt he was the only one who could, you know...He's a hot investigator in the industry now."

"Crocodiles? Give me a break." Then again, Nicholas had first met Barney when he'd had to chase Barney across Belize to catch him and get him to return a copy of Edgar Allan Poe's *Tamerlane*. Nicholas hoped this wasn't going to be another one of those jobs. One where he'd end up back in the jungle. He'd sworn off jungles.

"They say Barney was out with a guide, in the swamp or whatever. Ambushed by Nicaraguan pirates."

"Oh, come on!" Nicholas hated pirates more than jungles. People thought they no longer existed, but Nicholas knew better. Bandits in boats attacking other boats had never gone out of fashion, either on the high seas or coastal backwaters. What had gone out of fashion were the cutlasses, treasure chests, square rigs, and eye patches. Today's well-dressed pirates brandished RPG rocket launchers, jet boats, GPS tracking systems, and night-vision goggles. He'd read just the week before where a cruise ship off the coast of Somalia had narrowly escaped attack.

"Found his shoes, maybe one of his feet in a crocodile near the capsized boat."

"Like in its stomach?"

"Yes, yes." Nicasia glanced at him, her eyes red

and wet. "They shot it, cut it open. Like that time in the Corps when the tax collector vanished."

"But they didn't find the rest of him?"

"No."

"And they're not sure about the foot. Could be somebody else's foot?"

"Half digested. No prints." She sniffed again deeply, laying out a few more cards.

"That's convenient. You want me to look into this?"

"Not particularly. But you're the only one I know with backwater savvy. Nicholas, I've got to know for sure."

The bartender stuck her head in the door, eyeing the two of them speculatively, as though she were afraid she'd interrupted squabbling lovers.

"Uh, 'scuse me, Ms. Grieg. I got a party in this room soon. Last call."

"One of these." Nicholas held up his empty glass without turning, and the bartender disappeared. "Who at Newcastle retained Barney?"

"Drummond Yager. He's in New York, from their London office."

"Don't know him. When was this?"

"Barney left a week ago. I got the call from Yager day before yesterday. By the time I decided to call you, I discovered that you'd taken that particular day to get your ass in a colossal sling. Just like you, too, screwing up something even before it's started." Nicasia produced a hanky, blotting her eyes.

"Easy, Nicasia, I know I'm beholden to you for..."

"Damn right you are!" She flared. "Getting Fick to rep you didn't come easy. It took favors, and expenses, neither of which I could afford. Unless..."

"Unless? Unless I find Barney for you?"

"Yes. It'll be worth it if you find Barney." She pulled a plastic bag from her purse and tossed it across the table. A hairbrush and a blood-spotted tissue were inside. "Use it for prints, hair samples. The tissue's from a shaving cut. Use it for DNA."

The bartender barged in and pegged the drink down next to Nicholas.

"Here y'go, sport."

He glanced back at her swaying blond braid as she exited, leaving the door open.

"I'll look into it, Nicasia. But this could get expensive. I mean, DNA tests? And what if I've gotta mount some kind of safari in Costa Rica? You know, boats, arm a posse, that kind of thing. Or helicopters?"

"Send me the bill." She stood and walked across the room, stopping in the open doorway to glance back at Nicholas. "Almost forgot, Nicholas."

He didn't know what to expect from the odd smile on her lips. Was it spiteful or nostalgic? Maybe both.

"Happy birthday."

As Nicholas stared at the empty doorway, listening to her feet trot down the stairs, he figured he'd guessed about right: both. But life was too short for that kind of baggage. Travel light, he reminded himself.

He tapped a finger on the upturned joker and killed his drink. Thinking.

The idea of heading to Costa Rica to search for Barney was a loathsome prospect. Nicholas had had his fill of that life. The cities were blanketed in a haze of vile smoke from burning palm litter and garbage. The streets were nothing but potholes and junker cars, the neighborhoods chockablock with defunct construction projects draped in vultures. He despised the incessant din of crowing roosters, squabbling parrots, and howling dogs. The jungles were worse—thick with mosquitoes, leeches, humidity, and thieves. The rivers? Awash in crocodiles, toothy fish, parasites, and disease.

Yet his aversion to those environs went way beyond his entanglements with Nicasia. It was Devlin Smith, the double-dealing "mentor" he'd hooked up with after ditching Nicasia in New Guinea. Smith had sold him out to pirates, then watched, laughing, as the waters slowly rose up around Nicholas's sinking boat. Never mind that the pirates then double-crossed Smith and ran him over with his own boat. Nicholas's bitterness was not assuaged, and it became his defining moment as an adult. If you lose your life due to your own miscalculation, so be it.

How he ended up in New Guinea in the first place was another matter. His father had been a professional butterfly collector whose heart gave out while he was chasing spangled fritillaries in a field of marigolds. Nicholas liked to think he was of the same independent, single-minded stock, that there was a kinship between him and his dad. Even if that kinship was somewhat retroactive—the bond between them wasn't much in evidence while his father was alive. Nicholas had been a wheeler and dealer back then, antithetical to the mores of his aging beatnik parents. When he tapped the family's resources for an investment scheme that went bad, his dad worked incessantly to keep the family out of bankruptcy, and died soon after. Nicholas's mother blamed him for his father's death and moved off to Michigan, not speaking to him since. His only sibling, Garth, had only recently started talking to him again.

While Smith's betrayal was the defining moment of his adult life, the debacle with Nicholas's father's money and subsequent death was the defining moment of his youth. It's what sent him packing for the jungles and the Peace Corp in the first place.

So the Third World was his trial by fire, not to be relived. He needed somebody else to take on Costa Rica and the task of finding Barney for him.

But the day was young, Nicholas was tired, and there was much to do. He still wasn't completely extricated from Dr. Bagby's demise. And there was the matter of that missing Moolman canvass.

Downstairs he folded himself into one of the wooden phone booths and dialed a number. Got a recording, an announcement that was clearly read from a prepared script.

"You have reached Olbeter Investigations. The staff is unavailable to take your call at the moment, but if you'll leave your name and number, we'll contact you at the earliest possible opportunity." A series of beeps followed.

"It's Nicholas. Meet me as soon as you can, 113 15th Street. Or I'll call." He hung up. Olbeter didn't have a staff. Just bluster to make it sound like he had a going concern. Nicholas liked him well enough: he had style and some street smarts. But that didn't compensate for being your basic dope. Nicholas couldn't figure out how Olbeter stayed in business, though he found him useful, now and again.

He bit his lower lip, pondered a moment, shrugged, and dialed a Brooklyn exchange.

"You've reached Park Slope Investigations," a female voice intoned. "We're out of the office right now, but if you leave a message, we'll get back to you as soon as possible. BEEEP!"

Nicholas chuckled to himself. Maureen and Olbeter both making like they had an entire agency backing them up when they were both solo, like Nicholas. At least Maureen wasn't a dope like Olbeter.

"Maureen? Nicholas. Need a little help, thought a neophyte might need some work."

There was a clatter at the other end, then a click.

"Nicholas?" Her voice was huskier than usual.

"Never able to break that NYPD prowl-car snooze routine, huh?"

"Just got off staking the domicile of one Carlos

Esteban. So I nab him, drag him down to the INS, and wouldn't you know it? It's too close to closing, bring him back tomorrow, we'll deport him then. So I gotta hold this creep overnight. I'm not bringin' him home, so I camp out in the car all night with Carlos Esteban making kissy sounds in the backseat. Don't mess with me, Nicholas. I'm crabby. This isn't the night for drinks and dirty dancing."

"Still scrounging around for Immigration's Most Wanted?"

"Can we cut the bullshit, Nicholas? What do you want?"

"Got some work for you."

"Surveillance, I'll bet." She sighed.

"Meatier than that. Missing person, a guy I know who's presumed crocodile chow but..."

"Say what? Slow down, Nicholas."

"Barney Swires, white, thirty-six, five foot eleven, brown hair graying at the temples, deceptively youthful looks, kind of slouchy, blue eyes that seem to look right through you. Onetime civil servant and one of those guys who knows everything about anything that's underground in New York. Used to work for the Department of Transportation exploring old train tunnels, lost sewers, vaults, all kinds of abandoned structures underground. Well, yours truly nabbed him a while back. Turned out he was using some of these tunnels to break into museums and such. Decided to start his own museum in a storage locker in Queens."

"Never heard about this."

"Well, I didn't exactly turn him over to the fuzz. No money in that. I brokered the return of his cache to the insurance companies."

Maureen yawned. "You mean he hadn't hocked any of it?"

"Not this one. Saw himself as an art collector, not a thief. So he quit his city job and he's now on a new career path as a security consultant to banks and museums. When do you think you'll be back on your feet? Couple hours?"

Maureen yawned again. "Couple hours."

"I'll call you back at nine o'clock; fill you in once you get some coffee, a pencil, and some paper. I want you to take a meeting tomorrow at Newcastle."

"Newcastle?"

"The insurer. So let's get cracking."

Maureen let out a groan. "You're a ballbuster, you know that?"

Nicholas hung up and turned toward the bar.

"I owe you for the second drink."

The bartender glanced up from where she was washing glasses at a sink under the bar. "Catch me next time. 'Kay?"

Nicholas sucked the inside of his cheek, suppressing a smile. Policewomen were one thing, bartenders another. He pulled the netsuke peanut from his pocket and set it on the bar. "Hold this as collateral."

He left Gravy's, popped into a cab, and headed uptown. Time to canvass a few art dealers.

• • •

Similar to her downtown gallery, Beatrice's uptown exhibition space was ground floor, large, and white. Upstairs, her office/apartment had a picture window with a commanding view of Madison Avenue and a Ralph Lauren boutique. It was seven o'clock and she was pacing in front of the window with her pocket phone pressed to one ear.

"Yes...Yes...No...Yes...By this weekend. It has to be finished. I have an opening the next weekend, and we need time to get alarms installed and the exhibition erected...I don't want to hear that... that either. Do what it takes..."

Karen, BB's assistant, was sitting at an ornate desk against a bare brick wall examining figures and stabbing a calculator. Occasionally, she would sigh and shake her head. Karen was feline slim and almost always wore black leotards under whatever else she was wearing, which often wasn't much.

The doorbell chimed, and Karen looked up at BB quizzically. Beatrice looked back and shrugged. Karen pushed a button on a box on the desk.

"May I help you?"

"Nicholas Palihnic to see Beatrice Belarus."

Karen looked at BB, who waved bye-bye at her.

"I'm sorry, sir, BB is not in at the moment, and for security reasons, I have instructions not to allow strangers unannounced into the building. If you'd care to slip your card through the slot with your business stated on the back, she'll get back to you just as soon as she is able."

"Forget about the card. Take a message. You got paper and pencil up there, don't you? Tell her I see her pacing back and forth in front of the window, talking on the phone, and that I want to talk about Moolman. Got it?"

Karen looked up at BB, who squashed her call and walked over to the desk. With a demure smile, she reached out and ran one hand through Karen's hair. With the other she pushed a button on the box.

"Mr. Palihnic, I don't believe I've made your acquaintance." Like a cat being stroked, Karen nuzzled into the petting.

"Well, I'm giving you a perfect opportunity. Care to talk about Moolman?"

"Perhaps we can arrange another time? I'm quite busy."

"Five minutes, that's all I ask. You can time me."

BB removed her hand from Karen's swirl of blond hair.

"Coming down with a stopwatch, Mr. Palihnic."

Moments later, they stood together in the center of the large white exhibition space, which at the moment was hung with a number of orange, black, and yellow abstracts, as well as several constructivist pieces that contained a lot of egg cartons and marbles. BB slowly circled Nicholas as though considering the latest in found-art sculpture. If he was going to make waves, she'd bowl him over with a tidal wave.

Nicholas stood for inspection, arms folded patiently. This was the second of six dealers he'd had to visit, and he was prepared for the high-hat.

"What about Moolman, Mr. Palihnic?"

"Ever hear of me? I do a lot of recovery work for insurers." Nicholas adjusted his glasses.

"Yes, I suppose I have. In this morning's paper. I should call the police, you know that, don't you?"

"Was I in the papers?"

"Said you'd murdered someone. For a painting. A Moolman, perhaps? I can only assume you're trying to sell it to me."

"I didn't kill him, I didn't get the Moolman, and I don't sell stolen art. I return it to the insurer."

"For a percentage, yes, I know of your type. Making a very fine distinction between crook and investigator, aren't we?"

"Hey, I'm beginning to feel like a fireplug you're circling. You're not going to pee on me or anything, are you, Ms. Belarus?"

Beatrice stopped circling, her mouth twisted as though overwhelmed by a sour ball.

"Can we cut the chitchat, the power body language?" Nicholas spread his arms. "I heard that you deal in Moolman, along with other abstract expressionists. It's not like I've singled you out. I've got a bunch of other rug merchants to visit. I'm just trying to find out if anybody has approached you with it, that's all."

"If someone offered me a stolen painting, I'd report it directly to the police." Beatrice stood behind and a little to the side, where he could only make her out in his peripheral vision. "Besides, my interest in

Moolman isn't exactly common knowledge. What makes you think they'd come to me?"

"It's my business to know things like this, Ms. Belarus, and I have to assume anyone who took it would know how to unload it and to whom. So here's my card." She took it. He removed his glasses and they locked eyes.

"You sure you haven't come across a Moolman to-day?" Nicholas let the question carry a lot of weight. She was a hardball character, and he wanted her to know he could play. Beatrice was pale as it was, but he thought she turned just a tad paler.

"Nobody calls me *Ms. Belarus*, Nicky. It's BB." She stepped around in front of him. "No Moolmans today."

"People call me all sorts of things, but only one person calls me Nicky." He started for the door. "Call me if one turns up. I'll make it worth your while."

Nicholas let himself out, and as soon as he hit the windblown sidewalk his cell phone started to vi-brate. He found cell phones useful sometimes, but preferred the anonymity of pay phones. Everybody had caller ID, and even if you did block your num-ber, the wrong people could tap into your signal and listen in. A pay phone number told the callee noth-ing, and if you used a different one each time, was tap-proof. Nicholas's theory was that the less any-body knew about him or his whereabouts, the better. Very few people knew where he lived, and all his bills were sent to a post office box. He gave out his cell number sparingly.

"Nicholas, it's me."

Here we go, Nicholas thought. It was the distinctive voice of his brother, Garth, and the tone was familiar. Nicholas always kidded him there were only two Garth tones of voice. One was that of the disapproving big brother. The other was that of a helpful neighbor who would come over to borrow the mower but end up drinking beer. Nicholas wished today's tone were the latter.

"What gives?" Nicholas sighed.

"What gives is that I read in the paper that my brother was arrested for murder."

"Yeah, well..." Nicholas rolled his eyes, drawing his coat about him to shut out the cold. "I've been on a killing spree."

"You think this is some kind of joke?"

"Yes, it is a joke. The guy was dead when I got there, OK? What do you want from me, Garth? An apology?"

"No, Nicholas. I'm sorry." There was a pause on the other end. "It's just sort of a shock to read about your brother as a murder suspect in the paper. You could have called, you know."

"Been busy." Nicholas regretted giving Garth his cell number—this business of having family, of being big brothered, was cramping his style. "I've been working on extricating myself from the murder rap, and I've got a new project that's hot. What could you have done, anyway? Not like you could have bailed me out."

"Well…"

"Look, Garth, let's be frank here. You and Angie have been in a bit of trouble yourselves now and again, am I right?"

"Well…"

"OK, then." Nicholas took a deep breath and calmed. "You can't afford lawyers for yourself, much less for me. What are you going to do, come down to One Centre with a stuffed squirrel?"

Nicholas had his odd line of work, and Garth had his: taxidermy dealer. He wasn't a taxidermist, just a guy who rented it to the movies and TV and such. And, as it happened, Garth got into a jam once or twice when one of his stuffed animals turned out to be something someone was willing to kill for. That was how the brothers had gotten reacquainted a year ago. Before then, they hadn't seen each other since their dad's funeral.

"Please, Nicholas, don't even joke about squirrels, not after what we went through." Garth's tone had softened toward that of the beer-swilling neighbor. "I guess the family curse for getting in trouble is alive and well. You should come over Sunday, have a beer, or a scotch… hold on…" There was a muffled sound on the other end.

"Are you OK, Nicholas?" It was Angie, Garth's longtime significant other.

"Golly, Mother, I'm just super," Nicholas chirped.

"Oh, for Pete's sake," she scolded. "Shouldn't we be concerned?"

"Except that girl I took to the T-dance, well, she's pregnant, and we figure we'll steal a car and go on a crime spree across the flat states . . ."

"You're family, Nicholas. We're your family. If you need anything, anything at all . . ."

Nicholas smiled. At least Angie wasn't a complete ball breaker. No history between them. And there was something about the way she was completely unfazed by his bullshit, not to mention all her goofy expletives, that disarmed him.

"Angie, sugar, I've got a good lawyer, I've got a handle on this, and will get it all sorted out, so don't worry."

"You coming to dinner Sunday? You've missed the last three weeks."

Nicholas sighed. He was of two minds about having a family. He'd spent almost two decades divorced from it. Out of touch. Angie had made a project out of bringing him into the fold. He liked her, mainly because she seemed to like him for some reason. But she was a tourist approaching his beach, his island.

"Look, babe, our family isn't exactly the Waltons."

Angie laughed. "I'll bake an apple pie and put it on the windowsill if that'll make Sunday dinner more appealing."

"You win, as usual." Nicholas sighed again. Angie had his number and knew how to make him feel just a little like a jerk. "Anything to get off the phone and get back to business. I've got a lot to do."

"See you Sunday, then, at seven." There was obvious satisfaction in her voice.

"OK, Mom. Hey, has Garth been giving any thought to that insurance appraiser work?"

"We'll talk again Sunday," she said guardedly. Nicholas was trying to do a good deed. But because of past frictions, Garth was leery of any venture coming from him. Before getting into insurance investigation Nicholas had been involved in his fair share of shady enterprises, including the one that had ruined their dad's finances.

"Hey, I know he's suspicious, but believe me, Angie, this is completely legitimate. I'm just trying to throw some work his way." Anything to put Garth off the disapproving big brother act.

"OK, then, we'll see you Sunday." She obviously didn't want to discuss it while Garth was standing there. "Good night, John Boy. And happy birthday."

"Super." Nicholas disconnected the call, trying to suppress a smile. Garth and Angie's concern was alternately annoying and mildly amusing. Why? Maybe he had yet to realize he liked it.

Chapter 4

Sam and Joey Pazzo had been drillers for six years, starting the very day they collected their high school diplomas and joined their pop at Hoboken Drilling, Inc. They worked skid and flatbed rigs for soil sampling. The Pazzo brothers were scrappy, reckless workers, and they always drilled as a team.

Maimings are not particularly unusual for drillers. Either a truck outrigger chops off their toes, or a wrench slips from a brace and lops off a finger, or an overtaxed coupling shatters and pokes out an eye. The Pazzo brothers had suffered only the virtual loss of all fingernails, not from any accident, but from continuous manual labor without the protection of gloves. Bulbous yellow corns tipped their fingers like pads on the toes of a tree frog.

After a day's drilling, they'd smoke a joint or two

on the way back to their wives and their two-family house. Sam lived upstairs, Joey down. Their kitchen windows afforded a sweeping view of the Helix, the long spiral ramp into the entrance of the Lincoln Tunnel. After a light dinner of pasta, meat, and iced tea, they'd gather their body armor and sticks and head for the hockey rink. Their team was called "HoBroken."

The outcome of a typical HoBroken game was never in doubt. Droplets of blood stood out brightly on the ice. Final score? The challenger, Metallica: five bloody noses, one chipped dental cap, one broken tooth, one overextended knee, an undetermined number of minor contusions, two black eyes, and one probable concussion. HoBroken: two bloody noses, one knocked-out tooth, an undetermined number of minor contusions, three black eyes, and two probable concussions.

Sam and Joey suffered all the black eyes and bloody noses for HoBroken.

"Ice tonight was fuckin' awesome best!" Sam smacked his helmet into Joey's as the team dragged themselves back down the corridor to the locker room.

"Yeah! Slam!" Joey enthused.

Their teammates were not so exuberant.

"Fuckin' Sam! Why the fuck don't you pass the puck!" a fellow HoBroken admonished, pointing his stick.

"'Cause you can't shoot worth a fuck, that's what." Sam pointed back. "Fuck."

"Fuck you, Sam," another teammate accused, a bloody tooth in his hand. "You Pazzo brothers act like you're the only ones on the ice. Joey shouldn'ta passed all the way out to center field. He did that to get the puck to you."

"Fuck you," Joey retorted, then flashed a smile at his older brother.

"Yeah, fuck you," Sam agreed. "You guys wanna play ice or what? Out there, you gotta do what you gotta do to put the puck in the goal, end of story."

"Fuck you, Sam," several teammates muttered.

When they entered the locker room, next to the Pazzo brothers' lockers stood someone they didn't expect to see: a boyish-looking guy with graying temples, a brown leather flight jacket, a Greek fisherman's cap, and a cup of coffee. He was lanky, and he leaned against the lockers with the waggish ease of a hick-town gas-pump jockey, hands thrust into his front pants pockets. But there was a sparkle in his blue eyes that belied this pump jockey was a man with a plan.

"Whoa!" Sam exclaimed, arms spread in confusion.

"Fuck!" Joey remarked. "It's Barney."

"Fellahs." Barney saluted by bowing his head.

"Joey, remember that tunnel fuckin' job out on 41st Street? Fuckin' almost froze my hands off that day looking for that vault. Bent a rod that day, and the truck broke down. Barney, that was you who was the inspector that day, am I right?" Sam tossed his helmet on the concrete floor.

Barney nodded.

"You was the one at Third Avenue, looking for some old elevated train foundations." Joey pointed at Barney with his gloves before throwing them onto the growing pile of sweaty armor.

Barney nodded.

"And that other time, we were pumpin' away, Barney warned us we're drilling into an electric conduit, we didn't believe it. 'Member?" Sam shed his pads onto the heap.

"Yeah, well..." Barney crossed his legs, dug his hands deeper into his pockets. "That'd been a DC power line and you'd be Pop-Tarts, for sure."

Sam pulled his jersey up over his head. "What're you doin' here?" he asked, voice muffled.

"Well..." Barney pulled a hand out of his pocket and rubbed his jaw in thought. "I figured that the Pazzo brothers play hockey, and, well, they live in Hoboken. Hell, I just worked it out."

"What'd you come out here for? You coulda called the company." Joey looked confused, his muscular body swaddled only in a yellowed jockstrap. "I don't get it."

"Fuck, you didn't come all the way to Jersey just to see us play ice." Sam snorted, wiping some blood from his upper lip.

"Yeah," Joey agreed.

The Pazzo brothers exchanged confused shrugs and wandered off to the showers. When they came back, most of their teammates had left, but Barney was still there, admiring the splintered end of Sam's hockey stick.

"That's the third stick this season," Sam boasted.

"Uh huh." Barney nodded to himself, pursing his lips, eyes turning toward the ceiling tiles as though he were enjoying a sunset sky. "Say, fellahs. Might you be interested in, say, a little night drilling? Work on the side. Though to think of it, you guys look a little beat up, a little tired." Barney gently set the stick against the wall and shrugged. "Maybe you're not up to it."

"Night drilling?" Sam's frog fingers fastened the buttons on his shirt with remarkable agility. "Where?"

"Just a big open space." Barney dug his hand back in his pocket, squinting at the floor. "No utilities, really, so nothing volatile in the way."

"Sounds cool," Joey said to Sam. "Too cool."

"You got to figure we'd be drilling into about twenty feet of construction fill. Concrete, shingles, bricks, wood, some chain-link maybe, like that." Barney's blue eyes looked up from the floor. "Think you could handle that?"

"Fuck. Probably have to go with a double casing to get through it." Sam donned a down vest. Joey was lacing his Timberlands. "Wash out the borehole with mud. There water nearby to help wash?"

Barney's eyes returned to the floor. "Harlem River is less than a hundred feet away. Some fire hose would come in handy."

"How many holes, how deep?" Joey asked.

"Thirty feet or so. Don't know exactly how many holes, but I figure it's a week's work."

"Samples? Cores?" Sam hacked at his sloppy black curls with a comb.

Barney shook his head slowly, still staring at his feet. "No cores, samples on demand. No blow counts, so you can drive the casings any way you want. But you fellahs would need to drill four-inch-wide holes. Each hole gets sleeved with PVC pipe."

"That's cool." Joey took the comb from his brother and hacked at his loose yellow locks. "Cash?"

Barney looked them both in the eye and pointed a finger at them, like his hand was a gun. "Cash."

"Very cool. What's it we're looking for, then?" Sam shrugged, fixing a Salem in his lips.

Barney took a deep breath.

"A boat."

Chapter 5

It was one of those frigid, densely overcast mornings that forebodes snow. More than that, there was the unmistakable musk of ice in the air. In the country, this scent would have been tinged with the scent of wood fires from a cozy hearth. In Manhattan, the aroma was perfumed with burning bread from the legions of food carts that stoke their burners with stale pretzels.

Maureen McNary had decided to take a car service to Manhattan. Normally, she would have snagged the R train from Bay Ridge, but she didn't want her confidence marred by being late or having to hoof it. Being chauffeured has a way of putting a shine on your shoes.

And she hadn't spared the Power Suit, the one she'd always worn to court when she worked for the NYPD. Gray worsted wool with thin red pinstripes, the ensemble included a double-breasted jacket and a respectably short skirt with a conservative yet curvature-enhancing number of pleats. Maureen was not by any means stocky, but she was decidedly muscular, and she felt the Power Suit accentuated her more feminine qualities. The pinstripes were an exact match to her ruby red hair.

The address was on 42nd Street, across from Bryant Park, and well apart from the other insurance biggies down in the 20s. Probably, Maureen reasoned, because Newcastle Warranty was the biggest of the biggies. The town car pulled up to the curb and Maureen stepped gracefully out. As she strode across the sidewalk, she shot an eye up the giant white building, which had a strangely concave facade, an architectural motif that made the whole building look like it was holding its breath.

On the twenty-second floor, Maureen approached the oak-paneled receptionist's cubicle. The prim woman sitting there eyed her expectantly.

"I have an appointment with Mr. Drummond Yager."

"Your name?" The receptionist flipped open the appointment book.

"Maureen McNary."

"Oh, yes. I'll ring him. If you'll just wait there ..." She gestured toward two red leather couches. ·

Between the couches and above the magazine table hung a tattered Union Jack in an elaborate gold frame. A small plaque affixed to the frame simply said "TITANIC." *What a goof*, Maureen thought.

"Miss McNary?"

Maureen half expected some gap-toothed Terry Thomas character, and was not altogether disappointed. She was confronted with the chiseled countenance of a lean Englishman in his fifties, wearing a double-breasted herringbone suit. Severe silver hair was delicately plastered to his scalp, his complexion deeply creased with the kind of wrinkles one gets from hard climates. His overbite was made dignified by a strong chin and round wire-rimmed specs.

Maureen stepped forward and extended her right hand. He extended his left, and the handshake was awkward.

"Drummond Yager." He took his other hand from his pocket—and there wasn't one. Just an abbreviated palm with which he gestured down a side hallway. It looked like a cat's paw. "Shall we repair to my office?"

Maureen followed him down a short hall. Inside his office an ornate desk the size of a small boat consumed the space from the windows to just shy of the door. Behind the desk was a world map flanked by pictures of large salvage ships, submersibles, and bathyscaphes. Maureen folded into a red leather wing chair opposite the desk, crossed her legs discreetly, and produced a notepad from her bag.

"I understand you're here to investigate the instance of Barney Swires's unfortunate demise." Drummond leaned forward onto the expanse of his blotter, hand and nonhand side by side.

"Yes." She managed not to focus on his paw, looking him straight in the eye. "I need details, like where all this happened, the names of people on the scene, local police who handled the investigation..."

"Absolutely." Drummond nodded glumly like a funeral director and slid a thin folder across the desk. "It's all here in an internal report prepared by my department. However, there really hasn't been any police involvement. You see, in this particular area of Costa Rica, which is sparsely populated, there is only a sort of regional manager who looks into criminal matters. If it is deemed serious enough, federal investigators from San Jose get involved. In this case, the accident was considered open and shut. There were bullet holes in the boat, meaning he was shot at, no doubt by Nicaraguan pirates. Then there was the crocodile with Mr. Swires's boot in it. Appalling."

"Not for nothing, but you'd think the Costa Rican police would try to apprehend these pirates." Maureen waved her pen incredulously.

"Allow me." Drummond stood, pulling a retractable map of Central America down over the world map. From his breast pocket, he drew out a Mont Blanc pen, the white tip of which he used as a pointer. "You see here? This is Costa Rica. And this here? This is Nicaragua. The Rio Denada, the river where Mr. Swires was lost, opens to the ocean here in Costa Rica, but just upriver it becomes the border between Nicaragua and Costa Rica. The Rio Denada, unlike, say, the Hudson River, is braided: it has many side channels, back bays, and swamps where the pirates can hide. To find them, one would have to chase them back into Nicaragua, and this is something the Costa Ricans will not do." Drummond waved his paw hopelessly.

"And the Nicaraguans? They doing anything about these pirates?" Maureen adjusted her gaze.

"This region can only be accessed by boat and by float plane, or possibly trails that would take a week to traverse from the nearest town. The Nicaraguans really aren't all that interested in policing an area so remote. They have no economic investment in the area, and the pirates don't jeopardize their border or sovereignty. The only thing at stake are the Costa Rican fishing lodges that bring in American sportsmen."

"And the Costa Ricans, they're not concerned?"

"Up until now, the pirates had only been stealing boats from the lodges. Although these skiffs cost about five thousand dollars in Florida, the hefty import fees bring their cost up to twenty-six thousand a piece. The more boats stolen, the more boats have to be bought to replace them, and the more the government makes. And thus the more Newcastle Warranty loses in claims. That's why we hired Mr. Swires."

"These pirates…" Maureen tapped her pen on the pad. "They make a living swiping and reselling boats?"

"Drugs, mainly. They use the boats to navigate the river, move cocaine and marijuana from the highlands. Perhaps they sell a few of the boats to other fishing lodges. We really don't know."

"How come you called in this guy Barney? By what I'm told, his expertise was in preventing burglars from using subway tunnels and sewers to do break-ins. This seems kinda far out for him."

"Well, Miss McNary"—Drummond returned the map to the ceiling and reseated himself—"Mr. Swires's reputation in this business has grown rather formidably, and our LAD—"

"LAD?"

"Lost Assets Department. They recommended him to me. It was my understanding that his talents were, shall we say, very much along the lines of: it takes a thief to catch a thief. We gave him a try and, well..." Drummond's paw deftly tucked the Mont Blanc inside his jacket, as though tucking Barney's memory away. The folds of his face were pinched together in a mildly sad, if somewhat bemused, expression that Maureen thought odd.

"So where's this foot now?" Maureen cocked her head.

"The foot? Oh, you mean Mr. Swires's foot, from the..."

"The foot from the crocodile, whatever. We get that an' we can find out whether it belongs to Swires." Her pen was poised.

"Oh, I see, for DNA testing," Drummond said glumly, as though he were a funeral director and she'd chosen the cheapest casket. "Isn't that rather expensive?"

"Cheaper than a Costa Rican safari." Maureen pulled the Ziploc from her purse, the one Nicasia had given Nicholas. "We can match a tissue sample to hair or skin samples from this brush, perhaps to his blood on this tissue."

"A trip to Costa Rica? You mean, to search for Mr. Swires? Well, I daresay, even if that isn't his foot, his chances of survival in that environment…"

"Hey, you never know. He could have been taken captive. He could have received medical attention."

"My dear Miss McNary, the Rio Denada is teeming not only with crocodiles, but with alligators, not to mention half a dozen different kinds of vipers and coral snakes, including the highly temperamental and venomous snake known as the Bushmaster. The jungle is bristling with poisonous frogs, tarantulas, and banana spiders. The muddy shallows are awash with stinging catfish. During high tides, sharks move up into the river. Travel by foot through the coastal swamps and rain forest is an almost insurmountable challenge, especially if one is weak or injured. And the backwaters are populated only by thieves and murderers. What chance has a man who has lost a foot to a crocodile? And assuming, for the sake of argument, that he survived, he would be in no condition to move far from the place of the incident. Our people conducted a thorough search of the surrounding area and failed to discover his body—alive or dead. Assuming the foot is his, the chances of survival are, in my experienced estimation, nil."

"You have a lot of experience in being stranded in the jungle without a foot?" Maureen arched an eyebrow.

"Absolutely." Drummond held up his cat's paw and smiled back. "When I worked in our Port Moresby office, I was investigating something quite similar, actually, in Indonesia. Pirates took away our craft, forced us into the river, then attempted to run us over with our own boat. They made quite a sport of it. Propeller mangled my hand, or nearly so. My partner swam for help, but I never heard from him again. Some local fishermen found me onshore right where the ambush took place, two days later. By that time, I'd had to remove what remained of my hand because it had begun to rot." His smile disappeared. "Unpleasant in the extreme."

Maureen paled only slightly from the gruesome details. Ten years on the police force gave you an iron gut and a morbid sense of humor.

"I see." She snuck a side glance out the picture window, at the snow falling over Bryant Park. "So, Mr. Yager, when do I get the foot?"

His smile was forced, as though the bereaved had chosen cremation. "I'll inquire."

Chapter 6

Snow materialized in a hush out of an opaque sky, a brace of silent gulls dissolving into the gray. Barney put his hand out the window of the car, caught some of the flakes, and put his palm to his tongue. It was the taste of childhood, of sledding, of hot chocolate, of wet mittens on the radiator.

He parked his rental sedan in a small lot under the Triborough Bridge, under massive concrete arches supporting the bridge above. The lot was next to Icahn Stadium on Randall's Island, a sister to Ward's Island. They were two little river-bound satellites to Manhattan Island and the Bronx, stacked at the crotch of the East River where it split into the Harlem River and Hell Gate Channel. There was once a channel between the two islands, but it had since been filled. The islands' primary tenants were the Sanitation Department Training Grounds, a

Department of Environmental Protection water treatment plant, and the Manhattan State Mental Hospital. There were some ball fields on the north and south ends of the island, as well as Parks Department buildings. But mostly it was just a place where the piers supporting gigantic bridges and viaducts marched across the landscape like alien destroyers oblivious to what lay underfoot.

A backwater for secondary government facilities, the islands were a geographical afterthought—most New Yorkers couldn't even tell you where they were. Pedestrian traffic was nonexistent, and there were no sidewalks, no bars, no homes, no delis. Cars: infrequent. It was the kind of place where bad things could happen out in the open, but didn't.

Streamlined and turquoise, Icahn Stadium looked like a huge old 1950s diner from the front. Barney blinked up at the snowy structure, then lowered his gaze to a pay phone next to the stadium's sleek ticket booth. A cold breeze whispered in his ear. He considered the phone for almost a full minute.

"I shouldn't," he said aloud. "But I will." With long slow strides he started toward the phone.

There was a time when all that mattered to Barney was his collection. He'd always been more or less the quiet, thoughtful type, not subject to snap decisions or the feeling that he had to prove anything. But while a person may sometimes seem as unchanging as a dust-blown desert, there's always water moving underground somewhere.

Back in the day, his expertise in locating abandoned tunnels and vaults around the city was almost legendary. It was rumored that he was psychic, or had X-ray vision. After carefully researching and studying plans and historical records, he would go out to the street and just stare at an intersection, noting the location of every manhole, every pavement seam, every surface irregularity. Then he'd stroll the area, scanning the ground like he'd dropped a dime. When asked what he was looking for, he'd say: "History."

Sometimes he'd stop and feel the ground with the flat of his palm. Likely as not, there would be a troop of hard-hatted engineers in his wake, the ones who hadn't previously witnessed his talents muttering skeptically. He might circle the site five or six times like this, his audience growing impatient. Then he'd eventually come to a slow stop and say: "Paint."

Someone would hand him a can of spray paint, white, the kind that sprays upside down.

Then someone would invariably ask: "Here?"

He wouldn't say anything, just flash them his quick, patented secret grin. It was his characteristic sly smile that could have been bashful or boastful. Crouching, he would start to paint a crisp white line on the pavement.

When he was done outlining the vault or tunnel below, someone would usually ask: "Are you sure?"

The art of dowsing is invariably suspect. They didn't know that he'd done exhaustive research in advance.

He'd give them that secret grin again, squint, and say: "Pretty sure." It was at once facetious and conclusive. When he said *pretty sure*, there was no mistaking that he was absolutely positive.

He was always right. Always.

And that became a problem. Not for his job, but for Barney. It's fine to be good at something, even great. Even expert. But when you come to be characterized as genius at what you do, that's different. Often as not, genius is discovery without art. For said genius, it's as if you're doing a magic trick over and over. It's just a trick, but no sleight of hand. Just pure aptitude and instinct. But it can amount to the same thing.

Barney didn't realize the extent of his own malaise until the day he located an abandoned tunnel on Madison Avenue. It had once connected the basements of two mansions across the street from each other, one of which had become a private museum. He was with the construction crew when they cut a hole in the wall of a subway emergency exit tunnel and broke through the vaulted brick roof of the tunnel. They lowered a ladder, and Barney went down with his miner's helmet to take dimensions and photos. The tunnel was bulkheaded in either direction at the basement walls, though one protruded beyond the building line of the museum. When he came out of the tunnel, the crew was having lunch. Barney was curious about exactly where this tunnel extended into the museum and studied the lawn in front of it for some time before going in.

He paid the entrance fee and walked along the Victorian marble hallways until he came into a room of antiquarian books. He stopped in front of a glass case. On display inside was Edgar Allan Poe's *Tamerlane and Other Poems*. He'd never had any particular interest in collecting books, didn't read anything but books on New York history. A placard noted that *Tamerlane* was one of twelve known copies, valued around $200,000. He studied the floor for a moment, crouched, and put a hand on the cool stone. He stood and looked about the room. Then he looked again at the book. With his toe, he tapped lightly on the wood front of the display case. Hollow. He pursed his lips.

The display case, of course, was directly above the tunnel.

The skies didn't open in a gush of sunshine and seraphim choruses. Barney's revelation was just as calm, considered, and measured as was his ascribed genius.

Two days later, a story came out in the paper about the tunnel.

Two nights after that, in the wee hours, Barney slipped into the emergency exit hatch with a bag of tools and came back up four hours later, covered in dust, with the little brown book wrapped in a towel.

Back at his apartment, his kitchen glowing with the beams of sunrise, he unwrapped the towel and gazed for an hour at the book in his hand. Just holding it, his blue eyes alight.

He was apprehensive when a coworker ran into his little office around noon that day to report the theft, that burglars had used the tunnel he found to steal an old book. But as the days passed, it became apparent the police figured the crooks had read about the tunnel in the papers. Barney was never even questioned.

In future criminal endeavors, Barney didn't use his work projects. Rather, he researched and located tunnels adjacent to small museums or private collections on his own time. Vacant subway equipment rooms. Amtrak tunnels. Sewer chambers. Sealed building vaults. Abandoned aqueducts. Even heat-exchange culverts that led from downtown skyscrapers to the river. Most of these underground spaces were known to numerous people in and out of government: they weren't lost or abandoned, so he was never singled out.

He was careful to obscure any patterns that might be detected in his crimes. They were widely disparate geographically, anywhere within the five boroughs but as far away as Albany, which made it more difficult for various police agencies to compare notes. He stole a wide variety of mediums and genres. He used different tools. He left conflicting evidence of the size of the "gang" at work, from two to five, based on discarded work gloves, coffee cups, cigarette butts, gum wrappers, what have you.

It was often ridiculously easy to steal valuables

once a wall or floor was breached. As even the most cursory study of art theft substantiates, most such burglaries are more the product of initiative than daring and intricacy. Smaller museums and private collections often have rudimentary alarm systems and no guards after hours. No matter that they have millions of dollars in art and collectibles on hand. Just alarms on the doors and windows at night, so that if you don't come in that way, there's little chance of detection. For many successful thieves, alarms aren't even an issue: they walk in during the day and when no one is in the room use a box cutter to remove a painting in less than thirty seconds, roll it up, tuck it in their trench coat, and walk out.

And inasmuch as Barney didn't try to sell any of his acquisitions, the chance of getting caught after the fact was practically nil. That's where the garden-variety art thief almost always got pinched.

Like any worthwhile endeavor, the rewards of collecting this way proved complex but cumulative, and at times hard to peg. Mostly it had to do with *what it was* and *what it wasn't*.

What it was was tangible proof of his conquest, not just a notch in his belt. As he stole a Gauguin here, an Incan idol there, an extinct stuffed ivory-billed woodpecker over there, his collection grew. So did the stakes—it was dangerous, which, combined with his cunning, made it a thrill. It was about being a collector, which is something only a fellow die-hard collector can truly appreciate. Collecting is about the coveting, the obsession, the hunt, the acquisition, the accomplishment, the possession. But more than that, each piece had a life of its own, each one fueling his soul as though he were absorbing its life force. His collection was a kaleidoscope of history.

What it wasn't was stealing. Barney wasn't delusional—he knew that he would be seen as a crook if discovered, but he didn't see himself that way. The wealthy families and institutions he relieved of their possessions were not seriously deprived, especially as long as the insurance companies compensated the victims. It wasn't about money, since he didn't sell the pieces. It wasn't about notoriety, about reading of his exploits in the paper, though he did have to keep up with what the police were thinking, so far as he could.

Yet, it also wasn't entirely rewarding. Possessions make poor companions. Not many women would appreciate Barney's penchant for stealing rare works. To have a woman live with him, to know where he went, to find out about the storage locker with his tools and research, to find out about the other locker with the collection, was untenable. And of course, he could never be entirely honest with a woman. Truth was a barrier.

Then Nicholas Palihnic had hunted him down, taken it all away in exchange for half a million dollars and no prosecution. Nobody knew except the insurance companies and Nicholas. Barney was even able to keep his job with the city. He tried to compensate for the loss of his treasure by buying rare items, but by comparison, there was so little challenge. The job with Trident Mutual? Just like his genius at finding lost tunnels and vaults, his innate knack for gaining access to museums ably pitted him against would-be thieves. At the same time, his world began to fade. Malaise followed. In the morning, he couldn't think of a reason to get out of bed.

Nicasia had reversed that. With his collection gone, Barney could afford to let a woman get close, and in turn discover the rewards of opening his life, his heart, his trust, to another. They met at Trident Mutual, and their attraction was instantaneous, their bond deep, their love palpable and kinetic. He came to realize that the love of a woman was one of the most precious things he could ever have collected. It was like owning a rare work, in a way, and you only needed one to be happy. Love had a life of its own the way art had provenance, history. And like his collecting, it required Barney to give a lot of himself. The more he put in, the more he got. But love also filled a different void in him, one not only of the soul but of the heart. Keeping it filled—the way he'd kept his storage locker full of rare collectibles— grew to define him in a way that *objets d'art* never had. Never could have. Being with, even talking with, Nicasia kept that void filled.

But she didn't know the truth about his past. And she didn't know about his current enterprise. The truth barrier remained. If all went according to plan, Barney aimed to break down that wall once and for all.

• • •

As Barney approached the pay phone, he ached to hear Nicasia's voice. He hadn't realized how much it would hurt to be apart from her. So why didn't Drummond want him to call her or talk to anybody? What harm was there in calling? He'd just use his calling card and say he was in Costa Rica.

But Barney didn't know he was supposed to be dead.

He dialed and the receptionist answered. "Nicasia Grieg, please."

Her line began ringing. What harm could there be in giving her a call? Unless...

Barney scanned his surroundings, the parking lots and stadium behind the pay phone. There it was, a small red pickup truck with tinted windows, peeking from behind one of the Triborough Bridge's fat legs.

"Grieg here."

Barney's chest tightened at the sound of her voice, but he hung up without a word and went back to his car. He'd noticed that same red pickup, or one too much like it, parked across from his temporary digs in Pugsley's Point. Barney wasn't completely sure, but with all the loot at stake, his employers would be keeping an eye on him, wouldn't they?

Only one more week. Then he'd be back with Nicasia. One more week.

From the car's trunk he produced a satchel and slung it over his shoulder. Was getting involved in this venture a very serious error in judgment? He could, after all, just tell Nicasia about his past and be done with it. But there was something from his more distant past, something that happened in a Japanese garden—before the thieving—that needed to be settled.

The whiz of tires sang overhead on the Triborough Bridge, trucks grumbling and gurgling as they shifted their way out of the tollbooths above. He checked the contents of his satchel: eight wood stakes, a hand sledge, fluorescent red tape, a couple of black Marks-A-Lots, a handheld GPS device, and a folder of old blueprints. Car locked, he took his coffee cup from the roof and started toward the spot where Little Hell Gate Bridge once connected the two islands.

The City of New York had, at some historic juncture, decided to dedicate Randall's and Ward's Islands to the civic cause of handling refuse: solid, liquid, and human. The channel of water that had once divided the two islands had been completely filled in with debris by the Army Corps of Engineers. It had become overgrown with saplings and haphazard drainage ponds. Above the channel, aligned along the east side of the island, loomed the New York & Connecticut Railroad trestle, a striding monster with oddly Oriental accents and gargantuan balustrades. Aligned along the west side was the Triborough Bridge. A paved asphalt road at ground level that ran between the two and across the filled channel had obviated the necessity for the Little Hell Gate Bridge, and so it had been demolished.

Bag over his shoulder, Barney walked around to

the back of the stadium, to an entrance for an overflow parking lot along the Harlem River. The back
lot was several acres of broken macadam, dirt, and
occasional decorative shrubs. It looked like whoever
filled the channel between the two islands had lost
interest in the area where it joined the Harlem
River. Amid piles of overgrown rubble, slivers of water had yet to be filled with debris. Ducks sliced the
mirror surface of the slim ponds, moving quietly
away from Barney's approach. A stone seawall de-
lineating the edge of the filled channel was still in-
tact, forming one boundary of the parking lot. As
Barney looked along the wall, he could see the bay
where it joined the Harlem River and made a big
lazy curve north. A fancy modern-looking footbridge had been erected across the bay. It connected
the parking lot to a fence that dead-ended at the
mental hospital grounds on the other side. Someone
had had the bright idea to install little nature trails
that meandered from the ramp of the footbridge
down through the rubble and saplings. He wondered who came out to walk the trails in this no-
man's-land.

But it was there that he would find the *Bunker
Hill*.

He slid over a downed section of flimsy wood slat
fence, and into the scrub. It would be a little rough
getting the drill rig in there, but the Pazzos were resourceful and would be undaunted by such obsta-
cles. When he came to the edge of one of the ponds,
he turned on the GPS and waited for it to pick up a

signal. Because of all the terraforming, all the clut-
ter, and overlapped infrastructure, it was hard to
picture what the channel had looked like when it
flowed beneath the Triborough Bridge's legs.

Barney unfolded a blueprint entitled "U.S. Army
Corps of Engineers, East River Land Reclamation
Project: CLOSURE OF LITTLE HELL GATE
CHANNEL (August 1943)" to help get his bear-
ings. It was a crude plan view of Randall's Island,
Ward's Island, and Sunken Meadow—formerly a
grassy shoal at the channel's east terminus. Xs on
the plan showed where a line of boulders had been
placed across the channel, around Sunken Meadow,
and to the far side of Randall's Island. Also shown,
with little detail, were the Triborough Bridge sky-
way to the west, the trestle to the east, and the channel passing below both. Numerous faint symbols
resembling crosses were shown in Little Hell Gate
Channel. Lowercase italics identified these as
"wrecks hauled for fill."

Barney strode slowly away from the parking lot,
into the brushy rubble, eyes on the GPS, and came
to a stop when it beeped. He knelt and put a hand to
the ground. The *Bunker Hill* would be deep, and
hard to detect using his magic touch. On his hands
and knees, he crawled under some brambles, checking the tortured ground with his palm, trying to feel
a void. It wasn't a vibration or a mental picture that
he hoped to sense, but the lack of either. Like putting one's hand on an egg and knowing it's empty or
full, soft- or hard-boiled.

He pursed his lips, looked at a spot on the ground, and reached into his bag. He cleared away a tangle of twigs and leaves so he could drive a stake into the earth. But then he paused. His eyes latched on a glint in the dirt below, and instead he used the stake to pry a soda can from the soil. Just a gold soda can, not a pocket watch. Not the gold ring from the treasure box of an orangutan potentate he imagined it might be. He looked at it, and the secret smile grew on his face.

Barney was ten years old again, in the Japanese garden, and he could see Mr. Faldo's eyes twinkle as he said:

Be happy with useful work and what you have now, for you will not always have either. It is the path to a life of truth.

Chapter 7

The fete was held at a grandiose town house in the upper east 60s, practically walking distance. But BB and Karen took a limo. It was noon and lightly snowing, as it had been all morning.

The event? An opening for Xavier Gliche, the neoconstructivist hailed in *Newstime Magazine*'s spring "Art!" issue as the very latest genius of modern art. The gallery? Osman Strunk Gallery, the namesake of a New York gadabout and competitor to BB. The time? Well, the only reason it wasn't a twilight black-tie affair was that the work displayed was old and previously unsold. A clearance sale for an artiste on the slide.

"Why, Bea, you awful thing—here to steal Xavier from me?" Ozzy chortled. "Take him away, babe, and ol' Ozzy will come for you with a shotgun," he dared.

"Oz, would I do that to you? You remember Karen?" BB mused as to how Xavier might have been worth stealing a year ago. She handed her coat to a servant, but held on to her cell phone.

"Of course: Karen. You know, that hair! What a swirl, girl! Love it." Ozzy pressed goblets of Moët Brut into their hands and herded them up the broad marble staircase.

Karen's feline smile flickered. She reached out for BB's hand and got a reassuring squeeze.

"Always so special to have you here!" Ozzy whispered in BB's ear. "Find a winner, babe, and let's haggle."

By the time he got back downstairs another guest had arrived.

"I don't believe I've had the— Oh, I declare! Ozzy likes tweed as much as the next person, but there is a limit!"

"Name is Palihnic." Nicholas adjusted his double-breasted jacket, which was a somewhat original shade of rust. "And you're Osman Strunk. I found something you lost once."

Ozzy reaffixed his monocle so that he could examine the card Nicholas stuck into his palm.

"Really? Ha! I'm sure I would have remembered. Who in Allah's name is your tailor? Red Buttons?" Ozzy lifted a goblet from a passing waiter's tray, pressed it into Nicholas's hand, and wheeled him toward the stairs.

"For Galloway Group, your insurer." Nicholas

sniffed at the champagne. "Photo-realist, name something like Pompano? Jean Pompano?"

"Jeanie?" Ozzy led Nicholas up the stairs. "Oh, yes, that piece stolen from the basement. You recovered that? Where do you buy your shoes?"

"In Philadelphia."

"Oh, don't say it. Just don't. You buy your shoes in the cheesesteak mecca? I'm aghast."

"The shoes I get from an importer in the Bronx. I found your painting in Philadelphia, hanging on William Poole's wall. You remember your friend Bill?"

Ozzy snorted. "Bill was such a brat. Nice Italian shoes in the Bronx? To what is the world unraveling." Ozzy rolled his fingers in the air and ducked away into the crowd.

Nicholas surveyed his surroundings. The walls were hung with pieces from one of Xavier Gliche's particularly dreary periods: discombobulations of stovepipe, umbrella skeletons, barbed wire, and milk cartons featuring missing children. Corners were reserved for his brief venture into freestanding sculpture: stacks of rusty fuel tanks that not only looked bad but smelled worse. In contrast to the art, the room was newly painted white, with high ceilings and ornate trim. An uptown junkyard.

"Howdy." Nicholas stepped up to where BB was flattering some guy in torn jeans, sweatshirt, and bowler. Long, dirty gray hair shot out from under his hat.

"You must be Xavier Gliche." Nicholas forced a

handshake on him with one hand, downing his drink in a gulp with the other. "I don't think you've ever had any of your work stolen, have you?"

With the grimace of a man with a caper stuck between his teeth, Xavier turned away to where Karen was hobnobbing with a woman in a gold lamé pantsuit.

"Mr. Palihnic." BB toasted the air.

"I got your message. So you have something for me, or is there someone else here you'd like me to insult?" Nicholas slid his empty glass onto a passing tray of smoked oysters.

"Well, if that's a genuine offer . . ."

"I charge by the head. The first was a freebie."

"You take checks?"

"Just the rainy kind, and only with an alibi."

"Bravo." Beatrice toasted the air again.

"So you called me here to tell me something, and here I am."

"Yes. I wanted you to know that I made a few calls about Moolman. As a professional courtesy. But I'm afraid I haven't heard anything. Which Moolman was it again?"

"*Trampoline Nude, 1972.*"

"Well, I'll keep my eyes open. I put out feelers for you." BB brushed some imagined lint from her lapel. "But to be honest, I really don't follow Moolman's work at present and don't know any dealers that do, so I'm probably the wrong person to be helping you."

"C'mon, BB. What's with the coy act? Look, I

know you have a hungry client that you feed
Moolmans to like they were potato chips."

"Potato chips? Really?"

"At Christie's last month, you bought two
Moolmans for over five hundred thou, a good hundred and twenty-five thou more than they were
worth. Two weeks ago at Sotheby's you picked up
Legs Wide, 1975 for four hundred and fifty thou, a
good two hundred thou more than you should have
paid. These kinds of overruns wouldn't have been
unusual back when. But things have been staying
within estimates these days, unless you're talking
about Artschwager or maybe Lichtenstein or
Calder..."

"You needn't be didactic." BB took a pair of goblets from a passing tray and handed one to Nicholas.
"In my world, last month was last year. I move a lot
of art, Mr. Palihnic. And it's no secret that I'm an ag-
gressive player. What I want, I get. What I get, I either have a market for or I make a market for. I've
done my best to be of help to you. If you want to bite
my hand, I'll pull it away. What about the other
dealers you were pestering? Surely you found someone more versed in Moolman than I?"

"I'm not picking on you, BB. One dealer thought
maybe I had it, and I think he wanted to buy it from
me. He's out. Two others are out of town, one in
California having liposuction and the other at a spir-
itual liftoff at the Great Pyramids. Another was the
nervous type who confessed immediately to an in-
discretion with a runway model. And the last was in-

credibly forthcoming, showing me all his bank transactions, a collection of antique tin toys, and his catatonic great-aunt."

"Maybe you're barking up the wrong tree, doggie." BB's attention began to wander as she started eavesdropping on Ozzy's conversation behind her.

"Maybe. But I've got to believe that whoever took it plans to sell it. For that to happen, there needs to be a broker."

"Or maybe, doggie, a collector had it stolen, direct to his collection." She stole a glance at Ozzie and saw he was eavesdropping on her.

"I've investigated and solved . . . let's see, eighty-seven stolen art cases as of last Friday. Two were by collectors." One of them being Barney Swires. "Odds are against it."

Nicholas figured it was time to press his luck, see what happened. He didn't want to shove her. Just give her a little nudge.

"What I'm thinking is that maybe you had someone swipe it for you, BB. The day he got killed, the thief told me he had another offer. I thought he was putting me on. Looks to me like whoever it was just came and took it."

BB fixed an even, dull look on Nicholas. Her bloodred lips twisted in what he guessed was amusement. Like someone watching a hapless spider approach their shoe. He guessed she imagined him the spider. Just the same, he liked those lips. Sensuous.

"If you have the audacity to suggest that I, or an agent of mine, stole that Moolman..."

"You said yourself, 'What I want, I get.' I'm a suspicious person. These are hard times for most dealers. Yet you're opening a new gallery downtown. Some say you're heavily leveraged."

Her cheeks reddened, and her lips quivered as though she'd lifted her shoe and the spider ran under the radiator. One thing Nicholas figured she couldn't, wouldn't, and had never abided was impudence. Or the erosion of her reputation.

"That's enough, Palihnic. Karen?" It was clear that the audience with the queen was at an end.

Nicholas studied Karen's sleek form approach and take BB's hand. He tried to catch her eye but she kept her gaze on BB. Girlfriends, the nonplatonic kind. Interesting.

"Should I ever come upon stolen art," BB sniffed, "I would report it to the police, not to a natty character like you. You'll not bite my hand." With that, she and Karen glided from the room.

Ozzy fluttered up to Nicholas. "You have been naughty, haven't you? What on earth did you do to poor Bea?"

"I said I thought that she was overleveraged, that she was desperate, that she was making a lot of rash buys." She had the painting, all right. And he meant to find a way to make her surrender it to him.

"Congrats." Ozzy gripped Nicholas's shoulder and smiled wickedly. "You just made the permanent guest list."

"Ozzy?" Nicholas's eyes narrowed, his face gone foxy. "We need to talk."

"Really?"

"You wouldn't happen to have a von Clarke, would you?" He could simply ask BB to give him the Moolman, but that was a low-percentage play. Odds were in favor of blackmail as the tool of choice to make her cough it up.

"Do I ever!" Ozzy snapped his fingers over his head in triumph. "And wouldn't Bea like to get her mittens on it. Ha!"

Nicholas's face shifted from fox to wolf. "What if she stole it from you?"

Ozzy froze, his monocle swinging from its beaded chain on his chest.

"Bea? Steal?"

"You know, like that brat, Bill."

Sucking in his cheeks, Ozzy squinted his own foxy look. "Just what are you suggesting, naughty man? Billy lived here. He could waltz off with anything. And did."

"You live here, right?" Nicholas tapped his lips in thought.

"Why..." Ozzy's eyebrows knit in bewilderment, his mouth curled with curiosity. "Why would I steal my own von Clarke?"

"What if you did, and said someone else did, and she ended up with it? What then?" Nicholas waited for him to figure it out.

"Oh!" Ozzy looked like he was going to faint, and

put a hand on the wall. "Why would I do that to poor Bea?"

"Would she do it to you if she thought it would ruin you? Take out the competition?"

Now Ozzy gripped his chest as though expecting an asthma attack. He opened his mouth a few times to say something but obviously thought better of it.

"Well? Would she?"

Ozzy's melodramatics faded as he composed his deportment and put a thoughtful finger behind his ear. "Well, of course she would. It's a jungle. But I cannot afford to let the von Clarke go without moolah."

"You'll get what it's worth. Probably more. What if I told you I could get Bea to broker it for you and then hand you all the money? Fee free."

"Ha! Don't tease. So what's in it for you, m'boy? Hmm?"

"Well, it's like this." Nicholas drew Ozzy close, put a conspiratorial hand on his shoulder. "Sometimes you need a fish to catch a fish. We both get the fish and she's left holding the rod."

Nicholas changed bars almost as often as he changed phone numbers: often. Friends and acquaintances were kept abreast of his latest hangout and knew where to find him, but now and again there'd been those who'd sought to do him harm. Some thought him slippery, he simply considered himself cautious.

As far as bars went, he liked anonymous dives where nobody knew, cared, or would be able to remember him. He used them as neutral yet familiar meeting places that wouldn't spook a crook. Most of these dives teetered on the edge of bankruptcy, eviction, health violations, or all three. Dirty Bud's, Terminal Bar, and Tiny Tini Hut were among his past haunts.

Nicholas's current place of business was known simply by its address, "113" 15th Street. The main barroom was as dark as any Spanish grotto, each dingy booth lit only by a votive candle in a highball glass. In fact, the only electric light, other than in the bathroom, was a single 25-watt globe over the bar's deco proscenium. A single window illuminated the poolroom, which was off to one side. There was no table service, no kitchen. The joint was run by an ex-beatnik called Wax, a burnt-out guy who concentrated more on his jazz CDs than on his bartending.

"Hey, man," Wax said, his back turned. "What can I get yah?"

"Rolling Rock." Nicholas grinned. The ashtray in front of him was littered with joint nubs. A stoned bartender was his favorite kind.

"Right with yah. Now where did my man Davey Brubeck slide off to?" Wax felt around between the top-shelf liquors for the wayward CD with one hand. With the other, he snatched a cold bottle of beer from an ice bin and plunked it on the bar. "Happy Hour: Two-fifty. You hiding up there, Davey?"

Nicholas slapped three bucks on the bar and retreated to the dark recesses of a booth. For all Wax knew, Joseph P. McCarthy had just bellied up for a beer. Except for two uniformed UPS guys playing pool, 113 was empty.

When Maureen entered some minutes later, Nicholas watched her squint around the room before approaching Wax.

"Hey, sister, what can I get yah?" Wax had given up on the Brubeck disc and slid Duke Ellington's *Blues in Orbit* into the machine. A boozy tenor sax filled the room with a sexy rhythm.

"How about a Bud. Anybody else been in here? A guy in a tweed suit?"

"Happy Hour: Two-fifty. Not that I recall. Guy got a Rolling Rock little while ago." Wax pointed at a speaker. "Go, Jimmy, go."

Maureen slid three dollars onto the bar and watched as Wax started to roll a joint behind the bar. When her eyes adjusted to the dark, she took another look around the room and saw Nicholas tucked in the corner. She approached him. She smoothed her skirt at the hips and he looked away, grinning to himself like an alley cat willing a passerby to pet him.

"How do you find these places, Nicholas?" Maureen slid next to him in the booth. "I mean, every time you get a new dive, I think I've seen the lowest…"

"Hey, at least the name is the address. Easy to find, easy to remember." Nicholas smiled, admiring the cut of her power suit. "Not a bad neighborhood either."

Maureen's lips twisted up one side of her face. She kicked off her shoes.

"I saw our friend Drummond Yager this morning, spent the afternoon making inquiries. Wanna hear about it?"

"Been a while since we..."

"Took some buffalo wings up to your place and got sauce all over your sheets?" She gave him a sly look from under her red locks. "We going to talk shop, or what?"

"Maureen, what is it with us?" Nicholas slid a hand down her thigh. She shuddered. "Animal magnetism?"

"Yeah, like animals, I guess," she said breathessly.

113 was dark, the music was loud, and the bartender was thoroughly preoccupied. Nicholas blew out the candle.

Booty Wood did his thing on muted trombone. Matthew Gee Jr. chased his licks as first trombone. And by the finale of "C Jam Blues," Duke's band was rocking full force to the insistent wails of Jimmy Hamilton's clarinet. End of Side 1.

Nicholas and Maureen headed back to his place to play the flip side. And eat a little chicken.

Chapter 8

Drummond Yager stepped out onto the balcony of his Upper East Side high-rise. The night was chilly, and he fastened his quilted satin robe over his silk pajamas to guard against the cold. Smoothing his silver hair, he took a pack of Dunhills from a side pocket. With hawklike intensity, his predatory eyes surveyed the river, snow-dusted rooftops, and the overcast sky. The clouds glowed a dull orange from the city's sodium streetlamps. To his right, tramway gondolas bound for Roosevelt Island whirred and rattled past. From his shadowy perch, Drummond tracked them, rabbits unaware of his presence.

The flickering, humming expanse of the Queensboro Bridge loomed just beyond. Across the East River lay Queens, and to his left, upriver, he could just make out the bulk of the Manhattan

Psychiatric Hospital on Ward's Island. Where Barney would soon be drilling every night. Where Drummond's coup de grace lay buried. Yes, the view from his corner balcony was commanding, which was precisely how he felt. This job was the decisive one. It had been a long, rough road. Time to cash in.

Drummond had been away from the civilized world more than twenty years. As a dying expatriate once confided, the nether reaches of the planet have a way of "picking away y'soul like so many bloody ants." Drummond hadn't understood what the man meant. As he'd sat in moldering Vietnamese hotels, dank ship galleys, and guano-carpeted caves, he'd idly wondered how you'd know if your soul, being a rather flighty thing, had been picked away by ants or not?

Cambodia, the Gobi Desert, Irian Jaya, Somalia—in search of "lost assets" he'd traveled to harsh, inclement outposts so isolated from the civilized world that they seemed utterly devoid of compassion or empathy. He'd been witness to bizarre human, animal, and societal cruelties the likes of which newspapers rarely dared report.

When Drummond first began his travels, he'd regularly taken respite in civilized company, relating his bizarre travels in hushed tones to plantation owners and diplomats over brandy and cigars. But as the years waned, his gruesome tales turned into rollicking dinner table anecdotes that made the ladies blanch. The soiree invitations waned too.

Shunned by polite society, he immersed himself

in back-to-back assignments. After two straight years in jungles, swamps, and war-torn wastelands, a fateful expedition "went bad." His guide was dead from a snakebite to the eye, the bearers had deserted with the supplies, and Drummond found himself alone, lost, and jaundiced from yellow fever. At his wits' end, he sat cradling a heavy golden Buddha on a muddy riverbank, where he hoped death would somehow be swift. Mosquitoes thick as fur covered the back of his sun-burned neck, and he was hypnotized by the blinding sun rippling on the undrinkable water he craved. Perhaps the bearers were right—the fat little statue had been cursed.

It was then that Drummond responded to a tugging at his sleeve. It was a small boy, a stringer of fish by his side and a dugout canoe beached nearby. The boy smiled and held out a plastic bottle of clear water.

The water, fish, and canoe saved Drummond's life that day, though the encounter proved fatal for the boy.

That's how Drummond discovered the ants had picked away his soul.

Not long after his recovery from yellow fever, Drummond's tour of duty was ended abruptly by the home office in a cryptic dispatch commending him for his tenure. He knew a scaffold for what it was, and an assignment to New York could only mean one thing. They'd given him this one last assignment to keep him busy while they debated how to retire him. And with all that he knew, and all that he'd done in the name of Newcastle Warranty, they certainly wouldn't trust him to live out his days quietly as a pensioner.

"Maybe I'll be shot by a mugger, or be run down by a lorry, or have a fatal overdose of heroin," Drummond whispered to himself. Leaning on the balcony railing, he scrutinized the next batch of people rattling by in a gondola. Was one of them an operative from Newcastle, keeping an eye on him?

"Drummond, it is cold here." Silvi, his slinky Argentine protégé, slipped out onto the balcony. She'd thrown on a full-length fox coat instead of a bathrobe. Turning up Drummond's collar as he lit a smoke, Silvi took his gold lighter and fished out a Dunhill from the pocket of his robe.

"You laugh again in your sleep." Silvi tried to blow smoke in his face. "Never I see a man so laughing in bed."

He put an arm around her waist, gave her a quick, edgy smile. "Barney's on his way over."

"Who do you think he calls today on the phone? Barney has maybe a double cross?" Silvi inhaled deeply, squinting at Drummond.

"Perhaps I should ask him who he was calling," Drummond said dryly. "Although I rather think we'd do best not to tip our mitt, not just yet. You're sure he didn't talk to anyone?"

"No. Maybe he speaks only five words, he waits, he hangs up."

"Do keep an eye out for that redhead I mentioned,

the one who came to my office asking about Barney. I'm unsure of that one."

From the living room, a buzzer sounded.

"It is him." Silvi pushed away from Drummond and disappeared into the living room.

Moments later, Barney stepped out onto the balcony, looking from Drummond to the nightscape. "Nice view."

Silvi reemerged with two sifters of cognac.

Barney took his drink with a nod and waited for her to retreat to the warm apartment before he continued. "We're all set with the Pazzo brothers."

"What have you told them?" Drummond's eye flitted from Barney toward Hell Gate.

Barney dug his free hand into his pocket and leaned on the railing. Drummond looked at him, waiting for an answer.

"That the Department of Environmental Protection was concerned about the buried boats leaking fuel oil into the water table. Told them we have to drill at night because during the day the Fire Department uses the area. Their training center is right across the way. Said I was hiring the Pazzo brothers for a small kickback." Barney took a sip of cognac.

"Are these Pazzos reliable, Barney?"

Barney cocked his head in thought. "Drillers are a pretty erratic bunch; they take a lot of stupid risks. But if they didn't, we wouldn't be able to pull this off. Not like this. We'd have to cut them in."

"Did you stake out the boats?" Drummond finished his cognac. Barney took another nip at his own and winced.

"I found the boats. All a matter of which is the *Bunker Hill*."

"Found?"

"Pretty sure."

Drummond considered Barney's furtive grin. He wasn't sure what to make of it. He looked at him until Barney finally raised his eyes to his. The ice blue eyes didn't tell him anything either.

"Let's say these drillers, when they hit the *Bunker Hill*, bring up gold on their drill bit. What then?"

Barney put his snifter aside. "Told them there used to be a smelting plant on Ward's Island, that there's liable to be a lot of stray brass in the substrate."

Drummond looked away, out to the river. "These Pazzo brothers had better not find out what we're on about, Barney."

"If they do?"

"Then I'll expect you to take care of it." Drummond gestured to a plain black box on a lawn chair. This would be the test, a gauge of Barney's mettle. Yager still had doubts about this specialist Swires. After all, he was a technical person, a blueprint and yardstick man, who from what Drummond knew had no direct experience in criminal enterprises. Then again, LAD listed Barney as "recommended" on their freelancer database.

Barney turned to the box, pursing his lips, thinking.

"This what I think it is?"

Drummond didn't reply. Barney knelt, put a hand on the lid of the box, and opened it. Inside: a pistol. A big, silver automatic. He studied it a moment, understanding that he was in a bit of a predicament.

Drummond felt he'd made Newcastle's goals clear, and this only made it clearer. Here was a giant multibillion-dollar insurer against the ropes. A series of poorly timed natural disasters around the globe had Newcastle near bankruptcy. A hurricane in Florida, fires in California, floods in Europe, a drought in California, a tsunami in the Far East, mudslides in California. Drummond's job was recovering sunken assets. Only he had to do it clandestinely. Why? Because as soon as "lost assets" hit ocean bottom they became treasure, and out came the government's paw looking for the lion's share. Barney was to find the boats covertly and figure out a way to quietly extract the gold. And to keep the operation secret by whatever means necessary.

Had Barney realized that Drummond's idea of expedience might extend beyond the drillers? That Barney himself might be expendable once the gold was recovered? Did he suspect that Drummond might be working to his own ends? If he had such suspicions, Drummond didn't detect them.

Barney lifted the big silver gun out of the box and looked down the sights at a passing gondola. Then he resumed his place at the railing and grinned casually.

"This should do the trick."

Drummond arched an eyebrow—such a cavalier attitude with a gun indicated that there was more to Barney Swires than fifteen years of mapping tunnels for the city. But then, Drummond had surmised as much. Otherwise Barney wouldn't have gotten mixed up with insurance work.

"Extra clips are in the box." Drummond dragoned smoke from his nose. "It's loaded."

Barney cocked his head. "I can tell, by the weight."

Drummond still wasn't completely sure if his bravado with the gun was part bluff. "Take it in the box," he said, flipping his cigarette off the balcony with his truncated hand, his simmering demeanor intensifying. "The number has been filed off; it's virtually untraceable. When you're through with it, dispose of it immediately. If you throw it in the river, there won't be any fingerprints. Best to drop it off a bridge, into deeper water. But get it as far away from you as possible, as soon as possible after use."

"Uh huh. And when do I get the van, the containers, the industrial collector, and generator?"

"Silvi will deliver them to Randall's Island the night you find the boat, after the drillers leave. Or are dispatched." Drummond lit another Dunhill. "I expect a report every night when you finish, no matter what the time. If I don't hear from you . . ."

Barney turned and carefully fit the gun back in the box, closing it and tucking it under his arm. "I won't double-cross you."

"We're talking about a great sum of money, Mr. Swires."

"I wouldn't be able to move that much gold by myself." Barney rubbed his jaw pensively, then tilted his head toward the apartment. "What about her?"

"That's not an issue," Drummond hissed.

Chapter 9

Barney exited the Quik Park on 61st Street and made a right onto First Avenue. He drove slowly and in time to the green lights, toward 125th Street, the Triborough Bridge, and Randall's Island. He had an hour before the Pazzo brothers showed up at the drill site, so he was in no hurry.

He glanced at the gun box on the passenger seat, orange light from passing streetlights washing over it in waves. Probably not a good idea to drive around with a weapon on the car seat, and he had a notion to maybe make a right at 79th Street and toss the gun in the East River at the earliest opportunity.

But then he remembered something Mr. Faldo once told him:

"Riches are obvious, but the things of real value are those we often take for granted. Regret is remembering the precious things we threw away before we know they are precious."

Well, he hadn't been talking about big silver automatic handguns, Barney knew that. But still, Barney wondered if he should figure out some way to make the gun a resource instead of a detriment. Drummond had in mind that he kill Sam and Joey. But what else could he do with the gun?

Another Faldo saying came to him:

"Indecision is the mind's inability to reverse itself, and to reverse circumstance."

That one always confused Barney, but he got the idea that it was a suggestion to think outside the box, or try considering completely opposite options than those that seemed to make sense.

So what if he gave the gun to the Pazzos so they could kill him?

The Faldo episode had occurred when Barney was ten years old. It began when he stumbled upon a backyard Japanese rock garden. It was so strange and curious that he fancied it must be the work of gnomes or trolls, who would surely enslave him should he be caught trespassing. On his second visit, it was Mr. Faldo rather than any gnome who caught him sneaking into the garden. Mr. Faldo offered Barney some mint tea in lieu of a talk with the police.

While Mr. Faldo wasn't Japanese, the white-haired old gent always wore bamboo sandals and a kimono. He proceeded to show Barney all the intricacies of his rock garden: the pond, the fish, the rock lanterns, the ancient, gnarled little trees. He said Barney could return to visit anytime, but that he must respect the rock garden as a place of tranquility—which Barney soon learned meant a place to goof off without a television.

Every day after school, Barney would slip through the bamboo thicket that surrounded Mr. Faldo's house and watch the old man work in his garden. They didn't talk much. Eventually, Mr. Faldo asked for his help digging a hole and Barney figured that was the end of that. If he wanted to dig holes, Barney could go home and help his father with yard work. But Mr. Faldo simply looked at him and waited. Barney finally capitulated. After a few spades of loam, the soil spilled away to divulge a pocket watch. Barney brushed it off and saw that there was an old train engraved on the cover.

Mr. Faldo marveled at the find and said that the train depicted was the Orient Express. Examining it carefully, he whispered to Barney that it was solid gold and made in Kathmandu, which was on Mount Everest, the final destination of the Orient Express. It was extremely valuable, he said, so valuable that you could never sell it for what it was worth because nobody would recognize its true nature, no matter what you told them. Anyhow, Mr. Faldo said, there were some things that had more value than money.

Barney didn't believe that. Not until the man at the bike shop wouldn't give him a Sting-Ray in exchange for the gold watch.

A week later, Barney was helping to clean out Mr. Faldo's fishpond when he found a huge gemstone ring. Mr. Faldo gasped and said it looked like the Maharajah's Serpent, a ring last seen when the Visigoths sacked Constantinople. The stone was about the size and color of a crab apple, but more purple. Mr. Faldo said he'd never found anything like these treasures while working in the garden before. He stroked his white hair thoughtfully and put a hand on Barney's shoulder.

"You must be a very special person. These things—the watch, the ring—come from the other side of Planet Earth. They must have been trampled into the soil so hard by invading armies, or dropped so deep into a glacial crevasse, or have fallen with their owners into a fiery volcano so bottomless that they worked their way through the planet until they surfaced on the complete opposite side of the globe.

"What's more, my friend, I think you may have a special life ahead of you. Why have I never found these things, old as I am? These are things both of the past and of your life's voyage."

Barney took the ring to a jeweler, who told him it was a worthless fake, and when he returned to the rock garden with this news, Mr. Faldo laughed.

"Do you expect a jeweler to know history when he sees it? Both the history of the ring and yours that has yet to unfold? For that is the value of this ring."

Barney thought about that a moment before surmising there must be many more valuables in the garden. He proposed some major excavations and mining operations, but Mr. Faldo held up a hand.

"You come to my garden for tranquility, which is knowledge of the self through diligence. A man must have balance of mind between his accomplishments, that which he desires, and that which he must be. Possessions are nothing of themselves, only the product of our own history. Our destiny. And destiny is who we are and ultimately will be."

Barney spent several days thinking about that. He looked up the big words in the fat dictionary at home, but he still couldn't make sense of it. And through his next several visits, he anxiously dug, scraped, and cleaned. Disappointment soon followed.

"You dig and scurry like a little dog. You have lost your tranquility and will not find the treasures until you get it back." Mr. Faldo smoothed his white hair and wagged a finger. "Be happy with useful work and what you have now, for you will not always have either. It is the path to a life of truth."

But it all came to an end one Saturday morning. Barney finished the latest *Phantom* comic book and decided it was time to escape the house before his father put him to work. He could hear his father down in the kitchen, probably dressed and ready for lawn work. Even since his mother had left them years before, his father's pursuit of the perfect lawn, the flawlessly trimmed hedge, and razor-sharp edging of the front walk were all-consuming. He cleaned, dusted, and vacuumed the house late into the night. And for all his fastidiousness, the meals he prepared for them—including breakfast—were relegated almost exclusively to cold cut sandwiches and raw vegetables. Even at the tender age of ten, Barney wondered if his father had gone off the deep end.

In the downstairs hall, Barney tiptoed toward the kitchen doorway. He could picture Father's curled lip and knit brow, a pipe clenched in little yellow teeth, the file scraping the clipper blades with a clang. He figured there wasn't anything Father liked more than sharp pruning shears.

From past experience, Barney knew there was such a thing as being too cautious. Peek around the kitchen door too many times before making his break and Father would catch him. Look once, then go, and he cleared the first hurdle.

With a can of 3-in-1, Barney dimpled oil on the hinges, carefully pushed the screen door open, and let it shut quietly on a slice of Wonder Bread he'd swiped from last night's sandwich.

Over the back fence, behind the neighbor's near-perfect hedge, up a tree, and over a garage roof got him to The Gully, a wooded lot adjoining a concrete drainage channel and dry culvert. Barney liked the culvert, a long dark concrete box that went under the highway. He could look up and see light through manholes and side pipes above.

Once on the other side, he was in Creek Park. Crossing the creek on a single-strand bridge made from rope he'd stolen from the school gym, he clambered up the hill to Mr. Faldo's house.

Barney pushed his way through the bamboo and into the rock garden. Mr. Faldo's spade was lying in the middle of the path, and the goldfish skimmed the pond surface hungrily. He sensed something was wrong.

"Hey, whadda you doin' here? A sneak thief!" a lean man in a tight brown suit shouted at him from the porch, stumbling down the stairs. "My father's not dead two days and you kids come in here stealin'."

A big woman in a black dress, sunglasses, and huge red lips came out after him waving a hanky. Pointing a finger at Barney, her big red mouth curled back and loosed a shriek that put Barney's short hairs on end.

Bursting back through the bamboo, Barney tumbled down the hill to the rope bridge, certain that the man in the brown suit was on his heels. In his haste, he slipped off the rope bridge and into the creek, but he scrambled up the opposite bank and ran for the culvert. Hoisting himself up into a chute off the culvert, Barney crawled up in a drainage basin and hid, listening to tires roar on the highway until it was dark.

In his flight from danger, the ring and watch had been dropped in the creek, no doubt destined to wend their way to the jungled shores of Kalimantan and the treasure box of an orangutan potentate.

He wondered what had become of his destiny.

Chapter 10

Nicholas lived in an eighteenth-century three-floor walk-up on historically colorful Water Street. Old New York knew no more sinister block, one that had once boasted dives such as Kit Burn's Rat Pit, where nightly rodent stompings, bear baitings, and terrier fights drew in the local skells, cribbers, and plungers. At another joint, bouncer Gallus Mags would bite off the ear of any patron she deemed obstreperous. Then there was Allen's Dance Hall, where any and all acts of deviancy could be enjoyed while the proprietor pontificated from the Old Testament. Every single building on Nicholas's block had been a rank bordello where hapless sailors fell prey to panel thieves, Mickey Finns, and shanghaiers.

But the digs where Kit Burn's brother-in-law once delighted audiences by biting the heads off rats for a quarter was now a cozy seafood restaurant. Lofts that once held dance halls and turpentine saloons became spacious track-lit dwellings. Where once the streets reeked of alcohol and dung they were now awash in fish market aromas and exhaust fumes from the Brooklyn Bridge. Formerly teeming with sailors, merchants, and thieves, Water Street was now a quiet, unremarkable cobblestone street.

Nicholas's apartment looked like it had been decorated in a hurry sometime in 1957. All the furniture was retro and arbitrarily placed, like feng shui gone bad. While some was new, much was old. A floral print couch and red wing chairs with white piping sat at opposite ends of the living room. There was a kitchenette that looked like it had never been cooked in and a bar with chrome and black vinyl barstools. A flecked pink and turquoise Formica kitchen table sans chairs. Strewn with junk mail, it hunkered between the couch and the large black TV—the only contemporary furnishing.

Down a short hallway from the living room with attached kitchen was the only other room, a large closet that served as Nicholas's boudoir—a room just big enough for a bed, a bucket of ice, and a pile of chicken wings.

"So, how was your chat with whatshisname?" Nicholas handed Maureen a spicy wing.

"You know, we're getting the sauce all over the sheets again." Maureen stripped the wing in a single bite. "Any more wine over there? These wings are hot." She brought her knees up under the black satin sheets.

"I got a cleaner over on Fulton who does a bang-up job with satin sheets. There's a towel over here somewhere." Nicholas handed her the wine.

"So you ready to hear about my talk with Drummond?" She drank from the bottle, spilling a little across her ample, freckled chest.

"Sure."

"I asked him for the foot. This guy Yager wasn't too thrilled about getting it for us. Better get another bottle of that stuff, Nicholas." Maureen handed him the bottle and plucked a wing from the pile, her glowing back exposed all the way down to her garter belt.

"Anyway, that was quite a yarn, Swires being crocodile chow."

"So what do you think?"

"I think this guy Drummond has some act going. So I made some calls to Costa Rica. I bet you didn't know, but I speak Spanish pretty good."

"I'd guess you'd have to, busting Mexican deportees all day."

"Anyhow, I got switched around a lot, you know, until I talked to the policeman who covers the area where Swires got eaten."

"So what did the cop say?" Nicholas took a pair of lemons from the bed stand.

"He corroborated their story. Then I said, 'Look, Enrique, how much are they paying you?' He said two hundred dollars. So I wired him three hundred."

"You think you have a bottomless expense account, don't you?" Nicholas started to roll a lemon on her thigh. She grinned wickedly.

"Well worth it. Said he was paid two hundred bucks to stick with the story, but that was all he knew. So I called the fishing lodge where the boats were stolen, told them the cop spilled the beans and that as a reporter for Condé Nast I was gonna ruin the lodge if they didn't spill their beans. Know what they said?"

"What?"

"They hung up. So I call the cop Enrique again, say does he want more money."

"How much this time?"

"Two hundred. I asked Enrique to nose around, get the lowdown. Long story short? Barney was never in Costa Rica. He had tickets, but someone else flew down there, and this someone stayed in a hotel under the name of Swires. But the guy at the hotel described a 'tall Argentine woman' staying in that room. That worth five hundred and change?"

"Yeah, that was worth five hundred. But c'mon, how'd you get this cop Enrique to open up like that?" Nicholas bit off one end of the lemon.

"Phone sex." Maureen grinned. "That's what he wanted. So I said a lot of stuff like '*Oooo, muey bien, Enrique,*' and groaned."

Nicholas sprayed the lemon on Maureen's chest.

"Ouch, sssss!" She recoiled. "That smarts, Nicholas."

"I'll make it feel all better."

The doorbell rang then, and it was ignored.

Some minutes later, there was some knocking on the front door, which was also ignored.

When the door was kicked open, Maureen rolled out of bed and onto her holster. But she no sooner had the Glock automatic in hand than there was a stranger with a badge and a gun standing over her.

"Police. Drop it."

Maureen let her pistol fall to the carpet, drawing the black quilt from the end of the bed around her.

Nicholas reclined under the black satin sheets, arms folded behind his head, looking at the two detectives with mild annoyance. The detectives were familiar from his recent arrest: one detective was hatchet-faced, the other roly-poly. Maureen moved from the floor and sat on the edge of the bed, groaning with embarrassment.

Nicholas cleared his throat. "You have a court order of some kind?"

"Yeah." Roly-Poly held up a piece of paper. "Sorry to bust in on your love nest here, or restaurant or whatever, but we gotta search the place. And take you downtown, pal."

"What's this about?" Maureen brushed her hair from her face.

"You got a permit for that Glock, nude lady?"

"In my bag, in the living room. I'm an ex-cop."

Roly-Poly went to get the permit. Hatchet Face pointed to Nicholas.

"Put your duds on, pal." He unfolded his warrant. "Seems a certain party indicated that you approached her this afternoon about selling a certain stolen painting."

Nicholas's eyes narrowed. BB might have thought that she had Nicholas by the balls now, but he was grimly delighted. If she pulled this move, it confirmed for him that she was involved in swiping the Moolman, and that she wanted Nicholas out of the way. Push had come to shove.

Cigar embers lit red dots in the eyes of the high rollers who stood behind shabby curtains, ogling the stacks of wire cages backstage. Spanish whispers mingled in the gloom as owners and trainers fastened razor spurs to gamecock legs and brandished glinting syringes to drug the birds. Above, pin feathers floated among the rafters in swirls of tobacco smoke, the eager arena crowd below inebriated with the aroma of chicken shit and malt liquor, like some barnyard den of iniquity.

"*Dos. El dinero en el pájaro* El Cid." Drummond pressed two one-hundred-dollar bills onto an outstretched wad of money. The bookmaker eyed Silvi's leather-bound cleavage as he handed Drummond his marker. After buying a small bottle of Martel and two tiny plastic cups for thirty dollars at the bar, Drummond led Silvi along the smoggy hallway toward the blazing lights of the stage. They went up two flights of bleachers to a second tier. The crowd could get a bit rough on the main floor.

"Cuba, it is where there is the best fights." Silvi

106 BRIAN M. WIPRUD

knocked back a shot of Martel. "Cocks, in Cuba, they fight with both legs gone." She sighed, stroking his forearm with her nails. "You go to fights for many years? Drummond, you do not look the type."

"For many years." Drummond sipped his cognac, thinking about the arena in Chad where children were forced to fight to the death, and then about Panama. "Have you been to Club Gallistico?"

"Hmm. Panama City."

Drummond eyed her for a reaction. He knew from her dossier that she'd been the mistress of a certain Panamanian general as a young woman, and had fled when the Americans invaded to take the country back from Noriega.

She met his eyes. "Yes, the fights there are good. But it is not, um, it is too . . ."

"Civilized?" Drummond arched an eyebrow.

Silvi only nodded, but held her thoughts as the crowd roared. The ring judge stepped into the arena, two men toting pillowcased birds in his wake.

Five minutes later, the jubilant crowd howled. The birds were reduced to flinching feathery wads, the arena strewn with their blood.

A portly, white-bearded man had sidled up behind Drummond.

"Ah, Mr. del Solar. Excuse us a moment, Silvi."

Drummond soon returned to his seat, smiling thinly. "Apologies, dear Silvi, an old friend."

He noted her forced smile, but it was necessary to keep her in the dark about this part of the operation. Her dossier also included a few incidents when she'd been double-crossed before. It was Drummond's experience that such people were out to settle the score. She was to be trusted even less than Barney.

"Drummond, what will we do with Barney?"

"You can do whatever you like with him, darling." His eyes twinkled. "Just as long as he ends up dead."

Chapter 11

BB had been married, once upon a time. Met the guy in art school. When they graduated they lived on the dingy urban edge making art nobody would buy. She had an inauspicious beginning selling art posters. He lucked out and got a job at the Met, first helping to restore frames, then actual paintings. Then he got a grant to go abroad, and by the time he got back, Beatrice had wheeled and dealed a partnership in the poster shop, which now did framing and mat cutting. During their separation, however, they'd drifted apart. They'd both realized they were bisexuals and couldn't tolerate an open-ended marriage. They continued to live together platonically until BB started brokering local art from her store, at which time the profit margins ballooned and she moved closer to her buyers on the

Upper East Side. She never heard from him again, and never went back to seeing men.

The morning dawned bright and cold. Karen came into the bedroom, her pale body and tiny breasts starkly framed by a flowing green kimono. BB smiled slyly from over a section of the Sunday *Times* as Karen climbed back into bed with a mug of strawberry coffee, black.

"Anything in there about Palihnic?" Karen ran a hand through her blond swirl, trying to tuck some behind an ear. She handed the coffee to BB.

BB sipped it and turned another page.

"Not that I've been able to find."

"That was a fiendish thing to do, BB." Karen giggled, then knit her brow. "I'm not sure why you did it, though, sweetie."

"I won't tolerate him sniffing around, whatever the reason. Or his impudence." BB flipped another page. "Nobody gets away with that with me. That's how I got to where I am. Like a bad dog, he needed negative reinforcement."

She knew that Karen would panic if she knew BB had indeed arranged to have *Trampoline Nude, 1972* stolen. Luckily Karen didn't know a Moolman from her cute behind. And taking the painting from that slob Bagby, was that really stealing? He'd stolen it himself, hadn't he? No moral high ground there.

"Well, I guess they arrested him, right? So now they look for the painting. And if he doesn't have it?" Karen idly stroked BB's ponytail.

"I'm not sure. I guess if he doesn't have the

painting they won't have anything to hold him on, and they'll have to let him go. But if he's smart he'll know he should steer clear of BB."

"Do you think he stole it?"

BB shrugged, glancing at auction listings. "Did you see this in Friday's paper? The auction at Phillips?"

"Yes. I thought we might go this afternoon, if you felt like it. But when Palihnic is released, won't he come directly to you, angry about you telling the police . . . ?"

"If he does, he's a bigger fool than he looks. What's to keep me from calling the police again?"

"But he suspects you. He may even think the Moolman you shipped the other day was the stolen one." Karen pulled the elastic from BB's ponytail, and her black hair fanned out.

BB set the paper and coffee mug aside, slid her hand into Karen's blond swirl, and kissed her. "But it wasn't *Trampoline Nude, 1972*, was it? If I have to, I'll get a restraining order."

She pulled the sash from Karen's robe and looped it around a stave in the bed's headboard. "Palihnic is small fish, Karen." She tied one end of the sash to Karen's wrist. "I'm a big fish, and I eat the little ones." She pushed Karen back against the headboard and lashed her other wrist. "He comes too close, and I'll just gobble him up."

Nicholas stalked out onto Centre Street holding his belt in one hand and his shoelaces in the other. He squinted up at the morning's bright frigid sky, possibly casting a derisive glance at the heavens in response to his ill fate, and marched straight up to the limo.

The sardonic Greek awaited him, holding the back door open.

"Somebody don't like you."

Nicholas ignored him as he ducked into the backseat and began relacing his shoes. Another night of fun in jail, only this time he didn't get Thules "Slick" Fick at his arraignment. What Nicasia managed this time was a judge who made himself available to order Nicholas released if he wasn't charged. Mr. Patel did the lawyering this time, and got admirably tough with the folks in the DA's office. Charge him or let him go. And the cops had diddly. No painting had been found, and BB hadn't seen the painting in his possession.

So they'd let him go, but as he could already see from the back window of the limo, Detectives Hatchet Face and Roly-Poly were hot on his heels in a gray Crown Victoria. They followed as the limo headed up Centre, across Canal Street, where this whole episode had begun, and back to Gravy's.

"Macallan, on the rocks with a twist." It was midafternoon, and Gravy's was almost empty. Nicholas peeked out the bar's curtained window at the Crown Victoria lurking across Irving Place.

"The twenty-five-year or the eighteen, sport?" It was the same bartender, only this time her long blond hair was worn in a cascade down her back.

Nicholas's eyes narrowed. "Eighteen."

"Have a double." The bartender filled the glass. "Your girlfriend is up in Tammany Hall. Doesn't look too happy."

"I'm none too happy myself." Nicholas smiled weakly and winked. He turned and trudged up the stairs. "And she's not my girlfriend."

Nicasia didn't say anything when Nicholas entered. She just shook her head like a parent who'd all but given up on her teenager.

"My troubles notwithstanding," Nicholas began, tossing his coat over a chair, "we have made some progress on Barney. We know he probably never went to Costa Rica, much less got eaten by any crocodiles. He might just be alive, somewhere." He sat down opposite Nicasia at the big round table.

"We?" Nicasia swirled her seltzer.

"Yeah. I've got Maureen McNary working on this with me." He took a healthy gulp of his drink.

"Isn't she the one who used to be an NYPD detective in Brooklyn?"

"Yup. She went private. Does good work."

"Why'd she leave the force?"

"I dunno." Nicholas shrugged. "Her explanation had something to do with a stick with shit on both ends. That relevant?"

"Maybe I should just have her work on the case. Let you rot in jail for a change." Nicasia flashed Nicholas a catty expression. "I'm not yanking your nuts from the roaster again, Nicholas. Understand?"

"You know, I just might not be as deep in shit as

you think, Nicasia. I won't be back in the jug. It's somebody else's turn." Nicholas finished his drink and stood. "I'll call when I've got more on Barney."

"When?"

He stopped in the doorway. Nicasia kept her eyes down.

"Look, it could very well be that Barney purposely misled you about where he was going. It may even be that he wants us all to think he's dead."

"What do you mean?" She reddened, pushing her glass away. "Why would he do that?"

"I dunno, but whatever the reason, he may have buried himself. He's a pretty clever guy. It's not going to be as simple as putting a skip trace on him."

Nicasia kept her eyes trained on the corner of the room.

"Hey, Nicasia?"

Red-rimmed eyes looked up at Nicholas, and he flashed a reassuring smile.

"Barney is almost as lucky as he is clever. I don't think we've heard the last of him."

Nicholas trotted down the stairs, wondering if that were true.

The bartender sauntered toward him from the other end of the bar. "What's your name?"

"Nicholas." He put out his hand and she looked him over skeptically. But she shook his hand just the same.

"Judy. I work Sunday, Monday, and Tuesday."

Nicholas slipped two twenties across the bar. "No matter how shitty a day I've been having when I come in here, I'm always a happy camper when I leave. Why is that?"

She crossed her arms. "Judy thinks Nicholas has a naughty streak."

He laughed and turned toward the door.

"A mile wide."

"Hey," Judy called after him, waving the netsuke peanut in the air between her thumb and forefinger. "You forgot your nut. The collateral."

"My nut?" He flashed her a foxy grin. "I'll leave it in your capable hands."

He stepped out onto Irving Place, sucking in the icy air to clear his head. He needed to get rough with BB, and his scheme to make her cough up *Trampoline Nude, 1972* needed to be implemented ASAP. Blackmail is usually nothing more than knowing the truth about someone. He needed detailed information about her finances, and fast. Ages ago that took time. Now it just took smarts and a keyboard.

Next stop: Mel. And Dottie.

Chapter 12

There were a thousand things to do back at Trident Mutual. Nicasia's desk was surrounded by a wall of paper: reports, invoices, field dispatches. She couldn't walk away from her desk for ten minutes without an equal number of e-mails filling her in-box. The light on her phone, a demanding red taskmaster, would be staring expectantly at her. But Nicasia couldn't bring herself to go back to the office.

So she made her way to her refuge. A cab dropped her off at 23rd Street and the West Side Highway in a little parking lot for Basketball City. It was part of the Chelsea Piers Sports and Entertainment Complex, an array of four piers and warehouses that had been turned into a driving range, bowling alley, pool, track, marina, and brew pub—a vast and hospitable improvement over the car impoundment lot it had once been.

Twenty minutes after arriving and dressed in a neoprene dry suit, knit cap, and life vest, she captained her kayak out into the formidable Hudson River.

New Yorkers, as a rule, are suspicious of their rivers. For a century or more, the citizenry has been fenced off, blocked from approaching the water by industry and shipping. During recent decades, concerted efforts to provide access to the Hudson, in particular, had successfully opened a series of connecting parks and public spaces along Manhattan's West Side. Yet the stigma of a polluted, putrid waterway was entrenched in the public's mind, even though the Hudson's water quality had been much improved.

Nicasia was pleased that most New Yorkers didn't come down to her sanctuary—that was part of what made it special. Uncrowded. Views of the city from near water level provided a valuable perspective. True, a most impressive portion of New York's midtown skyline loomed above, an expanse of skyscrapers and urban hum that made her feel small. Yet at the same time, she had the river itself to provide counterpoint. She could feel the Hudson's current rippling beneath her, feel its tide pushing or pulling the kayak. The forces were a visceral reminder that the river had been there before the mountain of brick, before the skeletons of steel, before the pinnacles of the Empire State and Chrysler buildings.

The city was, after all, only another phase of the landscape, like a canyon or mountain, and would one day be gone, wiped clean by planetary forces profoundly superior to frail human architecture and engineering. But the river would remain. For Nicasia, being in her kayak on the Hudson was something like holding hands with God, her business facade and worries trailing off in the current behind her as she paddled along Manhattan's bulkheads.

But the river represented so many things to her. Including the time she had been saved from a river by Nicholas. Including isolation and strength.

There was something about Barney's quiet self-assurance that had struck her when he came to Trident Mutual. She remembered the exact moment they'd met, when Nicholas brought Barney into her office, when his hand met hers, when she looked into those eyes, deep blue pools in the ocean. He was self-assured and yet utterly unassuming. As he sat in front of her desk, casually and yet concisely expounding on the vulnerability of everything from museums to private collections, he picked up an antique door lock assembly from her shelf. With a dime from his pocket, he completely disassembled and reassembled the lock as he spoke.

He had a certain wisdom that was hard to fathom, and thus drew her to him—like a river. There were depths and currents and dynamics there that she couldn't see, couldn't touch, but felt just the same. The currents of his emotion and soul were strong, and they could be intimidating. And yet she felt soothed by his presence, comforted, unafraid to lower her guard. Like the currents on the Hudson, his strength carried her, supported her. He was open and honest of heart as no man she'd ever met. But not as open about his past.

Since he'd been gone, the river was the only place where she could feel close to him. But after meeting with Nicholas, knowing that Barney was probably alive, the river provided little solace or quietude.

Why would Barney purposely pretend he was dead? Was he not what he appeared to be? She knew more about him than he knew, but was there something else in his past that had caused him to perpetrate this charade? Was it something she had done?

Her heart was breaking. Deep down she knew the truth was probably that Barney had gone back to stealing.

She recalled a line from a book she'd read in college, by Henry Fielding.

There is perhaps no surer mark of folly than to attempt to correct the natural infirmities of those we love.

She'd remembered that line once before. There was a man who had led a life as a liar and con man, and she'd fallen in love with him thinking he would change. That man had been Nicholas.

Had she been foolish to think Barney—a thief— could have reformed?

The questions repeated themselves in a rhythm, like that of her hips and torso dipping the paddle into the dark swirling water.

Chapter 13

By four AM on their first night of work, Sam and Joey Pazzo had smoked a mess of Salems and completed two borings.

Park Police dropped by wanting to know what they were up to. Barney stepped to the stage. He explained that they were doing tests for the Triborough Bridge and Tunnel Authority. He showed them a forged letter he'd typed on TBTA stationery authorizing the work. When he worked for the city, he'd collected a wide variety of official stationery, even from the office of the mayor. Officially, the land belonged to the Parks Department, but Barney also showed the officers a doctored tax map which showed that they were drilling outside of Parks Department property, within the right-of-way for the Triborough Bridge, which loomed overhead. Why were they drilling at

night? Tidal fluctuation, of course. They were trying to determine the relationship between aquifer
and tidal fluctuations as they related to the level of
hydrostatic pressure and potential resultant differ-
ential settlement on soils surrounding the bridge
spread footings. The cops didn't know what he was
talking about, so they left, satisfied Barney was on
the level.

By that time, the Pazzo brothers were packing up
for the night. Joey was lifting steel casing sections
onto the truck, a rig that looked like a roll-away oil
well. Sam got angry with a reluctant bolt that locked
the derrick upright.

"Fuck. Fuck, fuck, fuck, and fuck!" Sam was
hanging from the wrench.

Barney leaned on the rig, hands deep in his pockets. "Locking nut stuck?"

Sam turned toward the light of a lantern and
squinted with disgust. His jumpsuit was smeared
with grease, mud, and white bentonite dust.

"Whadda you think? Some fucker who had this
rig before us stripped the fucking nut. Now it's stuck
tighter than a fucking coconut in a monkey's ass."
Sam dropped to the ground, grabbed a pipe wrench,
and pounded the locking nut, shouting foul expletives aplenty.

Joey came to his brother's aid with a drilling rod,
the hollow end of which they slipped onto the end of
the wrench for extra torque. Like a couple of acro-
bats preparing a springboard stunt, they stood on
the extended pipe end, arm in arm. The nut gave

suddenly and the Pazzo brothers tumbled to the ground, cursing.

Barney carefully scanned his surroundings for any sign of the red pickup that he was sure had been shadowing him. "We done for the night?"

"Yeah." Sam's frog fingers turned the locking nut free.

"See you here, tonight at eleven o'clock. Get some sleep before then."

"Yeah." Sam turned and rocketed the locking nut off into the East River.

"Hey, Sam," Joey complained. "Now we're gonna have to go back to the shop . . ."

"So we'll go back to the fucking shop for another fucking locking nut! Louie never gives us *our* rig . . ."

Barney cocked his head. "Your rig?"

Sam got a dreamy look in his eyes. "Yeah, we got a rig, back in the yard."

"Well, it isn't, like, ours," Joey added. "But we got all the wrenches, and a tap set, an' extra locking nuts, an' all. But Louie, our boss, he took it away from us, thought we were gettin' too, you know, like it was actually ours."

"Now we got this piece of shit." Sam tossed a pipe wrench onto the back of the truck, smashing a cardboard box full of glass sample jars. He didn't seem to notice.

Barney rubbed his jaw. "Anybody in the yard at this time of night?"

"Course not. It's in the middle of the fuckin' night."

Barney pulled bolt shears from the truck and grinned at them.

"Hey!" Joey smacked himself in the head, smearing grease across his brow. "You know what he's sayin'? We cut the lock off the gate, get into the yard now, we can switch trucks, go directly to the day job."

Sam looked puck-stunned. Then he smiled, gaps showing between his teeth.

"Barney!" Sam grabbed the shears. "You're a fuckin' genius. A fucking criminal genius!"

And so it was in high spirits that the Pazzo brothers headed for the yard in Hoboken. They switched trucks and got to the site of their day job, at the end of Borden Avenue in Queens, ninety minutes early. Enough time to catch some shut-eye. They were so full of themselves for having swiped their truck back, and so excited by the idea of their boss, Louie, finding what they'd pulled, that they couldn't sleep. Aerosmith's "Rag Doll" pounded from the AM radio.

"Fuckin' Louie's gonna absolutely blow his top." Tears of mirth filled Joey's eyes as he handed a joint to Sam.

"He'd shit if he knew we was double-shifting." Sam chuckled, drawing deeply on the smoke. "It's perfect. Out there, under the Triborough, who's ever gonna see us?"

"Fuckin' nobody," Joey asserted, coughing out smoke from his lungs.

"Imagine, drilling for a boat. What the fuck?"

Sam shook his head, sipping from the dwindling joint.

Joey tugged on his lower lip, suddenly deep in thought.

"Hey, whadda you think we're really drillin' for out there, Sam? I mean, sure, a boat. But at night? Something feels, y'know, fucking funny about it, is all."

Sam pondered this a moment, then shook the idea away.

"Nah." Sam handed the roach back to his brother. "Like what could there be out there, under all that crap? Concrete, shingles, bricks, wood, and crap-ola."

"I dunno. But I found this. Barney dropped it by accident." Joey shrugged, passing a folded piece of paper he pulled from his top pocket.

Sam finished pinching the remaining smoke into an alligator clip and traded it for the paper. Unfolding it, he quickly figured out that it was a section of newspaper. It was some list of numbers, with the word "gold" followed by lists of countries and prices.

"Know what this looks like t'me?" Sam waved the clipping at his brother. "It's a list of, like, prices for gold."

"S'what I thought, Sam. Think it has anything to do with what we're doin'?" Joey flared his lighter, inhaled, and the joint disappeared.

"Fuck, I dunno. Maybe if we sleep on it."

"Yeah. Maybe."

The cab of the truck was a haze of pungent smoke, and the Pazzos had gone half-lidded. Quizzing, and the cannabis, had made them weary. Arms folded, they nestled into their respective corners of the truck's cab. The sky behind them to the east glowed purple with dawn, shimmering hypnotically on the skyscrapers across the river in Manhattan.

Sam let his lids and chin drop.

Joey commenced snoring.

Reclining in her older brother's Caprice on 61st Street, Maureen yawned and looked at the glowing green numbers on the dash clock. 6:05 AM. She'd been staring at the front entrance to an apartment building since midnight, and had witnessed Drummond Yager in the company of a tall Argentine woman enter the high-rise around three AM.

"Here we are again." Maureen sighed at the dashboard. Nothing worse than a stakeout. She'd done quite enough of them both as a detective and in her "new, improved" career as an investigator. She shook her head, thinking how things never quite turn out the way you want. First thing out of high school, she went into the Coast Guard to get a GI bill, which mystified her family. Why not just join the Fire Department? Four of her five brothers were firemen, her dad and granddad had been firemen. *What, the NYFD not good enough for you?*

In the Coast Guard, she worked as an MP, so she

used her GI bill to go to a university in Boston for a degree in criminology. Her family could see where this was going. *You're going to become a cop? What, the NYFD not good enough for you?*

While in school in Boston, a friend convinced her to join her as an exotic dancer at a strip club called Foxies. It paid well, sometimes eight hundred dollars a night, and Maureen never had trouble paying for her textbooks or buying herself a car. She managed to save quite a bit of money, with the idea of buying a house back in Brooklyn. That's when she met Donny, a Boston firefighter, and they got engaged, which pleased her family. Then Donny got the idea to start a fireproofing company, and she bankrolled him. The business failed, and so did their relationship. That was the end of the bankroll, and all of this coincided with her graduation.

So Maureen returned to New York and enrolled in the NYPD. Her father and brothers weren't even impressed when she rapidly made her way to detective. But being a detective, especially as a woman, really began to wear her down.

To be sure, Maureen considered herself a tough chick and could hang with the guys without her nose getting all out of joint over the stray sexist remark. Hell, she gave it right back to them, which, coming from an all-male Irish-Catholic family, wasn't alien to her. But the last couple of years she'd gotten sick of it. And that didn't necessarily mean that she wanted to paint her toenails and get chatty with the gals down at some beauty parlor. Maureen guessed what irked her was that she wanted to be able to act any way she wanted.

The Caprice was getting cold again, so Maureen started the engine. She recalled an instance when a dozen roses had been delivered to one of the patrol-women at her precinct. The cops all gave the woman a hard time about it, insinuating that she would soon be on maternity leave, never to be seen again. Even Maureen laughed at the blushing pa-trolwoman, who'd stuck her thumbs in her belt and told everybody to fuck off. Maureen had stopped laughing when she realized nobody had ever bought her flowers. Not even Donny, that scumbag.

She didn't regret leaving the force. The idea of becoming an investigator bloomed when in the course of her work she discovered how many at-large illegal aliens had bounties on their heads, ei-ther from bondsmen or from the Immigration and Naturalization Service. She soon discovered that the INS made virtually no effort to round them up, and that it was often as easy as flipping through a phone book to locate the would-be deportees. Ninety per-cent of her targets assumed by her manner that she was a cop and did not resist. Tougher than waiting for them to emerge from their domiciles was trying to cash them in at the INS, an agency of bureaucrats who lived for their next coffee break.

Thermos in hand, Maureen poured herself a cup of coffee and moaned. "Nothin's easy," she said aloud, but wondered if it wouldn't be a whole lot easier with a partner. Maybe a bit less lonely too.

The doorman opened the front door of the apartment building and the tall Argentine woman strode out onto the sidewalk wearing a full-length silver fox coat. She headed west at a purposeful gait.

"Christ, that coat. It's the size of a comforter, woman that tall." As Maureen started the car, she figured this might just be the tall Argentine woman who'd taken the Costa Rican jaunt instead of Barney Swires. Maureen rolled the Caprice to the traffic light at the end of the block. She could see the Argentine fox standing on First Avenue hailing a cab.

"Damn." Maureen grabbed her cell phone from the passenger seat and dialed a number.

"Patrick? It's Maureen. Yeah, I know what the fuck time it is. You wanna make some money? Fifty bucks plus cab fare. I need you to stake out a guy... Well, skip school today. I'm your big sister, I'll write you a friggin' note."

Fifteen minutes later, Maureen had tailed the cab to 25th Street and a white brick apartment building with a glass block lobby. It stood among similar buildings across from a red brick armory. After about an hour, the Argentine fox reemerged, now wearing jeans, a black turtleneck, jean jacket, and a black baseball cap. She proceeded to walk down the block to Park Avenue, past a couple of Indian restaurants to a self-service parking garage. When she didn't emerge for some time, Maureen got antsy, shoved her old police placard on her dash, and parked the Caprice in front of a hydrant. She bought a newspaper and a cup of coffee for the casual look, then strode down the ramp into the garage. She waved at the attendant in the booth as she passed, who ceased gnawing his bialy long enough to squint at what he assumed was a regular customer.

Pretending to be engrossed in her paper, Maureen drank coffee while she corkscrewed down the ramps, eyes scanning for the Argentine fox. She did a double take when she noticed what looked like her target's cap on the ground next to a red pickup. The truck's bed was covered with a tarp. Maureen bent down to pick up the cap, and when she stood, a fist hit her square between the eyes, her brain blossoming with an explosion of flowery sparks. And just as she was trying to force her eyes to see, the swimming blue haze flashed white, her lungs went cold, and her limbs stiffened.

Instead of calling for help, her reflex was to try to yell what she was thinking: "Mace."

Back up in the booth, Bialy Man could have sworn he heard a cow moo. But he was distracted by the dark-haired babe in the red pickup holding out her ticket and a twenty.

Patrick McNary was sixteen, the fifth and presumably last of Maureen's brothers. He was the only brother yet to become a fireman, and he didn't have the guts—not yet—to tell them he wanted to be a cop like his sister. It sounded bad, and would surely earn him no end of grief. But he had it all planned. He'd tell his family he was taking the test to become a fire-man, but he'd really go for police cadet. And when he had his cadet's uniform and peaked cadet hat, he'd saunter into Minogue's Bar and they'd lose it.

Patrick's mind played through this scene again and again as he idly skateboarded the sidewalk on 61st Street across from Drummond Yager's building. He'd only been there a half hour or so when a tall silver-haired guy exited the building and turned toward First Avenue. He fit Maureen's description, right down to the folded face and round specs. Skateboard under his arm, Patrick pulled a comic book from his jacket and pretended to read it as he walked. He crossed the street, following Drummond.

Yager was moving slowly, and before he made the corner, an envelope dropped unnoticed from his pocket. Patrick scooped it up—it could be impor-tant, something Maureen could use in her investiga-tion. Some tiny tubular things were inside, and as he approached the corner, Patrick held it up to the light. Crack vials. He figured Maureen must be working on some kinda drug case.

At the corner, Patrick peered around the edge of a building. Yager was hailing a cab.

A hand fell on Patrick's shoulder. He turned, star-tled. It was a cop. Despite being truant, Patrick was relieved until the officer said:

"What's in the envelope, kid?"

Patrick was a kid, but no dope. He'd been set up.

Chapter 14

After meeting with Nicasia, Nicholas had gone home to his apartment, showered, and changed into a tan suit of very coarse weave that matched his mood: prickly. The game of wits with BB required him to make the next move. He had bait for his hook; now he just needed to find the fish he was angling for. What had become of *Trampoline Nude, 1972*? He assumed she'd moved it quickly, partially because that's what most people did when they stole a painting, but also because he'd heard she was strapped for cash. It was too hot to sell in the domestic market, so it was probably out of the country. Money would have exchanged hands, a courier would have been deployed—you don't drop a multimillion-dollar painting into a FedEx pouch. Once upon a time the sale could have been done in cash, large sums. No more. You'd have to look far and wide these days to find a millionaire, or billionaire, who does anything with cash, and they're the retail market for stolen art. For that matter, you'd probably have to look far and wide across America to find someone laying out two hundred in cash at Costco. A *Homo sapien traditionalis* is defined by the tool. A *Homo sapien modernicus* is defined by the transmission of data. The swipe of a card, the flip of a phone, the click of the mouse. Every move BB had made was stored, somewhere, electronically.

So it was that Nicholas found himself climbing the stairs of a Federal-style town house in the West Village. It was on Commerce Street, a crooked, quiet little road.

At the top floor the door was opened by Melanie Dormé, whom Nicholas referred to as his computer person. Some would call her a skip tracer. Some would call her a credit investigator.

Mel knew what she was: a hacker. And that her name was unfortunately close to that of "The Velvet Fog"—Mel Tormé.

"Well, haven't heard from you in a while," she said, greeting him with a smirk. Mel was petite, and today she was wearing a white tank top and black miniskirt. Her dark hair was cut short in a way that might make a person think she was French—if one didn't already gather that from her last name. Nicholas often mused that her olive-toned skin would fit in well on the Riviera. He'd known her for about a year, intimately for only a few months. He'd been referred to her after his last computer person was incarcerated for probing the Pentagon's database.

Nicholas handed her a small cactus, gave her a peck on the cheek, and moved past her into the apartment, a sunny loftlike space with a skylight. It was more like a painter's garret than a hacker's dark cave. From a side room came the sound of a TV. Cartoons.

"I've been busy, you've been busy..." Nicholas waved a hand in the air while he studied her computer center. It dominated the room. Looked like a time machine from an old movie. A high-backed swivel chair was surrounded on three sides by monitors, servers, data ports, all kinds of stark-looking equipment that was out of place in the sunny room. Little green lights winked from the bricolage like errant fireflies. Cables, phone lines, and wires poured forth from the back of the contraption, each neatly tagged with color fasteners.

When he turned back to her, Mel was eyeing the pincushion cactus and its small pink flowers. "Well, at least you brought flowers." She crossed the room and placed it among an array of much larger ones crowded in front of the window.

"You don't really want me for a boyfriend, do you?" He began to lean against the time machine.

"Don't lean on that! You might knock it over!" She prodded him away from her equipment. "I want you for my husband. Can't you picture it? A bunch of little brats in tweed PJs running around, me making you chicken wings and wine for dinner."

Her sarcasm left him undaunted.

"Oh, it's a family you want?" He stepped forward playfully, taking her by the hands. "Well, let's start immediately, then."

"Ha." She pushed him away, pointing at her ring finger playfully. "Where's the rock? No rock, no family."

"Starting a family requires practice." He grinned.

"Boy, you are something else." Mel snorted. "You know, I have to wonder how you got to be like this. You have serious avoidance and commitment issues."

"What, now you're Doctor Freud? I suppose it all goes back to my parents, how I'm emotionally stunted, not loved enough. Or was it the day I lost my pink security blanket?"

She smirked. "It's gotta be something like that, because you are a mental case."

"Or maybe it's not me, but you, Mel. Do you have *trust issues*? Hmm? Look, let's forget about all this psychobabble. I'm a charmer, Mel, and you liked to be charmed. Can I charm you tonight? I have a few things to do, but we could do dinner, I'll take you to one of those bizarre little plays you like on the Lower East Side..."

"It's Saturday night, Nicholas. I have plans."

"Plans? Really?"

"No, I don't, damn you."

"Well, now you have a date. What could be so bad about that?"

"I refuse to be that easy, that's what's so wrong

with that." She squinted, but her smirk dissolved. "Besides, I don't have a babysitter."

"A babysitter?" Standing in the doorway to the side room was a miniature seven-year-old version of Mel, wearing baggy red pants and a bright green T-shirt, white socks on her feet, and red plastic butterfly barrettes that were only partially successful in keeping her black locks out of her eyes.

"I don't need a babysitter, do I, Nicky?"

"Hey, sugar snap." He held out his fist, and she marched forward warily, bunched her tiny olive hand into a fist, reached up and bumped his with hers.

"Mai tai," they said in unison. It was their greeting, Nicholas's invention. Told her it was good luck. The way people greet each other in Fiji.

"Don't sugar-snap me." Dottie squinted at him suspiciously. "Nicky, you promised."

Like mother, like daughter.

Nicholas suddenly felt warm. He'd forgotten. What? Didn't know.

"I haven't forgotten, if that's what you're thinking," Nicholas fibbed. He glanced at Mel, who seemed to enjoy watching Nicholas being called on the carpet by her daughter.

"You said you'd get me a tookie tookie bird, and that if a little girl has a tookie tookie bird, she can stay at home all alone because the tookie tookie bird can dance and sing and juggle mice and make grilled cheese sandwiches, and is fierce as a lion and will protect its master no matter what, against burglars and thieves and pirates."

"I said that? I mean, yes, I said that, and it's true. Tookie tookie birds are hard to come by this time of year in New York. But I'm working on it."

"Are you sure?" Dottie's lip twisted. Her big black eyes bore straight into his, dark lamps of innocence and trust.

"If Nicky says he'll get you a tookie tookie bird, I'm sure he means it." Mel slid over to Dottie and wrapped an arm around her. "He wouldn't lie. Would you, Nicholas?" Sarcasm.

Nicholas could handle Maureen. He could handle Mel. He could handle BB, Nicasia, and Ozzie. Even pirates, if he had to. Real pirates, with guns and knives. Even evil, double-crossing mentors like Smith. But not Dottie. This was new. Oddly, he liked it. Like his relationship with his brother's gal, Angie, he didn't know why. Didn't want to know why. Think fast. Faster.

"OK, here's an idea." Nicholas put a hand on her head.

"This'll be good," Mel muttered.

"I can show you a tookie tookie bird tomorrow night. He won't be alive, but at least you'll get to pet one and see that it looks just the way I said it does."

Dottie's face went from March to June, all sunshine. "Tomorrow? Why not now! I want to see a tookie tookie bird! Let's go now! Mommie, can we go now?" She grabbed his hand from atop her head and pumped his arm excitedly.

Mel shot Nicholas a scornful look. "Nicholas, honestly."

"Really, Mel. I know where we can go see a tookie tookie bird. But we have to wait until tomorrow."

"Tomorrow?" Dottie whined. "But, Mommie..."

"That's enough, Dottie." Mel's tone put the frown back on Dottie's little round face. The girl slumped, draping herself on Nicholas's arm dejectedly.

"How about the two of you come to Sunday dinner with my family?"

Mel cocked her head, like she'd misheard. "Nicholas Palihnic has a family?"

"You bet. So come tomorrow night to dinner, with my family. My brother. He has a tookie tookie bird."

A bunch of things were on his mind. It would get Angie off his back about settling down, about making his life less arbitrary. A "girlfriend" would look good. Bring Mel to dinner, mix things up, make the dinner more tolerable. Garth would be less inquisitive of little brother's lifestyle, more solicitous to his "date." Mel: she'd think he took her seriously. Dottie: gets to see a tookie tookie bird. Garth must have something among all that junk that would pass for one. Nicholas hoped so. At the same time, Mel sees his "family." Were these kooks and their taxidermy something she wanted in her life? He and Mel kidded a lot. Nicholas didn't really think she wanted marriage. She just wanted to be taken seriously. Whatever that meant. You didn't need to understand women to get them to do what you wanted. Mostly.

"You *are* joking?" Second time in an hour a woman was looking at him like he was selling curealls from the back of a covered wagon.

"They have a tookie tookie. Garth collects taxidermy. Honest."

Dottie loosed a low moan. "Why do I always have to wait? I have to wait to get a falafel. I have to wait to get an Italian ice. I have to wait to go to the ice rink. Wait, wait, wait." She groaned: "What's taxi termy?"

"Animals that are no longer alive but look that way," Mel said, stroking Dottie's head. "I dunno, Nicholas..." She furrowed her brow and searched his eyes.

"Mel," he said, keeping a straight face, "I would be honored if you'd let me introduce you two to my family."

"Dottie, go back in and watch cartoons. I'll bring your snack in a little while."

Dottie slid off Nicholas like a wet rag, the embodiment of abject disappointment.

"Go on," Nicholas added, putting out a fist. "We'll go see the tookie tookie tomorrow. Be here before you know it."

Dottie bumped his fist with hers, mumbling, "Mai tai." As though trudging through a swamp, she disappeared back into her room.

Mel sighed and stepped up to Nicholas. Straightening his thin tie with her fingers, she said, "What time tomorrow?"

"I'll ring at precisely seven, a cab waiting."

"That's a little late for Dottie."

"Late?"

"She goes to bed at eight."

"Eight?" He tried to conceal his surprise. How could anybody go to bed at eight?

"Five would be better."

"Five? OK, five it is."

"If you're late, one minute late, I won't answer the buzzer. Got it?"

"Fair enough. So, now that we've settled that..."

"We're not having sex."

"Mel, I don't think of you that way." Eight. Well, if Dottie went to sleep at eight tomorrow, perhaps... "I don't see you just for sex."

"I know. You need information."

"I do."

Nicholas could tell Mel was uncomfortable with this whole turn in his tact and wanted to change the subject to something safe, like business. She slid from between him and the cactuses, climbing into her time machine. "You mean it, don't you?"

"About what?" Nicholas drifted behind her chair. "You mean tomorrow? I wouldn't kid about something like that."

Her hands hovered over the keyboard. "OK, so who is it you want me to gut?"

"Beatrice Belarus, gallery owner." He spelled the name.

Her fingers began clacking on the keyboard, and the New York City Department of Investigation database popped up. "You want everything?"

"The whole shebang."

Chapter 15

Seeing as how he was supposed to be in Costa Rica, Barney had pointedly rented an apartment in an obscure part of town. He wanted it close to Little Hell Gate, which necessarily meant at or near one of the three termini of the Triborough Bridge. One end was in Harlem, one was in the South Bronx, and the third was in Astoria, Queens. Nicasia's extended family was Greek and inhabited Astoria. They'd had a good gander at him during their Easter Feast, so Queens was out. And to set up in either Harlem or the South Bronx would make him the consummate "Urban Pioneer"—a title Barney felt sure would get him scalped by the natives. So he had to venture farther afield.

Back when he worked for the City, he'd become familiar with an insular Bronx neighborhood called

Pugsley's Point. It was within easy access to both the Bruckner Expressway and the Triborough Bridge.

Pugsley's Point was a crusty slice of suburbia where those of modest income had staked a claim to cheap white clapboard houses. The peninsula community was decidedly for the nautically minded, the salts and the sailors. Boats, grand or modest, graced nearly every narrow driveway, often dwarfing the little white houses. Weekends united the populace of Pugsley's Point in a lemming-like drive to the nearest boat launches, mere walking distance from any home. They towed their boats to the launches, parked their cars back in their driveways, revved up their Mercs, and blasted up to Long Island Sound to wet a line and drink beer.

On summer days Pugsley's Point became a ghost town. But in the winter, as when Barney took up residence, the entire populace was stricken with cabin fever as bad as any in Juneau or Nome. Boats were shrink-wrapped in their blue cocoons for the winter and men in yachting caps eagerly awaited the next *Boat Show Magazine* or *B&B Marine Products* catalogue. And, of course, they braved ice, wind, and snow to saddle the barstools at Mariner Jack's on River View Avenue.

Although he'd technically been away in Costa Rica for a week, he'd only been drilling for two nights. So Barney had found more than a few hours to spend at Mariner Jack's: The regulars already knew him as the boatless renter who lived on Hull Street, but they pretty much left him to himself,

making it an ideal place to catch up on research
while enjoying a good cup of coffee and a decent
burger. Drummond had given him a dossier on a
boat called the *Bunker Hill*, the channel between
Randall's and Ward's islands, and Hell Gate—a fork
of the East River that led to Long Island Sound.
He'd pored over the history lesson several times already. But exhaustive and sometimes repetitious
study often paid off.

The California Gold Rush of 1849 had created
the need for better, faster ways to move gold to the
East Coast. This was before hammers drove the
golden spike, so clippers competed for the shortest
sailing time around the horn. But clippers were
soon eclipsed by steamers on both coasts using a
Central American shortcut. A railroad was built
across the narrow Panamanian isthmus, shortening
the San Francisco to New York trip by two
weeks. Vanderbilt got into the act, built his own
Nicaraguan railway, and challenged the reigning
U.S. Mail Steamship Company and all others to
beat his service.

Competition was keen. Banks paid well for safe,
fast gold shipments, which were commonly in excess
of one million dollars. In a bid to win the gold delivery contract for a Boston bank, Vanderbilt challenged the New Haven Steam Ship Line's *Bunker
Hill* to a race from New York to Boston. And to
make the stakes equitable, Vanderbilt put an equal
quantity of his personal gold into the hold of his
steamer *Stuyvesant*. Each boat was loaded with

60,000 troy ounces of gold, which at the price of the day equaled $1,200,000. Converted to a contemporary price, that would work out to something well over $20,000,000 per ship.

The route they were to follow to Boston took them up the East River, through Long Island Sound and Block Island Sound, around Nantucket, and into Boston Bay. There was, however, a catch. To get to Long Island Sound from the East River, vessels had to pass through Hell Gate, a narrow, turbulent, rocky passage subject to reversing currents and tricky tidal fluctuations. Navigating Hell Gate, which divided Randall's and Ward's islands from Queens, required specially trained pilots to sail an S-curve of whirlpools around jagged rocks and deep holes. In the morbid fashion of the day, the most notorious rocks had been given nicknames like The Grid Iron, Hog's Back, The Pot, Frying Pan, Mill Reef, Governor's Table, and Negro Head. In a single month in 1848, upwards of fifty vessels were wrecked in Hell Gate—as many as seven in a single day. New York merchants lobbied Congress to clear the channel, but the blasting of Hell Gate's rocks didn't commence until 1866.

It was too late for the *Bunker Hill*. Conditions were horrendous on that morning of March 1855: fog, ice runoff, a low tide, and no wind. But a contract was in the balance. It's said that the *Bunker Hill* had passed the most treacherous rocks—Hog's Back, Frying Pan, and The Pot off Hallet's Point—and was pulling out of the S-curve when she was driven off course by an out-of-control schooner. She drew too close to the shore of Randall's Island and fetched up on a rock called Fat Annie. Now, although the *Bunker Hill* boasted an iron-clad hull, her paddlewheel smashed, dislodging the axle and taking on water at the shaft as she listed. Although the sails were hurriedly raised, there was insufficient wind to regain control. The *Bunker Hill* swirled back into the main channel and sank somewhere off Hallet's Point in a whirlpool eighteen fathoms deep.

Local tugboat captains were proficient at retrieving wrecks from Hell Gate's shallower traps during the brief slack tides. But deeper wrecks remained unreachable, and were covered in debris from subsequent rock-blasting operations.

Newcastle Warranty had insured the *Bunker Hill*. One hundred and thirty-five years after the accident, a crack unit of Newcastle LAD investigators was formed to collect data on the prospects for the retrieval of lost ships. When they tried to pinpoint the current location of the *Bunker Hill*, studying nautical charts and cross-referencing them with maritime records of ships that sank in Hell Gate, they found something interesting.

Just downriver of where the *Bunker Hill* sank was Hell Gate's most treacherous rock: Flood Rock. This obstruction was a jagged underwater extension of Hallet's Point on the east shore in Queens. At the behest of New York City, the U.S. Army removed Flood Rock on October 10, 1885. This feat was accomplished by digging a deep shaft in Hallet's Point and tunneling under Flood Rock. The project was unprecedented: 300,000 pounds of dynamite was packed into the tunnel and detonated, removing nine acres of solid rock in one dramatic explosion heard as far north as Poughkeepsie. It was the largest man-made explosion prior to splitting the atom. Hell Gate was instantly widened from 600 to 1,200 feet.

After this event, the area was resurveyed to assess what, if anything, remained to be blasted. The survey discovered the remnants of hundreds of unidentified wrecks, one of which was noted to be a steamer. The significance of its appearance after the Flood Rock explosion went unnoticed. Until recently. The Newcastle theory went that the explosion and cascading rocks had flushed the iron-hulled *Bunker Hill* from its original resting place and shifted it toward Randall's Island. They reasoned she was only loaded with two and a half tons of cargo, was principally made of buoyant wood, and yet had an iron hull that would have kept her from breaking apart. Computer modeling further demonstrated that this was all feasible.

Records showed that the wreck in question, along with numerous others, had been dragged from the channel's edge by the Army Corps of Engineers and deposited between Randall's and Ward's islands, after which New York City covered her with construction debris to connect the two islands with a landmass.

Barney was just opening Section Seven of the

report, "Medium of Exchange," the part about the gold being transported, when he realized he was being hailed.

"Hey!" A group of three boat junkies at the bar gestured him over eagerly.

"Buddy, c'mere. We got a boat for yuh." Alvin, a sallow carrottop, held up a local ad magazine.

"Me?" Barney stuffed the documents back in their folder.

"Yeah, c'mere."

He tucked the folder under his arm and sauntered over, a bemused glint in his eye. "Do I need a boat?"

Alvin sneered. "Yuh need a boat, all right. Yuh just don't know it yet. Look, buddy, right here."

Barney took the magazine, cocking his head at a circled classified. He sipped his coffee, coolly scanning the ad.

"Not much to look at," Alvin allowed. "Not much to look at. But it's in good shape, good shape. Just up the road, on Bronx River Ave. Got twin Mercs."

"Center console," one of his pals added.

"Comes with a trailer," the other pal said.

Barney rubbed his jaw. "I appreciate you thinking of me, but..."

"Five thousand. Bet yuh give him five thou, it's yuhrs." Alvin snapped his fingers, took a fresh beer from the barmaid, and handed it to Barney.

"Uh huh. Now, just exactly what am I going to do with a boat?" Barney's exclamation made the whole bar go silent. He scanned the room. "That is, I don't know anything about boats."

At this, the audience shook their heads dismissively and resumed their nautical chitchat.

"I do," Alvin assured him. "I'll show yuh where to launch, where to fish, where to buy gas."

"Don't forget the magazines," one pal chirped.

"An' the catalogues," the other pal said.

"But yuh gotta get a boat first, buddy." Alvin was practically begging.

Barney perused the ad again, pursing his lips. He had been intending to execute his plan on Randall's Island with a truck. But a boat might be better. He finally looked up.

"Let's say I buy this boat. Do I need a license?"

They laughed and shook their heads.

"Could I go anywhere I wanted?"

They laughed and nodded their heads.

Barney pointed his finger at them like it was a gun. "Even down to Hell Gate?"

They swallowed their beer hard with an audible, collective gulp.

Hell Gate's reputation died hard.

Chapter 16

There was no look of surprise on H Olbeter's face as he entered 113 15th Street. A dark Hispanic man of medium height and sturdy build, H sported a velvet-collared overcoat and shiny shoes. He stood in the doorway nodding while he carefully removed kid gloves, tugging at each finger separately, like some English gentleman entering his club for an evening of whist. When the gloves were stowed, he approached the bar.

"Anybody else in this place, my friend?"

Wax was shaking his head at a flashing chrome CD, evidently disappointed.

"Y'know, CDs replaced records 'cause of needles and skips. And they replaced cassettes 'cause these babies got no moving parts. But when one of these things goes haywire, man, you wonder why you ever threw your turntable on the trash heap." Wax glanced up at H. "Somebody got a scotch a little while ago. Might be over there somewhere."

"Martel, my friend, neat." H stroked one of his pointy sideburns and took in his surroundings. It was then that he spied Nicholas in the corner booth, behind the flicker of a candle, watching him.

"Very classy place you have here." H sat across from Nicholas. "You just hide back here and spy on your friends, eh?"

"And on anybody else who might be looking for me. Don't forget, I once got cornered in a bar by Psycho Lawyer Bob." Nicholas smirked.

"That loco took us to Belize." H sipped his Martel. "Where to this time, my friend?"

"How come it took so long for you to get back to me?"

"That was just the other day. What, I'm supposed to wait at home for your calls? I'm a busy guy, Nicholas, got a lot of very classy clientele these days."

"For instance?" Nicholas folded his arms, and his tan suit crunched.

"Confidential, my friend, all very confidential."

"Someone told me you were stooping to courier work."

"Stooping?" H smoothed his hair. "It so happens, Nicholas, that confidential courier stuff can be very lucrative—"

"Gofer work."

"—high-security work that requires someone who can really keep their eye on the ball."

"Like you, huh?" Nicholas shook his head and sipped his Macallan.

"It so happens, my friend, that I just made seven grand in four days transporting a painting to Hong Kong. Now, what you been doin', amigo?"

"Confidential."

"Funny thing. A little tweety bird told me you got yourself arrested for murder."

"Never a dull moment." Nicholas winced.

H smiled. "So while me and my lousy courier job put a cool seven grand in my pocket, your snooping got you jail."

"Seven thou in your pocket?"

"Sure, I'm gonna get it. In cash too." H flushed. Nicholas laughed.

"You mean to tell me you didn't get the money up front? Not even half?"

"BB's always come up with it before. She's been real straight." H swigged the rest of his Martel and tried to ignore the accidental disclosure.

"Really? I was at an opening the other day, at BB's invitation. We talked about *Trampoline Nude, 1972* and she mentioned she had a buyer in Hong Kong."

"Forget it, Nicholas. It don't work. The painting I moved? It was a Moolman, but it was not *Trampoline Nude, 1972*. It was *Trampoline Nude, 1978.*"

Nicholas shook the ice in his glass. "How could you tell?"

"Because it had a big 78 right in the center, that's what."

"OK, OK. But you can't blame a guy for trying, H. BB was acting awfully suspicious about Moolmans in general. I still think she may have it."

"My friend, she's a rich lady. She don't need to move hot..."

H looked at the folder Nicholas slid in front of him.

"What's this?"

"You know Mel Dormé, don't you?"

"Of course. 'The Velvet Fog.'"

"*Melanie Dormé?* With a capital *D*?"

"Ah, yes. Credit investigator. Very pricey."

"Mel dug that up for me, and you're right, it wasn't cheap." The promise of Sunday dinner hadn't brought her price down any. "It's about BB. Chase Bank account, loans, Visa, MasterCard, Diner's Club, Merrill Lynch, Fidelity Investments. Check it out, and you tell me where your seven grand is coming from. She's already written over twenty thousand in checks to her contractor this month and there's not a penny in the bank. She's overdrawn, and her credit is all soaked up. See, your plane tickets are on the next page, on Visa, which is maxed. BB hasn't cut a rent check in three months. She's strapped."

H flipped through the folder, then went back to the first page and squinted.

"But with my own eyes I seen the guy in Hong Kong wire two and a half million dinero to her account. Day before yesterday, I think." H rubbed a sideburn nervously.

Nicholas put the booth's lone candle on the print-out and pointed.

"See here? It all went to Christie's and Sotheby's." H squinted at the folder again.

"I think I must drop a dime on BB, see where my money is at." H scowled, flipped open his cell, and made tracks outside to get a signal.

Nicholas sauntered up to the bar for another Macallan, smiling. Wax was nowhere to be seen, so he tapped himself a short Guinness while he waited for the bartender's return. The debriefing of H hadn't been a complete accident. Mel had not only supplied Nicholas with BB's complete financial portfolio but her recent telephone records as well. Nicholas had recognized H's number, listed on the morning after the painting was swiped. Just another reason he kept changing his own phone number. Any skip tracer, credit investigator, or hacker worth their salt could splay a person's life out like so many cold cuts at an office party.

Nicholas's real coup, though, was H's description of *Trampoline Nude, 1972*. Moolman was noted for being a clever and playful artist. The theory behind his Trampoline Nude Series was that the title led to preconceptions about the paintings' contents. People saw nudes, they saw the trampoline, all in abstract, of course. What Moolman had painted was merely the abstraction of a pineapple and a pair of bananas on a carving board, therefore proving the point that people see what they want to see, or are told to see. Especially when the subject is sex.

The numbers in the paintings were another precocious aspect of Moolman's work. It was both a comment on the fact that people are always ascribing numbers to paintings, by way of price, thus losing the sense of actual aesthetic value, and a play on people's natural inclination, again, to ascribe the painting's title with the content. For example, *Trampoline Nude, 1972* had a large "78" painted in the center, right on the pineapple's belly.

Nicholas knew where the painting was: Hong Kong. But that information alone wasn't going to get him his finder's fee. The trick would be figuring out a way to get it back to the U.S. and into his possession. The only way to do that would be to make BB get it back.

Maureen not only had to suffer sore joints from the effects of the Mace and a puckered purple eye socket from the punch, but she also took a lot of grief getting Patrick off the hook.

"If your mother was alive today . . ." Dad brogued over the phone, as much a threat as a lament. She was using the desk phone of a certain Detective Brady. After being pinched, Patrick had told the police at the local precinct that his sister used to be a cop. She'd gotten a "courtesy call" from Brady and had to do some fancy explaining to get her brother off the hook.

"Dad, this was all my idea; I take all the blame."

"You know what killed your mother, don't you?"

Dad never spared the big emotional guns. Maureen flushed, freckles burning on her cheeks.

"Yeah, Dad, I know. You remind me just about every time I see you. It's like I took a knife and stabbed her, right? It was me becoming a cop that gave her cervical cancer, right?"

"Don't you take that tone with your father! Talking about your dead mother's privates! And to think that after all the years at Holy Redeemer and Mass every Sunday that a child of your good mother's could turn out—"

"Cut it out, Dad! Cut the Catholic guilt trip, OK? I'm gettin' Patrick out of this, OK? I'll have him home in a few hours. So have a Bud and choke on it." Maureen slammed the phone down. Detective Brady looked across his desk at her.

"The Catholic guilt trip?" Brady's mouth twitched, and he took the toothpick from his lips and put it behind an ear. He was a big man, with dark hair and eyes—like a football player with a holster under his arm. On his forehead was an indentation and scar from where he'd been shot in the forehead as a beat cop. A small-caliber bullet that had barely penetrated his skull.

"But what's a good Catholic like him got against cops? God himself is police commissioner." Brady crossed himself and winked.

"Dad was a fireman, four of my five brothers are firemen. I was *supposed* to be a fireman." Maureen tried to unclench her jaw. It was making her head ache and her eye throb.

"So where'd you get the shiner, McNary?" Brady put the toothpick back in his mouth. Maureen sighed as she saw Patrick being led into the squad room. She shrugged wearily.

"I gave up my shield for a PI license, Brady. And I've learned they don't call 'em shields for nothin'. Thanks again. I owe you one." Maureen handed him her card and stood. Brady took his feet off the desk.

"OK, you owe me one. How about dinner?"

She thought he must be kidding, but he wasn't. Was he asking her out? She stared at him, mouth agape.

"You asking me out? Or do you want me to buy you a steak?"

"Yeah." Brady gave her a smile. "I'm asking you out."

This quarterback was asking her? The girl with the shiner? She didn't exactly feel like a Dallas cheerleader.

Maureen put a hand on her hip, shaking her head at the floor. "Can I ask a dumb question?"

"Shoot." His dark eyes looked up at her, even and deep. Not cold, not hot. Deep.

"Why is it guys pick the worst time to hit on me? It's always when I'm hungover, or have the flu, or am in an emergency room, or . . ."

"How about Monday?" Brady stood, sliding her card into his pocket. He was now looking down at her. A damn sight taller than Nicholas, that was for sure. She suddenly wondered if he was the kind of man who picked up his women and set them on the bed. Her feminine reflexes kicked in. A sly, flirty grin worked up one side of her mouth.

"Ring me Monday. I'll let you know." She tossed her hair as she turned away, and she left the room with a bit more swish than usual.

Maureen led Patrick downstairs and outside to where police cars were parked all over the sidewalk. Her borrowed Caprice was squeezed between a couple of squad cars, and they had to slide into the car through barely open doors. Without a word, Maureen pulled three Buds from under the seat and handed one to Patrick, who hesitated only briefly before popping the top. The way Maureen was brought up, it was a matter of course that you occasionally gave a teen a beer. The common Brooklyn wisdom went that it was better to have your kid—or kid brother—learn something about drinking with adults around. Besides, he'd earned it.

Rush hour had begun, and FDR Drive was a veritable speedway, tightly bunched cars at high speed jockeying for the Brooklyn Bridge exit, tires squealing as the pack cornered the Corlear's Hook bend. As the Caprice ascended the South Street Viaduct, the sun's orange beacon flared briefly from between the forest of downtown skyscrapers. In the rearview mirror, uptown was in twilight, a Canadian front pushing in a stern-looking assault of clouds.

"So what happened to you?" Patrick asked finally.

Maureen leaned on her horn and bullied her way into the right lane just before the exit.

"What do you think?"

"I think you got clobbered. You talk to Dad?"

"Shut up an' drink your Bud. Your sister's tryin' to think." Where the ramp inexplicably turned from two lanes to one, Maureen jerked the wheel right. A screech and a protracted honk from the guy she cut off faded away. Yeah, she'd gotten clobbered. It was the kind of thing that made her feel particularly aware of how much her ass was on the line without some backup.

Of course, if Brady had been there... She still couldn't believe he'd so casually asked her out. Red hair. Must be the red hair. Some men just have a thing for it.

"OK." Maureen pushed Brady out of her mind, and began an internal dialogue as she sipped her beer. "OK, so I took it on the chin. That's done. What have we learned, other than I could use someone watchin' my backside? These ain't no dummies we got here. The Argentine fox, Mr. Yager, smart cookies both, know they're bein' watched and know what to do about it. I underestimated them, that's all. But now's not a time to get pissed off; now's a time to make my next move. So, she won't be goin' back to Yager's place, that's for sure, an' he's gonna be watching so we can't really follow. What's next? I'm not gonna find this Swires guy by puttin' an ad in the paper. But say he's still alive an' doin' a job for Yager, then he's gotta contact him, right?

"Shit. If Yager thinks he's bein' followed, you can bet he's not gonna go meet Swires in person. So either the fox contacts him in person, which maybe she wouldn't do for the same reason, 'cause she knows I followed her to her place. Dollars to donuts they now communicate only by phone. At home, or the office? These guys are gonna have tap checks on their phones. As soon as a call comes through, they're gonna see a little red light go blink-blink. Of course, Drummond would have caller ID."

Maureen shook her head, punching the accelerator to beat out a cab for the left lane of the bridge.

"Whoa. Wait a minute," she said aloud, smiling at Patrick. "Caller ID."

"Huh?" Patrick crunched his empty beer can and tucked it under the seat.

"The McNarys got pushed around today. Tonight I push back." Maureen finished her beer, crunched the can, and tucked it under the seat.

BB was on her way home from the Phillips auction when her phone bleeped. She put her Christie's catalogue on the limo seat and answered.

"Yes?"

"Hi, sweetums."

BB cocked an eyebrow.

"Mr. Palihnic. Calling to offer me another stolen work of art?"

"I know all about how you moved *Trampoline Nude, 1972* to Honk Kong via a certain courier named Olbeter."

"You might have a hard time proving such an absurd notion." BB suddenly felt warm.

"Perhaps. But understand that it's not necessarily to my advantage that you hang for this. So before you set the cops on me again, I think we should powwow. What say dinner, someplace civil to encourage us to be on our best behavior?"

BB had to think about this. Even if H bit the hand that fed him, his witnessing the painting was not hard evidence. But it could make things a tad uncomfortable, and it could make the papers.

"I mean, this whole thing, provable or not, might be just the sort of thing your competitors might want to believe, if not run through the gossip mill," Nicholas continued. "And let's not forget all that mess in Milwaukee a couple years back, respectable art dealers caught red-handed beating someone up with a baseball bat. How much time did that woman Karos get? Ten years? No need for you to end up like her. I'm not in the business of turning people in to the cops. No profit in that. For either of us."

"Mr. Palihnic, I'm coming to realize you're less like a dog and more like a cat. You're annoying, often despicable, but nonetheless a curious little animal."

"Don't forget cuddly. Cafe Loui, at eight? It's right in your neck of the woods, and I've made the reservation."

"Hope you don't object to being stood up."

"I'll wait. *Ciao.*" Nicholas hung up.

The limo pulled up to BB's uptown studio, and she disembarked. Moth-sized flakes of snow fluttered down from the sky. She disengaged the security system, locked the studio door behind her, and climbed the stairs to her apartment. The light was blinking on her answering machine. She hit the play-back button and kicked off her shoes.

"BB, this is Olbeter, just calling to let you know that everything went smoothly. But you already know that, I'm sure. Any other time I can be of service, you know where to reach me. Please let me know when I can send someone by for the fee, uh, tomorrow?"

Bleeep.

"Bea, it's your old friend Ozzy. That nice Mr. Palihnic dropped by today—I tell you, he's a treasure. A wealth of information about what's stolen, that sort of thing. Great gossip. You wouldn't believe the places things have been stolen from, and the people involved. Fascinating. He said he had a real juicy one, but that he couldn't tell me what it was. Said you knew about it, and that he could only tell if you said it was OK. I'm calling for the poop, babe. Do tell."

Bleeep.

"Good evening, BB, it's Irwin Inquith, in Hong Kong. I just got a most curious call from somebody named Palihnic. He said he was a friend of yours, and that he'd be coming to Hong Kong and wanted to see what I had. But he was very confused, BB, very confused. He said he was sure you said I had *Trampoline Nude, 1972* for sale. I said I did not, that he must have misunderstood you. Naturally, I said nothing about our sale of *Trampoline Nude, 1978*, all things being confidential, don't you know. Anyway, if you get a chance, could you give me a ring? 'Night."

Bleeep.

"It's Karen. Thanks again for lunch and the auction. I'll be staying home tonight, going through my mail, feeding the cat, you know. So don't wait up. Remember, you have got to make some magic this week, sweetie. I didn't want to ruin our time today, but I looked at the books again yesterday and you need cash, Bea, or there's going to be real trouble. No fooling. Come up with something fabulous. I know you will. You always do. Bye."

Bleeep.

The machine's evil red eye stopped blinking. BB was by now stripped down to her black stockings and panties, her hair loosed from its clip. She scowled. She was agitated, but also increasingly titillated by the impending danger. She was looking forward to reining Nicholas in.

Ernesto, the doorman of 501 East 61st Street, had a large, waxed handlebar mustache. It was eight o'clock and he was admiring his greasy whiskers in one of the lobby's numerous mirrors when a redhead in blue coveralls pushed through the front doors. A toolbox hung from one of her hands, an orange utility phone hung from her belt, and snow dusted the hood of her parka. A Verizon identification card was clipped to her breast pocket, and she jabbed at it with a thumb.

"Phone company."

"Can I help you?" Ernesto's handlebar wobbled.

"Yeah, I need to see the junction box." She stepped past him and looked down the corridor. "It in the basement?"

Ernesto tapped her on the shoulder. "There is a problem?"

"Mrs. Brandenburg and Mr. Tannenbaum both said they been getting crossed lines. Call 'em. They'll tell you." She walked over to the doorman's desk and dropped her toolbox on the floor.

Ernesto picked up the house phone but was unable to reach either party. Little wonder. Earlier that evening, Maureen had looked up Drummond's exchange in a reverse phone directory on the Web and got a mess of other phone numbers belonging to the residents of 501 East 61st Street. When she was a block away from the building she dialed one after another until she'd got two that didn't answer.

Hesitating only briefly, Ernesto shrugged and led the way to a basement stairway.

"Past the laundry room, all the way at the end near the gas meter."

In her years as a police detective, Maureen had on occasion been involved in wiretaps, which at first she'd assumed were highly complex. However, the technicians were only too glad to show the buxom redhead the breadth of their knowledge. A typical explanation went something like: "See this thing?

Well, you clip this to the peg, then you press this, and listen into this. And if you wanna record something, you plug this thing inna the phone thingy with the clips and push 'record.'" Only slightly more complicated than stringing lights on a Christmas tree. When she quit the force, Maureen had invested twelve hundred bucks at the 007 Shop over on Christopher Street for the gadgetry, and this was the first time she'd had a chance to use it. Sure, it was illegal, but the information wasn't going to be used for evidence but to be a fly on someone's wall.

She found the junction box, rigged her device on two long wires, and tucked the gizmo discreetly behind the metal cabinet.

But her mind wasn't entirely on the task at hand. Where would a man like Brady take her to dinner? *He damn well better call.*

Chapter 17

Blue light splashed on the walls from behind a phalanx of palmettos. The floors were black, the walls white, the marble columns fake. Hurricane lanterns wired with flicker bulbs created wobbly orange domes of light at each table. *C'est Cafe Loui.*

BB's beaded clutch dropped on the table like a lead maraca, and she sank into the seat opposite Nicholas. She wore a simple black strapless cocktail dress, and her hair was loose for a change. Half lidded, she looked Nicholas over without a word, her demeanor alight with all the enthusiasm of one confronted by an IRS audit.

"Wine?" Nicholas smiled amiably.

BB declined with a wave.

Nicholas shrugged, his tweed suit crunching, and

poured some wine for himself. "And here I thought you would be relaxed, ready to talk turkey."

BB pulled the wine bottle from its bucket and poured herself some wine. *Still with the games*, Nicholas thought.

"Well, I think you should know right off that my idea in buying you dinner is to concede the match." Nicholas heaved a theatrical sigh. "I've been beaten."

"How so?" BB folded her arms, obviously not believing a word of it.

"I'm saying, I don't want to go to jail anymore. I'm saying that . . ." Nicholas drew closer to the lamp and lowered his voice. "I'm saying you got the painting out of the country, I can't prove you did it, I don't know where it went, and even if I did, I couldn't get my hands on it." He pulled back and gave a big, noisy shrug.

"You were a busy boy this afternoon. Made some calls. What's this really all about?" BB flashed a sour smile. "Extortion?"

"That?" He waved it off. "It was just to get you to show up. Would you have shown up otherwise?"

BB's smile withered, and she busied herself with a napkin before asking, "What about the man you murdered? How's that working out for you?"

"The DA can't make it stick. Not that they aren't trying. They're tailing me most of the time these days."

BB tensed.

Nicholas continued. "But not now. I ditched them in a bowling alley on University Place."

"So?" Her sour smile returned.

"So here's what." He leaned in confidentially. "The Moolman was a recovery job for which I would have cleared twenty thousand. Nothing to ruin my life over. Not worth it if it were to ruin our relationship."

"Relationship?"

"Sure." Nicholas grinned. "I believe we have a potentially constructive relationship. You buy paintings. I get paintings."

"You think so?" BB attempted a casual laugh, but it came out rather like a hiss.

"Sure. I come upon stuff all the time. Which reminds me, don't you occasionally pick up the stray Herbert von Clarke?"

"Von Clarke?"

He slid a hand into his breast pocket and pulled out a Polaroid of him holding a bright green and purple canvass.

"All I want is twenty percent and it's yours."

She reached for the picture, knocking over her wineglass. "Shit!"

A von Clarke about this time would put her solidly in the black. Nicholas knew that she had a buyer right up in Tarrytown who would pay three and a half million easy for one of this guy's lush, vibrant abstracts.

Nicholas made the photo vanish, leaning in with his napkin to help mop the tablecloth. His hand brushed hers, and it was sizzling.

"So, do you want von Clarke's *Day After Day*, or not? I have to move fast on this one, and there are other interested parties. But I thought this might bury the hatchet between you and me."

"Where did you get it?"

"Let's just say I found it, and leave it at that."

"You stole it?"

"No. I recovered it."

"Then the insurance company will want it back."

"Not this one. It happens every once in a while. Along with what I'm looking for, I recover a painting that isn't on any hot sheets. Have Karen check it out."

A waiter arrived.

"Oh, I see we've had an accident." He snapped his fingers at a distant busboy. "Let me move you to another table."

BB stood. "Why give it to me?"

"I'm asking you to broker it for me because you can get a lot more than I could. Everyone knows you're the best dealer in town, get the highest prices. I'm making out even at twenty percent."

"Don't bother with the table," she said to the waiter. She looked positively chalky in the blue light. "We have to leave. I'm sorry." Grinning thinly, she turned and made for the door.

Nicholas threw two twenties on the table, shrugged at the waiter, and followed her gamely.

Outside, it was a windless night, and big, moth-like snowflakes fell straight down, accumulating into a gelatinous mush on the sidewalk.

"So, what's it going to be?" He watched BB as she hailed a cab. She slid in, leaving the door open. Nicholas climbed in next to her. He thought about asking where they were going, but decided he'd just wait and see. She was still thinking. So let her think.

She needed that painting, that was clear. But not on his terms. She was the alpha dealer, she called the shots. He couldn't wait to see what shot she came up with.

They didn't speak for the block-and-a-half drive back to her studio. She led the way up to her apartment, and only when she turned, took his head in her hands, and kissed him did those dark eyes in that pale round face latch on to his.

She'd almost forgotten how different it was, kissing a man. The jaw felt wide and powerful, pricking her cheek with its fine stubble. And when Nicholas's body moved to hers, his hands grasped her by the rib cage in a way that both startled and aroused. And that damn suit of Nicholas's was like grappling a bale of hay. BB didn't necessarily like the whole sensation— it was unpredictable, and even wrong, though sometimes sex is better that way.

Nicholas was only a little surprised. He was attracted by forceful and deceitful women. Not only did it often translate into sexual assertiveness, but it posed a challenge to maintain the upper hand. A chess master has no time for novices. His dinner with her was all about gamesmanship, and inserting sex into the gambit was a bold move on her part. And of his: bishop for the queen, to force her to start sacrificing pawns and maybe facilitate checkmate in a blunder.

This woman took what she wanted. Fine. Let her think that she's taking him for a ride. She was sexy, so why not sex?

In the midst of being pushed back onto her desk and scattering stuff onto the floor, he had an unexpected thought. Of Mel, and Sunday dinner the next day. Dottie. It didn't make him want to stop what was going on. Safe to say men were pretty hard-wired when it came to sex. Nicholas in particular. But thoughts like that were like having your mom at the prom. He managed to supplant that with the notion that Karen might walk in on them at any moment.

Chapter 18

The drilling rig bounced and groaned as it tried to withdraw the drill bit from the bore-hole. Water frothing at the edge of the hole suddenly disappeared. They all knew what that meant. The water was draining off into a void of some kind. Barney came forward with the Coleman lantern, his eyes meeting Sam's.

"We into something?"

Sam nodded and flicked his cigarette away into the darkness. He shut off the water and pulled the hydraulic lever side to side in an attempt to free the bit from whatever it was stuck on some twenty feet below. He pulled another knob and the two piston-like stabilizers on either side of the truck pressed into the ground. Metal grinding metal rang along the drill rod until it came loose suddenly.

Sam looked at Joey, and they looked at Barney.

"Let's put on a sampler, see if we can get ahold of something," Barney suggested.

The Pazzos uncoupled the driver motor, hauled the drill rod out of the hole and up the derrick. They replaced the roller bit with a split spoon sampler and fed the drill rod back into the borehole. The sampler was an eighteen-inch hollow tube that could be split lengthwise and was used to recover portions of soil.

Guiding a cylindrical 300-pound weight onto the protruding drill rod with the help of a motor-assisted rope on the derrick, they proceeded to hammer the drilling rod into the earth.

Minutes later, the sampler was retrieved and Joey slammed it against the side of the truck, trying to get it apart. When it split open, Barney leaned in with the green glow of the Coleman.

"What the...?" Joey grimaced, fanning his face with his hand.

Sam just looked askance at Barney, who pulled a handkerchief from his pocket and held it over his nose.

The sample consisted of a yellowish-green and exceedingly pungent spongy material, sandwiched between discs of red wax. At the very bottom of the sample was a chunk of wood.

"Uh huh." Barney nodded. "That's cheese, all right."

"Cheese?" Joey spat. "Cheese?"

"Very old cheese. Covered in wax, like in a wheel

or ball, so it was watertight. This piece of wood at the bottom is either part of a crate or deck wood. Some of the boats here had cheese as cargo."

"You knew we might hit fuckin' cheese?" Sam blinked incredulously.

"Uh huh." Barney grinned. "Didn't think it was worth mentioning."

Sam and Joey looked at each other, then looked at Barney.

"I don't think this is the boat we're looking for, fellahs. But let's drill through it here, checking the wash water that flushes up from the hole for anything unusual."

Sam snorted. "We've drilled in about every fucking street in this city, and we've found all kindsa shit. Bones. Seashells. Arrowheads. Glass of every color, metal of every kind, and everything from chalk to fuel oil to Pampers and phone books. But we never, ever found fuckin' food."

"We never found cheese, that's for fucking sure," Joey added.

Barney betrayed a sly grin. "First time for everything, fellahs."

In the cavernous shadows below the Triborough Bridge, Silvi lowered her binoculars and squinted into the distance. The scene reminded her of the first time she came to America, startling the hell out of some night fishermen when she and forty other refugees beached at Fort Lauderdale. God, that stinking little boat! Better than a firing squad, she kept telling herself. Raising the binoculars again, she could see Sam start to lower the derrick while Joey loaded pipe onto the truck.

Silvi picked up her cell phone.

"Barney is finished for the night. He must call you soon."

"Did they find anything?" Drummond cleared his throat.

"Barney put PVC pipe into this borehole. When he puts pipe in the hole, it means he has found the ship, yes?"

"Absolutely. When he calls, we'll see if he at least found one of the boats, and if it's the correct one. But with daylight in a couple hours, they won't have time to extract the gold."

"Drummond, how are we to take this gold? Maybe if Silvi knows your plan, she can help."

"How so?"

"What if he finds gold tonight? I am right here, I maybe kill him and take this gold."

There was a pause on the other end as Drummond mused over that possibility.

"You mean drive back here with the gold, don't you?"

Silvi flushed.

"But of course." Stupid, stupid, stupid. She reproached herself yet again for talking too much, which was what had gotten her into that jam with General Passamigo in Panama. She'd had to go and suggest that they stage a false assassination of Passamigo as an excuse for a junta. Her bosses never liked her ideas, good though they might be. She guessed it was because egotists were neurotics. But she'd be damned if this deal would sour on her.

"No, Silvi, this game is my invention, you see? We'll do it my way. Don't worry your pretty head about it. We'll get the gold."

Silvi and her pretty head felt patronized, and she had trouble keeping an edge off her voice.

"Yes, it is your game. I follow him home, then get some sleep. I call you tonight."

Drummond was about to say good night, but Silvi had already hung up. He let the cordless drop into the pocket of his robe, smoothed back his hair, and poured himself a snifter of *jamu tuak*, a sort of Malukuan brandy to which he'd grown accustomed while searching for one of General Yamashita's caches of WWII plunder. There was little doubt that *jamu tuak* contained opiates, which sharpened Drummond's cunning. It was while under its influence that he had first killed, albeit in self-defense. But it takes a special resolve to use a *kris* to its best effect.

After a brief respite of river gazing on the balcony, Drummond slid the phone from his pocket and dialed a number.

"Hello, may I speak with Mr. del Solar?" He flicked his gold lighter at a Dunhill.

"Hold on," a young man said.

"Hello." The accent was Spanish, but especially sharp for that early hour.

Drummond exhaled smoke. "Put the plane back in the hangar for the night."

Chapter 19

The following afternoon was one of February's brighter, though no less frigid, incarnations. The previous evening's slush storm had covered everything in two inches of foamy ice, like vanilla cake icing.

Barney stepped onto the concrete stoop wearing a terry bathrobe, the screen door slamming behind him. Alvin had just trailered a boat into the driveway and was honking his horn.

Barney sipped from his mug of coffee, eyed the boat, then eyed Alvin's expectant face. "Didn't say yet that I'd buy it."

"*She*. Yuh call a boat *she*, buddy," Alvin chided. "Don'tcha know nothin'?"

Barney plodded down the steps to take a closer inventory of the twenty-foot-long vessel. Her wide V-shaped hull was white fiberglass, and not without patches and dings. The windshield had a crack and part of the gunnel railing on one side was missing. On both rear flanks she sported the caricature of a devil and the boat's name.

Barney tossed his cold coffee on the ground and set the cup down on the stoop. He climbed the side ladder. *"Devil Dog?"*

The bucket seat was a disaster, upholstered almost exclusively in duct tape, and the entire blue interior needed repainting. A voltmeter in the dashboard had ice on the inside of the gauge, and the canvas Bimini canopy in the rear wasn't merely mildewed but sprouting mushrooms. All the stainless steel fixtures had a hint of rust.

"Didn't take very good care of the *Devil Dog*, did they?"

"Little elbow grease is all it'll take to make her shipshape." Alvin shrugged it off. " 'Sa fixer-upper. Look at the twin Mercs, buddy!"

Barney cocked his head doubtfully and went aft. There were two relatively new-looking forty-horsepower outboards.

"This thing run? No mechanical problems?"

"It's cold, but about high tide." Alvin scratched his stubble. "Get yourself dressed. We'll take her for a spin."

And in an hour's time, they were backing the *Devil Dog* into the East River a couple of miles upriver from Hell Gate. A bunch of other cabin-fevered boat zealots had come out to watch the operation. The sun hung low and orange over the river to the west, but a brisk wind robbed the air of whatever heat it afforded. Snorkel parkas, earmuffs, and stocking caps replaced the usual array of cheap yachting garb. The spectators huddled around a fire burning in a trash barrel like Eskimos at a weenie roast.

Alvin launched the *Devil Dog* from the trailer and guided her to a dock by a rope on her bow. Ice around the pier shattered as the hull came alongside.

Barney stepped aboard carefully, scanning the deck. "Well, it floats."

"She. *She*," Alvin scolded, blowing into his hands. He hopped aboard and took Barney around to the various parts of the boat, most importantly things having to do with priming the engines, throttle settings for starting, and turning the ignition key. Barney took it all in, as did the curious, hungry-looking audience on the dock.

Next, Alvin unfolded a chart and pointed with a mitten.

"We's here. See, where it says 'Pugsley's Landing.' Now, this here is the East River. Down here is Manhattan, and up here is Long Island Sound. This here's yuhr compass. When it says north or east, yuh's headin' out to Long Island. When—"

"It says west or south I'm heading for Manhattan." Barney nodded. "Uh huh."

"Good, I see yuh got a good sense of direction. Now, see all these little numbers? These are how deep at low tide. And see these little triangles?

These is buoys. Now listen careful. This is real important."

"Real important," the Eskimos murmured agreement.

"Buoys is of two colors. Red an' green. Y'wanna keep a red buoy on the right when yuh're returning. 'Red Right Returning' at all times when passin' through channels, marked right here in dotted line. Yuh go outsida the channel, yuh can't be sure what'll happen. Now tell me, out loud, where do yuh keep the red buoy?"

"On the right, when returning, so I stay in the channel."

The Eskimos on the dock all nodded approval.

Barney rubbed his jaw. "How do I know when I'm returning?"

"Goin' toward the City is returning, goin' away is goin' away. See, this stuff is not real dif'cult, buddy."

"What about at night?"

"Night?"

"Uh huh. Say I want to go out at night."

Alvin shrugged a few times, his face scrunched in confusion. "Where you goin' at night, buddy?"

"What about at night?"

Alvin sighed, as if confronted by a stubborn child. "They got lights, but..."

"You mean the buoys? The buoys have red and green lights?"

"Yeah."

Barney glanced at the controls, the charts, and

then took in the expanse of the river. His eyes finally came back to Alvin. "That all there is to it?"

"That's it. 'Cept one of these days, if yuh feel like it, the DMV'll give yuh papers for her." Alvin flapped his arms, then straightened his captain's hat. "OK, cast off. Let's see if Barney can get her started."

Barney primed the engines, settled into the driver's seat, made sure the one lever was in neutral and the other was on "START." He turned the key awhile before the engines coughed a blue cloud of smoke and erupted to life.

The Eskimos applauded, their mittens going *fwop fwop fwop*.

"Where to?" Alvin beamed. For a change, Barney didn't have to think long.

"The Harlem River."

Ice from the previous night's storm clung to 14th Street's lamp poles, lights, and awnings, all ablaze and glittering with the glow of the setting orange sun. Nicholas climbed out of a cab at Broadway and made for 15th Street, dodging slush puddles and slick spots. He stopped at a pay phone. BB picked up on the third ring.

"Skinny Nick may never be the same, you know that?" Nicholas said, thinking about another body part while rubbing his wrists where she'd tied him to her desk.

"I'll rip Skinny Nick clean off if you don't sell me that von Clarke," BB said dryly.

"Got it. Parking lot for the Randall's Island pool, say eleven tonight? Make sure the check is certified, or it's no deal." He hung up.

When Nicholas immersed himself in the gloom of 113, he found his favorite booth occupied.

"Gotcha." Maureen's face flickered in the candle glow.

Nicholas slid in the booth opposite her, careful not to jar the somewhat overtaxed Skinny Nick. He was relieved to see Maureen didn't look in any mood for bedroom barbeque.

"Looks like you're getting somewhere." Nicholas gestured at her eye.

"Yeah, but it's costin' me. Spent yesterday afternoon pulling favors to get my kid brother outta jail. I had him tail Drummond and he got framed-up."

"And I always thought you worked alone."

"Ever think of taking on a partner, Nicholas?"

The gulp of Macallan went down hard.

"No." First Mel, now Maureen. "Why?"

"Why not me?"

"I pass on work when I get more than one person can handle."

"Sure, but you're skimming a profit off me, and I'm doing all the work here. Not for nothing, Nicholas, but I feel like I'm back on the force, except with no backup. The reason I gave that shit up is you don't get anywhere. There's always another murder, always another stupid crook. Wears a person down."

"Maureen, I don't get enough work for two people."

"Put and take, Nicholas—dollars to donuts you would if you had more manpower. Just think about it, OK?"

"I'll get you another beer." Nicholas went to the bar, worried about Maureen.

When he returned, he set the fresh beer down and slid across from her again.

"Maureen, I know what you're saying. There's times when you need a team. But we're working as a team now, aren't we?"

"Gee, thanks, Coach. I don't need a pep talk, I need you to put yourself in the game here and help me out. I tapped into Yager's caller ID, got a phone booth on Randall's Island from which somebody called him at three forty-five this morning." Maureen sipped her Bud and hissed a belch.

"What makes you think it was Barney?"

"I tailed Yager and his girlfriend, trying to see if they would lead me to him. But they made me. I got pegged." Maureen pointed to her shiner.

"Ouch. You have any bio on them?"

"None on her. She's Argentinian, tall and sexy in a sort of cruel way. Yager is English, thinning silver hair, overbite, glasses, deformed hand. He spent time in some foreign country or something."

Something about what she was saying tugged at

Nicholas's memory, but he couldn't place it.
Maureen continued.

"Don't know her name, ran his with friends at
NYPD and it came back empty. I'm thinking it's an
alias. Is it usual for insurance companies to work
with such shady people? Present company excluded,
of course."

Nicholas ignored the slight. "When there's a lot
of money at stake, they sometimes don't care how
they get it. The biggies, I've heard, have dirty tricks
squads, but I've never run into them personally.
Sounds like this guy Yager is one of them."

"Anyway, they're smart enough not to meet
Barney in person anymore." Maureen took a big
gulp of her beer. "But by the time they knew I
was following, I don't think they had any time
to keep Barney from calling. So when I bugged
Drummond's phone, I got four numbers. One from
Newstime Magazine looking for a subscription, one
from his girlfriend's cellular, one from somebody
named del Solar in Lake Komatcong, New Jersey—
he's a commercial pilot—and one from this phone
booth. The last three were between three AM and
four AM."

"What makes you think—"

"Just listen a sec, will you? I went out to Randall's
Island. Nothing there, really, except a stadium. I
lifted some prints from the pay phone. We may not
have Swires's foot, but we got his thumb. I matched
a latent to a thumbprint on the hairbrush you gave
me. I did it myself, so it's not a lab ID. But, Nicholas,

they're real identical. Central pocket loops on both his thumb and forefinger, right hand."

"Yeah, but what was he doing out at Randall's Island?"

"Dunno, but we better stake it out for a while. But not me, not up-front and alone. Drummond and his girl know me now."

"What's out there?"

Maureen looked at her notes.

"Just the Parks Department, a sewage treatment plant, a fireman's training center, a Sanitation Department training center, a bunch of ball fields, and a mental hospital. Think he'd be trying to bust out an inmate, some witness, something like that? I dunno, Nicholas. Not like there's any bank vaults around." She polished off her beer.

H Olbeter was suddenly illuminated standing next to the booth, tucking his gloves into his coat.

"Evening, Nicholas," H said, while gazing at Maureen.

"H, meet Maureen McNary, a highly skilled investigator." Nicholas winked at Maureen. "And Maureen, this is H Olbeter, a highly skilled investigator."

Maureen slid out of the booth and shook hands with H briefly, favoring him with a scant smile.

"What's the H stand for?" She took her coat from a peg and was surprised to find H helping her put it on.

"Honest, or heroic, or even he-man," H quipped.

"It stands for the fact that he was orphaned, and

in the paperwork they lost all but the initial of his first name," Nicholas said.

"Have fun, guys. Gotta get some sleep." She headed out the door. "Midnight tonight, on the island, Nicholas. Don't be late."

Don't be late. *Mel.* Nicholas glanced at his watch. 4:17 PM. Whew.

"Maureen, huh?" H took Maureen's spot opposite Nicholas. "Irish?"

"Yep. She's the one I got in your place, while you were away."

"My friend, I'd say she was somewhat attractive." H rubbed a pointy sideburn thoughtfully. "Muscular, with a black eye, and yet attractive. Give me her number."

"Park Slope Investigations. It's in the book. Look, I didn't call you here to play *The Dating Game.* What are you doing tomorrow night?"

"You need me, you got me. What's up?"

"I seem to remember you telling me you had a pyrotechnic license."

"Sure. Long time ago, I used to work in the film business. Rigged explosions some. Mostly supplied and supervised shoot-outs for cop shows. You ever see that show *Crime Story?* Ah, but the work was too unpredictable."

Nicholas rubbed his hands together.

"You still have the equipment for that?"

H looked uncertainly at his glass, spinning it between thumb and forefinger. "Yes, but we'd get in big trouble if we don't get a permit from the NYPD."

"You remember how to do it, right?"

"Of course."

"Sure?" Nicholas reached out and stopped H's hand from spinning the glass.

H looked up and blinked, his eyes turning indignant. "I was the best."

"Was?" Could he trust this dope not to get him killed?

H pulled his drink out from under Nicholas's hand and knocked it back.

"Who else you going to get? So you going to give me her number?"

"Maureen's?"

"Or is she your stash?"

Nicholas rolled his eyes. "I'm not into buying any real estate."

"Say what?"

"Women are like real estate, H. Maureen is a cabin in the woods—always there, secluded, you know you can always go there but would never think of living there."

"And I heard you an' Mel were..."

Nicholas shook his head. "She's the beach place. Great location, only good when it's sunny, but you never know when a hurricane—in this case a dependable man and dad-type—will wash it away. So it's not wise to invest in the beach house."

"Met her kid once, on the street." H smiled. "Cute. Mini Mel."

Nicholas was hitting his stride.

"Single mothers, they're like freestanding wood-frame houses, lotta shifting in the structure makes them suspect. Hips displaced from childbirth, most of them have lost their wiggle, both figuratively and literally. And then there's the wrinkles of consternation knit perpetually into their brows from parenting."

"My man, you have given this some thought, haven't you?" H was chuckling.

Nicholas slid out of the booth and reached for his coat.

"But the ones you have to be really careful of are the ones that look too good to be true."

"Those are the best kind!" H stood, finishing his drink.

"I'm talking about women a little older. Around forty. You have to ask, if they're so perfect, why are they still single? Some turn out to be haunted houses—one night's stay and you run screaming. 'Trust issues' and paranoia come out of nowhere, ghosts from past relationships. Others turn out to be fixer-uppers with so many hidden emotional problems, and possibly physical ones, that you realize you might as well have torn the house down and started over. Or bought another house entirely. Let's go."

"You are one sick monkey, Nicholas." H laughed, following him to the door. "So what kind of house are you?"

"Me?"

"Yeah, you."

"I'm a fourth-floor walk-up. Not too expensive, good exercise, breezy, sunny, don't want to lug too much furniture up there. Not the kind of place where you raise a family. Most women get tired of climbing the stairs."

Chapter 20

Angie opened the door and her chin dropped.

Garth stopped dead in his tracks in the bedroom doorway, beer bottle in hand.

"Ah, good ol' Sunday dinner!" Nicholas chimed, giving Angie a peck on the cheek. "Mel, this is Angie, and that over there is my brother, Garth."

Nicholas flashed a smile at his brother. Yup, Garth was in his usual attire: white shirt, sport jacket, chinos, sneakers. Wild blond hair barely held in by gel. How could a guy who looked like some high school drama coach be his brother?

"I'm Dottie!" The little girl burst from her mother's side and ran pell-mell to Garth. "Where's the tookie tookie?"

Angie mechanically tucked some of her short blond hair behind one ear uncertainly.

"Hi, it's a pleasure to meet you." Mel took Angie's hand, then smiled at Garth. "Wow. You have quite a place here."

Garth stared down at the little girl, whose excited black orbs were ogling him. He looked behind him as though retracing his steps might erase this mirage.

Dottie threw her hands out and stamped a foot. "Well?"

"Dottie!" Mel glided forward and put her hands on Dottie's shoulders. "That's not polite. Hi, Garth, I'm Mel. She's just excited to see the bird."

Garth shook her hand, blinking. "Hi. Nicholas has told me so much about you." Polite, but inaccurate.

"Has he?" Mel was obviously trying to contain her surprise.

Dottie's eyes drifted from Garth, refocusing. She twirled. Taxidermy was everywhere. The ceiling was filled with birds, wings spread: eagle, owl, pelican, ducks, goose, dove, turkey, hawk, flamingo ... The walls were covered in heads, most with horns: elk, deer, moose, antelopes of every description. On low bookcases were the smaller mammals: beaver, squirrels, badger, woodchuck, platypus, mink, mongoose, weasel, martin, otter, bobcat, lynx, porcupine, fox. And guarding the floor around the walls were larger full-body mounts: coyote, wolverine, wolf, tapir, wild pig, dik-dik.

"A lion!" she squealed, dashing over to a male African lion mount. She stared with wonder into its open, befanged maw. Dottie had fallen through the looking glass. "Way cool!"

Garth shot Nicholas a "what are you up to now" look, then turned his attention back to Dottie.

"That's Fred the Second. Got him just recently."

"Does Fred bite?" She held out a finger toward the lion's mouth, ready to pull it away in case he snapped at her.

"Fred's biting days are long gone. You can touch his mouth."

Her hand drew close to the fangs but pulled away.

"Look." Garth reached down and put his whole fist in Fred's mouth.

"Do you live here?" She was still staring at Fred's mouth.

"Yes, Angie and I live here."

"Way cool! Can I live here too?"

Nicholas leaned in to Angie. "Do you guys have a toucan, or some other exotic bird? I promised her she'd get to see a tookie tookie bird."

"Nicholas, you didn't say you were bringing any-one," she whispered.

"That's why I moved it up to five. Dottie has to be in bed by eight."

"In bed by eight, huh?" She eyed him suspiciously.

"Should we leave?"

"No, of course not, it's just that . . ."

"They don't eat much."

"It's not that, idjit, we have plenty, but . . ."

"You must have a tookie tookie bird here

192 BRIAN M. WIPRUD

somewhere ... Dottie would be real disappointed if you didn't."

"I see, a tookie tookie bird." She squinted at him. "You're up to something, Nicholas, aren't you?"

"Me?"

She let a few beats pass, then raised her eyebrows. "Be careful, Nicholas. It could backfire."

Angie turned from him to Garth. "Garth, you want to offer our guests something to drink? I have to go in back a minute."

"Sure, sure ... wine, beer, or"—Garth gestured to Nicholas—"scotch?"

"Wine would be great." Mel smiled, looking a little nervously at Nicholas.

"I'll have a scotch," Dottie said absently, transfixed by the lion. "That's what Nicky always has."

Nicholas followed Garth behind the counter as Mel tried to draw Dottie's attention to the other animals. The apartment had once been a soda shop. It had a checkered tile floor, and one side of the room was dominated by a long black bar.

"OK, Nicholas: is she, like, your girlfriend?" Garth whispered.

"She's a girl and she's a friend, so I guess that makes her a girlfriend," Nicholas whispered back.

"And the little girl, Dottie ... she's not ..."

"No, she's not mine. Mel is a widow. Poor bastard bought it in a motorcycle accident just after Dottie was born. Mel's in computers, does background work for me."

"You know, Nicholas, you're like Tom Terrific."

"Tom who?"

"The old cartoon show? You remember the tookie tookie bird but you don't remember Tom Terrific? Tom was a smart-ass like you who could change himself into something else. Anything else. But even if he was a toaster he had that same hat on, so you knew it was Tom, even if other characters in the cartoon were fooled."

Nicholas was mildly exasperated. "Garth, I'm sure I have no idea what you're talking about."

"I'll bet you do." Garth poured two glasses of wine, glancing over his shoulder at Mel and Dottie. "Cute, both of them. Very."

"I know." Nicholas had found the scotch and a glass. "Got any juice for Dottie?"

"Apple OK? I think we have some concentrate."

"Perfect. Looks like scotch." Indeed, Nicholas thought. No doubt this Sunday dinner would have the desired effect. Leave in two hours or so, put Dottie to bed, fool around with Mel for a while, leave in time to grab the rental car and make his two appointments on Randall's Island. One with BB at eleven for *Day After Day*, the other at midnight with Maureen to finger Barney. "You give any thought to that appraising job?"

"I've got work."

"This pays well, Garth. Travel. Expenses. It'd mix things up a bit. Try it. If you don't like it, then don't take any more work."

"Who is this for again?"

"Big insurance companies. They're loaded. Just

say the word and I'll put you in touch with the right people."

A door slammed in the back, and from behind a curtain a little wiry man with graying hair and a sharp goatee burst into the room. He was wearing a belted boxy sport coat with absurdly large shoulder pads.

"Allo, I ready! Nicholas, we must drink—" He stopped, thunderstruck, as though Mel and Dottie were an apparition from heaven itself. "My Gott! Nicholas! Eetz very nice! You not tell to me you have vooman! And little girl, to be pretty!"

"Mommie, what's wrong with him?" Dottie stared up suspiciously.

"You must be Otto." Mel held out a hand. Nicholas had told her about Garth and Angie's eccentric Russian handyman. "I'm Mel, and this is Dottie."

Otto grasped her hand and held it to his chest. "You go to beach? Very nice at beach."

"Otto!" Garth scolded.

"Beach to go very, very pretty veemin," Otto protested. "Mal is very pretty, so beach to must go to be nekked."

"Mel, don't mind him." Nicholas scrunched his face dismissively. Good, she was getting the full freak show. "Just don't go to any nude beaches."

"Nude beaches?" Mel was stumped.

"Ah!" Otto gasped and dropped to his knees to get a better look at Dottie, who promptly hid behind her mother's legs. "Dah-tay! Like small deer with spots come from mother's bottom, gentle big eyes of her. Not to be afraid of Otto! Look! I do very funny, yes?" Otto proceeded to do a trick where he dislocated his arm and twisted it behind his head at a bizarre angle.

"Otto." Garth handed Mel her wine. "I think you're scaring her. Dottie? I have your scotch."

A little olive hand reached around her mother and made the cup vanish.

"Who wants to see a tookie bird?" Angie emerged from the back room.

Dottie's head peeked around Mel's legs. Angie entered the room holding a black bird about the size of a large chicken standing on a piece of driftwood. It had a large, hooked red beak and a bunch of ridiculous curled feathers atop its head, a tizzy of sprouting question marks. While some might have called it a tookie tookie, it was commonly known as a curassow, denizen of South American jungles.

"That's a tookie tookie?" Dottie dashed past Otto and up to Angie. "Can I hold it? Please?"

Glass of scotch tinkling with ice, Nicholas took the bird from Angie and crouched so Dottie could pet it. Mel betrayed a wistful smile.

"Do you remember the sound the tookie tookie bird makes?" Nicholas asked.

Dottie filled her tiny lungs with air: "*AW! AW! EE! EE! TOOKIE-TOOKIE!*"

Angie leaned in to Garth and stage-whispered. "Who is this imposter calling himself Nicholas?"

"Tom Terrific."

Chapter 21

Barney leaned against a towering steel column in Astoria, Queens, watching a row house from the shadows of the subway above. The front windows were lit, the shades were up. He could see the living room clearly, filled with yellow light and people. More arrived every few minutes, greeted with hugs and kisses by a plump, elderly woman. Sunday dinner at the Griegs'.

Sure enough, a black town car pulled up to the house, and Nicasia stepped out. She stood there for a moment as the car drove off. Her hair was pulled into a long French braid. She stood looking at the house, like she was deciding something, then turned suddenly in Barney's direction. He rolled to the other side of the column, smiling to himself. She looked great. It was all he could do not to break cover and wrap her in his arms, absorb her smile and her eyes, sink her body into his, smell her hair. Did she feel him close to her? Was that why she'd turned? If she called out his name, would the night and the shadows suddenly turn to daylight?

But he couldn't show himself. What with Drummond and the gun and Silvi watching him from that red pickup, he didn't dare get Nicasia involved. Oh, he'd snuck out of his house, left that red pickup parked down the block back in Pugsley's Point. No two ways about it, those people meant to kill him. And he didn't doubt that they would do the same to anybody else who got wind of what was going on. He didn't want them bringing Nicasia into this. If things didn't go as planned, they could kidnap her—or worse—as leverage against Barney.

He peered around the pillar and saw that Nicasia had turned back to the house. He watched her kiss her mother, then waited as the door closed, shutting him out in the cold, severing the beat of his heart from hers.

Chin raised, he scanned the hazy night sky, finding a flickering star, a spark of determination from the heavens.

Just a couple nights more, he hoped. *And then I'm coming home.*

Nicasia hadn't wanted to come to Sunday dinner at her folks' place in Astoria. But with Barney missing, she didn't know what to do with herself. She couldn't spend all her time kayaking. As her mother used to say, "I didn't know where you were! I was worried awful!" Funny how we became our parents.

Immersing herself in her family had seemed like the thing to do when she left Manhattan. She wasn't so sure now as she stood on the sidewalk in front of the house where she grew up. It wasn't exactly the quietest neighborhood, what with the elevated subway train right across the street. She turned to look up at it. She thought about how often sunlight spilled through the structure, making patterns on the living room wall. A train would come by and cause a strobe effect as the sun flashed between the cars. Nicasia had never liked the way it looked at night, when it looked like a striding giant ready to step on their house.

The stuffed grape leaves and moussaka were waiting, but she paused outside a second longer and caught her breath. She hadn't seen anything. But she'd felt something, like a wind move right through her chest.

"My God," she whispered, clutching her coat front. Was that Barney's ghost she felt? Or was Barney out there somewhere thinking about her?

A tear rolled down her cheek, her dark eyes scanning the cold city sky. A star above wobbled faintly through the haze. A dim light, a faint hope.

"Barney, come home, damn you, come home."

"Nicasia?"

She turned.

"Hi, Mom."

"Why are you standing out there in the cold?"

Her mother peered from the circle of porch light into the gloom.

Nicasia went up the walk and kissed her mother. "Just looking."

"Well, come in! I didn't know where you were. I was worried awful."

Silvi trained her binoculars on the woman getting out of the town car. Just a silhouette. She noted the license plate of the limo and the address of the house. Would Barney come out of hiding? Was this his family's home? There was some sort of party going on inside.

No. She didn't think so. This was most likely his girlfriend. Even better.

Fool. Barney thought he could give her the slip, but he was just another one who underestimated her. Like Drummond.

"What's the matter, Nicholas?"

He pulled away from Mel. "What do you mean?" When a woman has a problem, she asks the man whether he has one. Amazing.

She sat up on the couch and did a quick sound check to see if she heard anything from Dottie's room. Then she put a hand tenderly on his chest and looked up into his eyes, her face illuminated by street light from the windows. "Thanks for tonight."

"No thanks required. It was my pleasure." He put his hands on her hips. "Is something wrong? Did Otto freak you out?"

What the hell could be wrong? They'd done the family dinner thing, put Dottie to bed, even sang her the Tarzan song, and now Nicholas and Mel were in the clinches on the couch. Textbook.

"Nothing is wrong. But something is...different."

Nicholas just cocked his head.

"I don't know how to explain it. Maybe it's just tonight. But...we still have our clothes on. And we've been kissing for a long time...we've never kissed this long."

"Great, let's take our clothes off, then." He began unbuttoning his shirt.

She rolled her eyes and smoothed his shirt across his chest. "It's just that...you're kissing differently."

Flummoxed, Nicholas did his best to maintain his affable expression. It was always best not to say anything. Not until he knew what to say. This could go anywhere.

"Maybe I'm imagining it. But do you feel something for me? No, stop! I see you calculating. Just wait a second, and tell me what you truly feel."

Minefield. To Nicholas, the man who tells a woman how he truly feels hands her a mallet with which she is liable to clonk him over the head—often. Was he to tell her that he felt like having sex? Was he to tell her he didn't feel like formulating specific feelings for analysis? If he were candid, he'd say he felt like he liked things just the way they were, but he knew she didn't, which was why he'd staged the whole Sunday dinner thing.

His plan had backfired, just as Angie had suggested. Somehow, Mel was starting to be able to see the shores of his island. He stood and picked up his jacket and tie.

"I guess I'd better go."

She bowed her head. "That's what I thought."

"Mel, you know me well enough—I'm not that kind of guy. I don't have what you're looking for. I wish I did."

Nicholas rolled the tape back. Did he just say that? Guess it sounded good.

"You know that if you or Dottie ever needed anything, I'd be here for you." Where did that come from? Funny enough, it felt like the truth. Well, it could work. Couldn't it? The truth? His instincts had, after all, rarely betrayed him.

"Thanks, Nicholas." Mel put her hand over her mouth and looked toward the window. Bars on the window sliced up the street glow, casting shadows across her and the room. A police siren sounded from Seventh Avenue and faded. "Thanks for telling me the truth. I knew, for all the games that we play about you being the cad that you are, and me liking it, that there's a decent guy under it all."

Nicholas cleared his throat, shifting his weight from foot to foot. His instincts weren't giving him anything. "Don't be so sure."

She chuckled softly, the dew of tears in her big eyes.

"OK, Nicholas. Have it your way."

He tried to look away but couldn't.

"I don't want you coming around anymore. Ever."

Nicholas had been punched before. He'd been beaten. He'd been kicked, knifed, and grazed by a bullet. He'd been prepared for those, because he'd known he was in danger. He had no idea he was in danger with Mel—not just because of the way she felt, but because of the way he suddenly felt. And the wound was a surprise that stung like no other.

He had no breath to speak even if there were something to say.

So he left.

As he hustled down the street to catch a cab, he reflexively glanced to the sky as if for divine guidance, and noticed a star's light cutting through Manhattan's gaze. Didn't see that very often. So he stopped and gave it a second look.

It was moving.

He snorted and continued on his way. Just a plane headed for LaGuardia.

Chapter 22

Barney's fingers throbbed, his heart pounding as the titanic humpbacked Hell Gate Bridge drifted overhead. The glitter of the Triborough Bridge lay just ahead. It was like navigating a space capsule around intergalactic mother ships.

"I'm coming home, Nicasia, coming home." Since the night before, when he'd seen her silhouetted in the porch light, that had become his mantra.

On the boat with Alvin, at slack tide, Hell Gate Channel had seemed rather tame. But night and a dropping tide had transformed the channel into a roar of unseen serpents. Barney's eyes burned with the river's myriad smoky reflections from factories on Hallet's Point, the FDR Drive, and Shore Boulevard. He blinked hard, searching for the flashing red beacon of Hog Back Reef in the black void that loomed beyond the bright lights of the Triborough Bridge.

It was supposed to be close by on his right, just past Negro Point. But the aft red and green lights of oil barges intermixed with the red and green beacons, which were further cluttered with the flicker of distant traffic lights on East End Avenue.

Were the barges standing still? Were they moving toward or away from him? The tide's audible draw clawed at the *Devil Dog*'s hull, the cold night tingling with the roar of tortured fathoms and the sucking, hissing sound of whirlpools and eddies.

Barney's mind swelled with images from Hell Gate's historical litany of treacherous and unforgiving power. And yet here he was, in the dark, in a boat, piloting the channel for only the second time. His inclination was to pull out of the fast-flowing channel, away from the big ships and toward the shore of Ward's Island, toward the river's kinder currents where he might stand a chance of swimming to shore if the *Devil Dog* fetched up on Heel Tap, Big Annie, or Holmes Rock. But he'd stood on shore there and seen the jagged lurking rocks. That same inclination had been the ruin of many a ship. So he throttled back and attempted to coast through the channel as slowly as possible. Completely disoriented, Barney couldn't be absolutely sure where he was, except that he was in the jaws of Hell Gate.

Well, it was all or nothing now, no turning back.

"Hog's Back." Barney's eyes flashed at the light, imagining that the rhythmic splash was river against the rocks. He spun the wheel.

"Red Right Returning." He pointed the boat for a

red light to his right, trying to give what he assumed was Hog's Back Beacon a wide berth.

The *Devil Dog* hit an eddy spinning off a bridge pier, and Barney was suddenly looking back upriver, sliding backward. He spun the *Devil Dog* about, his eyes dilating as the boat came to bear on the looming hull of a tanker. The ship's struggling engine churned the river with the determined chop of impending demolition.

Sweat fairly jumped off his brow as he cut the wheel in the other direction and throttled in a circle away from the tanker. Another eddy twirled the *Devil Dog* toward an approaching light—the tanker's tug. A warning blast sounded from the tug, and Barney whirled the boat back upriver, throttle pushed full. He'd drifted much farther toward Hallet's Point than he'd realized, mistaking the red bow light of the tanker as Hog's Back. In a wild burst of water, Barney cut across the bow of the tanker, which passed at a pebble's throw to his left.

"Red Right Return," Barney fairly cursed. "Nobody told me there was a red light on the bow of every boat on the river."

When the tanker and its wake passed, Barney was again in the dark, panting with exasperation. Dead ahead, the sparkling line of the FDR Drive was blotted out and he suddenly realized where he must be.

"Mill Reef." Barney squinted at the shadow ahead, looking upriver to where a thin bridge was emerging from behind Ward's Island. He spun the wheel and steered the *Devil Dog* back toward the materializing bridge, which he recognized as the Harlem River footbridge. Just beyond that was his destination. He opened up the twin Mercs, figuring the less time spent in Hell Gate the better.

Once in the Harlem River, his way was brightly lit by the FDR Drive, though he was still leery of getting too close to Ward's Island. As the grim hulk of the Manhattan Psychiatric Hospital passed on the right, he gently motored his craft into a shallow bay and up to a dilapidated stone seawall adjacent to the Icahn Stadium overflow parking lot. Even though the boat was only a couple hundred feet from the drilling site, it was low enough that in the dark it wouldn't be visible from there.

Barney collapsed into the torn captain's seat. Pulling off his cap, his fingers trembled as they raked his wet locks. His jaw muscles ached from clenching, and his eyes were bloodshot from strain. He wondered if he had the pluck to attempt a return voyage, if that somehow became necessary. In truth, he wasn't exactly sure how the whole thing would play out. His scheme was organic, flexible.

It was early yet, just about nine PM. So he went for the thermos of coffee, just to calm his nerves. A few sips later he realized he'd rather drink his coffee on dry land. He slipped a gangplank from his gunnel to the bulkhead and tromped through the thin blanket of crusty snow across the vast, empty stadium parking lot toward the lights of the Triborough Bridge looming ahead. Turning the corner of the stadium, he found the van Drummond had promised in front of the main entrance. The keys were under the back bumper, and he used them to unlock the back doors.

The equipment was all there, so he figured he might as well put some of his plan in action. He drove the van around back of the stadium, across the overflow parking lot, and parked next to the athletic field fence and a pile of fine gravel the stadium maintenance crews used to keep the runners' track in shape. He plugged the collector into the generator, stood the open barrels in the van, and put one of the collector's hoses into a barrel. Starting the generator, he proceeded to vacuum gravel from the pile into the barrels until they were all almost full. He then drove the barrels across the parking lot to the *Devil Dog* and used a hand truck to ferry them across the gangplank into the boat.

The plan in motion, Barney then drove the van to the drilling site and parked. Five minutes later, the Pazzos' drill rig appeared under the Triborough Bridge and turned into the overflow lot. The rig backed into the drill site and Barney helped the Pazzos back it into place without driving into any trees.

"How come you got a van today, Barney?" Joey lit a Coleman lantern.

Sam started the rig's generator, which coughed and gurgled to life.

"Borrowed it from a friend." Before they could ask any more questions, Barney brought forward a rectangular black box and handed it to Sam. It was the box Drummond had given him.

Joey came over with the lantern. "Whoa."

"Fuck." Sam smiled.

"You guys want it? It was sitting in the parking lot, pretty as you please." Barney eyed their reactions carefully.

"No way." Sam frowned, closing the box and shoving it back into Barney's arms. "That's a hot gun." He crunched back through the snow to the rig and began pushing levers.

"Whatever." Barney walked to the edge of the light and threw the box and gun into the brush. When he turned back to the rig, he saw the brothers quickly look away from where the gun was tossed.

No sooner had they set up than the water frothing from the borehole vanished into the ground. The roller bit had punched into another void. Without a word, Sam screwed on a sampler and Joey manned the driving hammer. Fifteen minutes later, Joey was opening a sampling tube. Barney approached with the lantern.

"Looks like wood, some metal, some glass'n shit." Joey sneered.

"An' some gold," Sam snorted sarcastically.

Barney's eyes caught the buttery yellow glow of gold beads.

"Must be some of that brass'n shit you said we might find," Joey said, tossing the contents on the ground.

"Must be." Barney smiled. "Let's start another hole, but case this one with PVC. No sense in going farther into that one, but if we don't find anything in the others, maybe we'll come back and drill down."

Barney saw the Pazzos exchange a furtive glance before Joey asked: "How will we know when we find what we're lookin' for?"

"Be cool if it were gold, huh?" Sam's eyes strayed toward the darkness where the gun lay.

"That's why I'm here. I'll know what we're looking for when I see it."

While gold in the form of bars is eminently stackable and transportable, it was not always practical. Not in the 1800s, anyway. For accounting and transaction purposes, it was sometimes desirable to measure out precise quantities of gold. The raw material (a combination of flakes and nuggets) was sloppy and awkward to handle. Pouring a steady stream of molten gold into water, however, was a quick way to reduce the metal into fairly uniform pellets, which was the form preferred by many East Coast banks when obtaining gold from California in the days before a West Coast assayer's office was established. Gold pellets prevented any monkey business like lead-filled bars or bars of nonuniform karat.

As per the Newcastle Warranty report, Section Seven, "Medium of Exchange," the *Bunker Hill*'s hold had been loaded with approximately 250 burlap bags of gold pellets.

Chapter 23

Nicholas picked a desolate parking lot on the far side of Randall's Island from Little Hell Gate, directly under the noisy Harlem River span of the Triborough Bridge. He stood next to his rental car and a dirty mountain of snow, an old tweed overcoat buttoned tight to his neck. Cold as the night was, and with such short hair, he should have worn a hat. But just as he didn't use umbrellas, he didn't wear hats either. Besides, he hardly felt the cold.

I don't want you coming around anymore. Ever.

It was over. No more Mel. Easy come, easy go.

I don't want you coming around anymore. Ever.

Over and over and over. Time to go AWOL, Nicholas, so go, already. But the exchange with Mel played like a looped tape.

What was it about Mel? Why was she special? If

Maureen had said *adios*, he would have shrugged it off. Was it because she'd rebuffed him? That had something to do with it. Much more than that, he couldn't fathom. He was still uncomfortable with some of the things he'd said.

I don't have what you're looking for. I wish I did.
I'd be here for you.

"Let it go, you idiot," he growled to himself. He needed a clear head for what was afoot.

Fifteen minutes before he was supposed to meet Maureen on the other side of the island, and just as he'd begun to wonder whether BB had stood him up, a cab curved down the ramp from the bridge. It was obscured from sight by buildings and bridge abutments, then reappeared coming his way. It stopped on the main road, discharged a passenger, and sped off.

It wasn't BB, which was not necessarily a surprise. But Nicholas was surprised to recognize the approaching silhouette.

"Of course," he admonished himself, rolling his eyes.

Shifting the carpetbag from one hand to the other, the Chinese gent in the porkpie hat stepped up to Nicholas and scrutinized him. The same gentleman Nicholas had run into in Dr. Bagby's Chinatown vestibule. Of course: it was this guy who'd stolen the painting from Dr. Bagby. He'd had *Trampoline Nude, 1972* in his carpetbag. The bag Nicholas had handed back to him. The painting had been right in his hand and he hadn't even realized it.

"You have the painting, yes?" Porkpie smiled, displaying a big gold bicuspid.

"Yes, in the trunk." Nicholas eyed the loose sway of the carpetbag. That night in Bagby's vestibule, Porkpie had had more than the painting in that bag. He'd had whatever he'd used to kill Bagby. Probably still did. "Got the money?"

Porkpie pulled a bank check from his sleeve. "Must see painting." That gold tooth flashed again like Satan's wink.

"Right." Nicholas nodded approvingly at the check. "Let's get the painting, then." Producing the keys, he turned his back on Porkpie and shuddered. Car tires thrummed overhead on the bridge deck.

Porkpie drifted behind him and out of his peripheral vision. But the car was carefully positioned, and streetlamps from the bridge ramp cast Porkpie's shadow on the trunk as he drew near. Just as soon as Nicholas popped the trunk lock, the transmitter in his ear buzzed, and H said:

"Watch it!"

There was a whoosh that burst into a bang when it connected with the trunk lid; Nicholas wheeled, stumbled, and fell to the ground off to the right. Porkpie regrouped immediately.

"Just say the word and I'll take him down with one shot," H said in Nicholas's ear as Porkpie ran at him with the butt of a steel pool cue. But Nicholas's hand was already on the gun in his overcoat pocket.

An explosion in Nicholas's coat pocket stopped Porkpie in his tracks. Dropping the pool cue, he pawed his shirtfront, looking for blood, for the hole where the bullet hit him. Finding none, he looked toward Nicholas. Nicholas had shot himself by accident.

Behind a cloud of blue smoke, Nicholas was clawing at his overcoat and gasping. Buttons popped and rolled on the ground as he flung open his coat, exposing a gush of gore that splashed to the pavement.

"Oh God, oh God," he muttered, groping the air with one hand. The other hand was busy trying to put out the growing fire in his coat lining.

Porkpie goggled Nicholas's supine, writhing form, then furtively glanced at the crate in the trunk. With his eyes back on Nicholas, he pulled the keys from the trunk and tried to slam the lid closed. The damage from the cue prevented it from latching.

Time for the clincher. Nicholas lurched up, then bit down hard, and blood coursed from his mouth. Like one of Peter Cushing's better performances, he gasped and fell back to the ground slowly, one hand surreptitiously splashing blood on the fire in his coat lining.

"Holy cow," Porkpie spat, shaking his head at Nicholas as he snatched the bank check and pool cue from the ground. Then he climbed into Nicholas's rental car and sped away, the trunk lid bouncing open and shut as he went.

Nicholas had intended to count to one hundred, but he got as far as thirty before wrenching off his coat and running for the snow pile. Pressing a ball of snow to the burn on his thigh, he limped back to his smoking coat and removed the transmitter.

"You got him?" Nicholas turned and spat the spent blood cartridges from his mouth.

"Can't miss him, the trunk open like that. Right on his tail, my friend. You OK?"

"Yeah, H, I'm OK. Think you put enough blood in that pack? It was like the Hoover Dam bursting from my gut. Sure this isn't the first time you rigged this setup?"

"Done it hundreds of times," H said flippantly.

"And did you set a hundred coats on fire? Mine's still burning." Nicholas retrieved a change of clothes from a duffel bag he'd hidden in a pile of snow.

"Mr. Bitch N. Moan. I gotta go, cover the man here. Call later."

By the time Nicholas had his shirt off, he was beginning to get a serious chill. And standing around in boxer shorts in February was no day in Cancún. He tore the duct-taped charge and blood pack off his stomach and threw it aside. Dressed and in his good tweed overcoat, he was still shivering uncontrollably. So he took a couple nips of Macallan from a flask to warm him and hustled his way toward the stadium.

I don't want you coming around anymore. Ever.

Nicholas hissed to himself: "Travel light."

A camera with a telephoto lens was clamped to the steering wheel, and Maureen swung it away from the Argentine fox's red pickup to the lamp glow way down by the bridge. She zoomed in as tight as she could and snapped off another photo for the hell of it. Even if she didn't bring Swires in, she could at least prove she'd located him. That was the brand of thoroughness, the kind of professionalism, that Nicholas never seemed to practice. Maureen didn't even think he owned a camera. What kind of partner would he make?

"He's not even a PI, for Christ sake," she whispered to herself. "But the asshole does make a lot of money."

And here he was, getting in on the passenger side.

The dome light was disconnected, so Nicholas sat down on a pile of newspaper and an apple. He grimaced and handed Maureen the apple. "What's up?"

"You're late. You got dirt or something on your face." She grabbed him by the chin. "What you been up to?"

"One case at a time, kiddo." He pulled his head away and wiped at his jaw with a hanky. "What's coming in over your spy scope?" He leaned over and put an eye to the camera.

"Nicholas, this looks like blood all over the back of your head!" She pulled a wad of napkins from the dash and mopped his hair.

"Would you stop? It's fake blood. I can't see with you pushing on my . . ."

"OK, OK . . ."

"Who else but Barney and Athenian sea captains wear those Greek fisherman caps these days? Sure looks like Barney from here. What's he doing?"

Maureen shrugged.

"About an hour ago, a drill rig drove away from here. Barney made like he was leaving, too, then he pulled the van back around and stuck that thing in a hole in the ground. Not for nothing, Nicholas, but your elbow is puttin' my leg to sleep here." Odd. Nicholas was in her lap without so much as stroking her thigh. Which reminded her that Brady hadn't called. *Shit.*

Nicholas took his eye from the camera and settled back into his own seat. "I saw the drill rig parked by the ramp over there. Two guys smoking a joint. So they haven't really left yet." He squinted off into the distance. "It looks to me like Barney's filling barrels with whatever is down in the hole."

Maureen's cell rang and her heart skipped a beat. She'd been waiting all day for it to ring. For Brady. It wasn't so much that she liked him—oh, he was handsome enough. Like a teenager, she was just thrilled that somebody "doable" had taken notice of her. And like a teenager, the prospect, the anticipation, of him calling, had made it very important that he did. But who the hell could it be at eleven thirty? Not Brady. Maybe her kid brother was in a jam. The number was blocked.

"McNary?"

Her heart froze. Only a cop would call a woman by her last name. "Brady?"

"Sorry for the late hour, and not calling sooner. Things got crazy here at the precinct. You know how it is."

Nicholas gave her a sidelong glance. "Maureen, we have business. Better lose that call.

"It's OK, Brady. I had another engagement tonight." Maureen was conscious that she was sounding too businesslike—a cop's reflex when talking to another cop. So she softened the tone. "I'd forgotten about dinner anyway."

There was a pause on the other end.

"Dinner?" Nicholas shot her another sidelong glance.

"No excuse," Brady said. "A man calls when he says he will."

"So, I guess you owe me one?" Maureen fairly purred.

"What is this? You talking to Moondoggie?" Nicholas grimaced. "Look, Gidget, could you please hang up and get back to what we're doing?"

"Is that your date?" Brady asked flatly.

"No, just a friend." Of course, she said it like she was covering. Never too soon to use jealousy to your advantage. "I'm being rude, so I should get off the phone."

"But I owe you one." Brady said that just the way she hoped he would—with a tinge, just a tinge, of desperation. "I'm off duty tomorrow night."

"Tomorrow? I'll have to check and don't have my calendar. Call me tomorrow?"

"OK, I will." Brady sounded determined. "Good night, Maureen."

"Good night..." She didn't remember his first name. He'd hung up anyway.

"Ahem?" Nicholas cleared his throat, pointing out the window. "Yoo-hoo, Gidget? We've got some company. Look over there. Here, use the binoculars."

Maureen suppressed a smile as she put the binoculars to her eyes. *He called.*

"That's the Argentine woman. She's got a huge fox coat, really gorgeous. Works for Drummond, and she's the one who went to Costa Rica." Maureen had never owned a fur coat or been to the tropics. Daytona Beach didn't seem to count. She found herself slipping into a speed fantasy about going to Jamaica with Brady.

"I remember. The slinky Latin number. So she's watching Barney, to make sure he does what he's supposed to do for Drummond. Swires has got himself quite an audience. Us, her, and the drillers."

Nicholas's smile faded suddenly. "I wonder if he knows?"

Then he seemed to have another thought. He pulled out his cell phone, dialed, and waited. "Ozzy? You can call the cops now."

Maureen gazed out the window. *He called.*

The drill rig sat empty near the ramp up to the Triborough. The Pazzo brothers had gone to see what was what.

"It's like he's vacuuming stuff outta the hole, Sam!" Joey peeled back into the shadow of the bridge pier. "Think he's, like, pullin' cheese outta the ground?"

"Cheese, Joey?" Sam sneered. "Just shuddup and lemme think about this a sec, OK?"

Moments later, Sam snapped his fingers and smiled.

"That list of gold prices!"

"Yeah?"

"Don't you get it? That brass we found?"

"You mean it was real fuckin' . . ."

Sam's eyes twinkled in the shadow. "Fuckin' gold, Joey!"

"How we gonna get it?"

"Same way we play hockey."

Chapter 24

Sealing the last barrel, Barney wiped his arm across his brow and tried not to peer into his surroundings. He hoped all his players were out there, somewhere. Minutes earlier, he'd checked the trash pile—the gun box was missing.

He drove the van around to the back of the stadium and over to the bulkhead where the boat was parked. The *Devil Dog* sat lower than before, and Barney checked his pocket watch. Full low tide was an hour away. At full low tide, the *Devil Dog* might be stuck in the muddy bottom of the Harlem River.

Using a hand truck, he carted a barrel down to the boat and used the contents to top off the barrels he'd hidden there with gold pellets. While he figured each of the barrels weighed about 200 pounds, filled top to bottom with gold they would weigh more. So he turned down the lantern and poured buckets of water into each barrel to bolster their heft. Then he went about sealing them.

When he was through, he trudged back ashore, set the lantern on the van's bumper, and picked up his thermos. Now if they'd just give him enough time to finish a cup of coffee and take a breather. He took a sip. Nope.

"Mr. Swires." Drummond Yager's Argentine companion wandered in from the darkness, black patent leather boots flashing beneath the huge fox coat.

"Silvi, hello, I uh..." Caught with his hand in the cookie jar.

"Drummond, did he say you must get a boat? I don't think so, Barney."

"I, uh, well..." Gee, Mom, I wasn't going to eat any of the cookies.

She stood not three feet in front of him, arms folded, legs apart so that her eyes were almost down to his level. She raised a finger and started pointing, counting silently.

"You know, I see...forty barrels? Twenty in boat, twenty in van. That make it too many barrels. Should be maybe only twenty, Barney. How come so many barrels?" Her eyebrows mocked him.

"What are you doing here, Silvi? Does Drummond..." Barney leaned back against the van to put some distance between them.

"No, he is not here." She took a step forward and put an arm on his shoulder. Her eyes inspected his, then her lips attached to his.

Barney pushed her away, but her hands held him to her by the belt. "What's this all about, Silvi?"

"Boat barrels have gold, or maybe van barrels have gold, eh? So you tell Silvi where is the gold—boat or truck?" She kissed him again, and almost made off with his bottom lip. "Barney, you are a double-crossing bastard, with nice blue eyes. I like that very much."

Attractive? Barney supposed she was, like a model in a magazine. But close up? Tall, severe-looking. All in all, she scared the hell out of him.

A catty smile slinked across her mouth, and it looked like kitty was coming in for another bite. Barney felt a sudden jolt of pain to his forehead the instant before his brain flashed white and his knees gave.

"Wow, what a bashie!" Maureen gasped, eye fixed to her camera.

"It's called a coco-nobby." Nicholas was glued to the binoculars.

"A what?"

"When somebody smacks your head with theirs. It's called a—"

"In Brooklyn it's called a bashie. I thought Swires was gonna get lucky there at first. Think we should go over and..."

"No, no, no, not yet... bingo! Look over there. Guess who else just dropped in? This is too good to be true. I hope you brought your gun, Maureen."

Maureen sighed. Nicholas didn't even carry a gun. Pathetic.

Silvi loved doing that. Men could be such delightful idiots.

She stepped up to where Barney lay on the ground and put a boot on his neck. This time, Silvi wasn't going to be cheated. This time, she was going to enact the double cross that she always warned her employers about—and got punished for. Barney gagged helplessly as she fished through his pockets and came up with the van's keys. She'd leave this little man for the dogs. Drummond would punish Barney for botching the job, unless of course he thought Barney was a part of Silvi's scheme. Either way, he would kill him, so she didn't need to.

"What a novel tableau."

Silvi checked her reaction of surprise as Drummond sauntered into the circle of light.

"Good thing you are here, Drummond. Our friend, I think he has ideas. Barney brings a boat, you see, with twenty barrels."

Drummond gave her an enigmatic side-glance from under the hood of his fur-lined parka. Snatching up the lantern with a dip of his paw, he went to the van's open doors and pushed on a barrel or two—clearly too light to contain gold. Then he went to the boat, and when he couldn't budge those barrels, he popped a lid. He held the lantern high.

Standing on the bulkhead, Silvi's dark eyes glowed

yellow as Drummond dug into the beads to check their depth.

"That's it, Drummond? We have it?"

Drummond fished around in his coat pocket and drew out a small pistol. Silvi's heart sank as he pointed at her. Then he smiled, raised it to the sky, and pulled the trigger.

Hot red balls of flame streaked into the sky. Flares. She looked back at Drummond in confusion.

"My dear Silvi. Can you explain why you didn't call me when he discovered the gold, as I instructed you?"

"I see he is up to something, so I come to see. I cannot tell you what I do not see." A plane zoomed low overhead.

"Too bad, really." Drummond produced a road flare, ignited it, and set it on the gunnel of the boat. "You see, I've spent fifteen years at Newcastle Warranty. An excellent employer. Really. But an employer nonetheless." He stirred the gold beads, admiring their dull luminosity. "During my tenure, I've recovered over nine hundred ninety million dollars in lost assets, and reaped a cumulative salary amounting to under four million dollars, including bonuses."

"Drummond, we must get barrels back to my truck and..." Silvi was grabbing at straws, but Drummond ignored her.

"So what with benefits, let's say four million plus. All right, now add that to my pension. Perhaps a million. That's five million, in return for almost a billion dollars. Why, that's one half of one percent. A paltry finder's fee, wouldn't you say?"

The roar of an engine echoed in from the river, pushing a rush of cold air.

"But this way, my cut works out to a smidgen under three percent, a rather modest finder's fee, all things considered." The glow of the gold left his hooded eyes as he resealed the barrel.

She knew he'd intended to rip off Newcastle, but now she realized that he would probably stiff her too.

"Yes, now we maybe both get money we have long waited for," she interjected confidently.

Drummond eyed her a moment from the recesses of his fur-lined hood, and smiled weakly. "Of course. But do you think that I'm *really* doing this for the money? No, not for the money."

Flood lamps flashed behind him as a seaplane roared upriver toward the cove. Propeller wash blasted a spray of glittering river water in its wake.

"Fifteen years, my hand and my soul frittered away in every filthy nook of this stinking planet all to recoup Newcastle's bad wagers. And now they have a mind to retire poor old Drummond. It was a pact with Lucifer from the start," he shouted over the plane's roar. "Fair's fair: the *Bunker Hill* for my soul."

He loosed a peculiar, nonchalant laugh that made Silvi shudder. It was the laugh he'd made in his sleep.

•   •   •

"FREEZE!" From behind the pickup, Maureen trained her Glock at Silvi. If she was going to shoot anybody, she wanted to shoot the woman who'd coldcocked her. Perhaps get herself a fur after all— the hard way.

Nicholas walked breezily past Maureen, the antithesis of her SWAT-style entrance.

"Hi, folks." He smiled and waved at the assemblage. Under the big yellow wing of a twin-engine float plane, Drummond, Silvi, and the bearded pilot who must be del Solar were hoisting the last of the barrels up into the plane from the *Devil Dog*.

Nicholas leaned over Barney, who still lay sprawled on the snow. He could see his pupils moving under his closed eyelids.

"Faker." Nicholas smiled and turned back toward the tableau. They squinted in his direction.

"The lady back there with the gun used to be a cop. She's a good shot, so no monkeying around, OK? We don't want anybody getting hurt." They didn't move, but Nicholas could feel them scheming. "C'mon, I want all you nice people to keep your hands where I can see them and come ashore."

Drummond put a mitten on his hood and yanked it back, his overbite quivering in amused awe. "Why, if it isn't Nicholas Palihnic! I'd venture you're a better swimmer than I imagined."

"Smith?" Nicholas did a double take. "Devlin Smith?"

"Yo, Nicholas." Maureen kept her finger firmly

on the trigger. "Let's say we cuff your old school chum and his pals, OK?"

"My, Nicholas, it has been a long time since we did business." Drummond let his hands drift downward.

"Keep those hands up, Smith," Nicholas warned. "It hasn't been that long. I can only imagine how you got out of that scrape in Borneo. I saw that boat run you over, I saw the blood in the water."

"And you left me for dead," Drummond scolded. "That wasn't a very nice way to treat your mentor."

"Oh, yeah. Like the way you watched as those bastards sank my boat? So what is it you're after this time? Some giant gold Singha? A U-boat full of platinum? Lost Jesuit diamond mines?"

"If you're here, you must know what's in these barrels," Drummond said coyly.

"Surprise me. It's been the same-old-same-old all day long."

"Twenty three million dollars in gold."

A gunshot cracked through the sky, then another: a window on the van exploded.

Nicholas dropped to the snowy ground, almost knocking the wind out of himself. Safety glass from the van's burst window rained down on him like tiny ice cubes.

"Nicholas!" Maureen shouted from the other side of the van, and between its wheels he could see her murky form wrestling with someone.

From the plane, Drummond bellowed something, but Nicholas's view was blocked.

He scrambled to his knees next to the van and popped his head around the other side.

"Slam!" Sam Pazzo checked him in the gut with a hockey stick.

Nicholas buckled to the ground, pain like a thumping bass drum in his stomach. Through eyes blurred with tears, he spied Barney scrambling for the bushes. Once again, Nicholas flashed bitterly, he was getting trounced in one of Swires's fiascoes.

Joey was standing right behind Sam, holding Maureen's own Glock. He handed a big silver automatic to his brother.

"Fucking nobody fuckin' move!" Sam shouted, pointing the silver automatic at Nicholas, at where Barney used to be, then at the vacant boat. He was bouncing up and down with agitation, his eyes blazing with hockey fervor.

"Yeah, nobody!" Joey was swirling in circles, pointing the Glock in an even sweep of his entire perimeter. "Sam!"

"What the fuck is it?"

"The dudes on the boat: where'd they go?"

Drummond, Silvi, and del Solar had vanished.

"Who the fuck cares? C'mon!"

Sam led the way as the Pazzos trotted toward the boat.

A loud whine emanated from the seaplane. The propeller started to rotate.

Sam and Joey hopped onto the boat's gangplank.

Smoke erupted from the engine, and the seaplane roared to life.

A hand darted out of the plane to close the door, but Sam reached out and grabbed it. Drummond spilled out of the plane, on top of Sam and into the boat.

The plane's engine howled.

Silvi appeared in the doorway, a sawed-off shotgun in her hands. But Joey grabbed the barrel as it went off. The buckshot shattered part of the *Devil Dog*'s railing with a clang. With his other hand Joey gripped her by the coat and yanked. She stumbled and fell to her butt. The shotgun clattered to the pontoon, rolled over, and plopped into the water. Joey tried to climb over her into the plane, and she latched on to his collar. But she wasn't tussling with any amateur; he coco-nobbied her before she could bashie him. By this time Sam and Drummond were on their feet struggling onto the aircraft's pontoon as the plane twisted toward the open water.

Maureen stumbled over to where Nicholas lay on the ground, and they watched Drummond, Joey, Silvi, and Sam claw, punch, and grapple their way onto the plane.

"It's like *The Three Stooges*." Nicholas coughed, trying to get his breath back. "OK, the four stooges."

Maureen dropped to her knees next to him. "Like a WWF tag team match, but no folding chairs."

Like an overwound toy with a bent wheel, the plane lurched away into the river, legs, arms, and feet wiggling from the doorway. With all the weight on one side, the plane was listing, and the *Devil*

Dog—tied loosely to one of the gunnels—seesawed behind like a pull toy duckie. Red tail and wing lights blinked against the night, the shouts and curses of the brawl echoing across the channel.

"There goes twenty-three million in gold." Maureen sucked on a loose tooth and spat some blood.

"Yeah, well, mission accomplished just the same. We got Barney. But there they go."

The plane stormed down the Harlem River, lifting off just as it passed under the footbridge and veering sharply away from a passing tugboat. Silhouetted against the glittering city beyond, water fell from the pontoons like sparks. The tug's searchlight caught a flash of Silvi holding on to a pontoon strut, her fur coat flapping in the wind.

The plane's landing lights passed over the *Devil Dog* in the middle of the Harlem River. Drummond could be seen standing on the bow, tall and stoic as any British officer of the fleet; he didn't even shake a fist as the plane flew over. His parka hood denied anyone the satisfaction of his expression as the boat gently sank beneath him. It was a performance that would have done Admiral Nelson proud. Except that this was not a display of man's heroism in the face of defeat, but of avarice's profound pique in the face of meddling rogues. The swirling icy waters gradually bubbled up Drummond's body and over his head.

Nicholas broke into laughter, clapping his hands.

He shouted: "I guess it's your turn to go down with the ship, Smith!"

"I don't think he heard you," Maureen gasped, still out of breath from her struggle. "Why is the boat sinking?"

"That wasn't for him." Nicholas smiled bitterly. "That was for me."

"But I don't get it—why's the boat sinking?"

Nicholas shrugged. "I guess maybe the shotgun blast blew a hole in the bottom of the boat."

Barney strolled from the nearby bushes, fingering the bump on his forehead. Maureen and Nicholas watched as he ambled over to them, blue eyes of innocence connecting with their gaze of distrust.

"Guess they got away." Barney flashed his secret smile. "What are you doing here, Nicholas?"

"Barney, you scare me." Nicholas took a deep breath. "Next time you get in some kind of jam, have Nicasia call someone else."

"Nicasia? She had you come look for me?"

Maureen sighed. "She thought you were..."

"No, don't ruin my surprise, Maureen."

She turned less sanguine. "Hey, would somebody mind telling me what the hell just happened here?"

"Why would she send you to look for me?" Barney rubbed his chin, confused.

"Oh no, you first. Fill us in, boy genius. I know you're just dying to tell us what was going on around here."

Barney stirred the snow-crusted ground with his foot for a second, hands deep in his pockets. He pursed his lips and tilted his head toward the water's edge. "C'mon."

Maureen and Nicholas shambled after him to where the gangplank floated at the river's edge. Barney knelt next to a gnarled tree where the boat had been tied. A wire was attached to it at the waterline. Winding the wire around and around his hand, he finally reached its terminus, which was attached to a large rubber plug. In the dim half-light cast by the bridge, he held the stopper out for inspection.

"I drilled a big hole in the bottom of the boat. When the boat pulled away, out came the cork, so the boat sank."

"What?" Nicholas and Maureen said in unison.

Barney tossed the wire and stopper back into the river, wiping his hands on his jeans as he stood. His eyes scanned the river.

"I don't think we have to worry about Drummond. Even if he could survive the icy water, the current would have carried him a ways downriver. Don't think we'll see any more of him tonight, anyway. And if he survives, he'll be after the plane, where the gold is."

Nicholas and Maureen exchanged a curious glance.

"Is that what you were vacuuming from the ground?" Nicholas peered closely at Barney.

"Uh huh." Barney fingered the lump on his forehead again. "From a boat that was buried here, by accident, a long time ago. Gold in pellet form. Just sucked it out." He made a popping sound with his lips. "Put them in barrels, loaded them onto the boat."

Maureen swept a hand back toward the van.

"What about those barrels?"

"Hmm." Barney cocked his head at the ground, scratching the back of his neck as though he'd missed a tough shot in eight ball. "You see, there were two sets of barrels, one with gold, one with gravel and water. Things didn't quite work out the way I figured."

"You tried to double-cross them, but they were watching, and those punk drillers figured you out too. They got the gold, you got the gravel, am I right?" Nicholas raised his eyebrows. And his voice. "And you let those crazy, double-crossing punks get away with twenty-three million in gold?"

Barney dug his hands deep in his front pockets. "Well..."

Nicholas didn't think he'd have the gall to finish the thought. But he did.

"...it's only money."

"Guess what, Barney?" Nicholas wasn't going to let him have the last line, oh no. "Drummond told Nicasia that you're dead."

Barney jumped like he'd been stung by a bee.

Nicholas smiled—as he suspected, Barney had no idea. *Just let him scheme his way out of this one, smug bastard.*

"That's why we're here. She hired us to find you. Or your body. So the fun's not over yet, buddy-boy."

Nicholas slapped him on the shoulder, a little harder than was necessary. "Not only do you have to explain to Her Highness Nicasia that you deceived her, but you and I have a little unfinished business. I owed one to Nicasia, so I found you."

Nicholas started back to the car, Maureen in tow.

"*You* found him?" She laughed caustically.

Barney was left standing dumbstruck at the water's edge.

"Now *you* owe *me* one, Barney." Nicholas turned, still walking, the beams of the van's headlights making his shadow long, sinister, and black on the snow. "I've got a little job for you, first thing tomorrow. We'll pick you up at seven thirty AM in the parking lot by the stadium here."

Maureen put a hand on Nicholas's arm, bringing him to a stop, their breath making frosty plumes in the frigid air.

"Barney going to be OK?" she whispered.

Barney stood where they left him, staring at the ground.

"What do I care? He got himself into this mess, he can get himself out of it."

"And Drummond. You can't mean to tell me he was your mentor?"

"If it weren't for him I might still be in the Peace Corps."

"You? In the Peace Corps?" Maureen snorted. "Surprised you didn't start a war somewhere."

"Hey, that wasn't entirely my fault."

•   •   •

Barney waited until he saw their headlights swing around the lot before he pulled a handheld marine radio from one jacket pocket and a signal strobe from the other. The strobe was about the size of a coffee cup. He set it on the ground and turned it on. The strobe flashed a blue circle of light around him.

He jabbed a few buttons on the radio.

"Come in, Charlie X-ray, over."

The radio crackled with static, then blared:

"Charlie Zebra, we read you loud and clear."

"Rendezvous at..." Barney checked his watch. 12:47 AM. He certainly needed to have the deal all done by the time Nicholas returned. No time to call Nicasia. She was asleep, anyway. That he would have to deal with by the light of day. "Four thirty AM rendezvous. Do you copy, Charlie X-ray? Over."

"Roger that, over."

Barney pulled a handheld Web device from his pocket and switched it on.

"There will be a blue beacon on the bank of the Harlem River where you can come ashore. I'll tell you exactly where by four AM, over."

"Roger, Charlie Zebra, will await your transmission at four, over."

Barney looked at the screen of his Web device, touched a few buttons, and brought up his overseas bank accounts. Still listed as "AWAITING TRANSFER."

"Are you ready to transfer the funds as arranged?" Not only would he see when the money popped into the account, but he would receive an e-mail confirming it.

"Roger, Charlie X-ray, over." The voice was flat.

"Remember. The merchandise will be wired with explosive charges." Well, at least they would think it was. "If the transfer doesn't go through, I blow it all up. No double cross. Over."

"Roger and out."

Chapter 25

Porkpie tipped his hat as Karen closed the front door to the uptown exhibition space, which was alight with midmorning sun.

Still wearing her satin bathrobe, BB admired the von Clarke where it leaned against the wall. "Dreadful frame."

"Bea, you're absolutely brilliant," Karen said, tightening her robe. "That's the same man that brought the Moolman, isn't it?"

"That's right." BB played with a smile as she looked over the back of the canvass. "Yes, the same clever fellow. He helps certain people unload paintings discreetly. That way nobody knows they're going bankrupt. Anyway, Moolmans I know." BB waved a hand at the canvass. She didn't mention that she'd also had the clever little man murder that swine Nicholas. "Von Clarkes are your department. Authentic?"

Karen lifted the painting and examined the back.

"See here? Herbert often jotted things down on the back of canvasses, like phone numbers, grocery lists. Mm hmm. Flemish linen canvass." Then she flipped it around and looked at the front.

"Oils applied with the mixture of brush and palette knife strokes. Classic. This is *Day After Day*." Karen shook her head in wonderment at what might seem to the untrained eye a study of purplish bruises on granite. "This will certainly put you in the black. Should I call Mr. Axelrod?"

BB glanced at her watch. "When I got the buzz on the von Clarke last night, I put in a call to the studio just as soon as Axelrod was off the air. Said he'd be home this morning. Call a limo. I'll drive the jazz up now."

Twenty minutes later, BB stepped over the *New York Times* on her doorstep. Taking it along for the ride was only a passing thought. Even if she had, the item on B4 may not have caught her attention. The headline read "Robbery at Strunk Gallery."

As a network anchorman and host of *Probe*, Peter Axelrod was perhaps one of the most recognized men in America. However, none of his public would have recognized him first thing in the morning. That chiseled hair became a Dippity-do fright wig, and a few martinis put blood in his eye. Caps on his teeth glowed slightly blue by his bathroom's fluorescent light, and capillaries in his nose traced out a subminiature road map. He preferred seeing himself on TV, which was the way he wanted everybody else to see him. Before BB's arrival, he spent some time powdering his nose and touching things up.

Decked out from head to toe in purple Patagonia, he went spryly to the first floor and opened the refrigerator. Removing the bottom crisper trays, he exposed a safe. A clever place for a safe, he thought, and it was his idea, after all.

Moments later, he left the kitchen with one hundred thousand dollars in a sealed plastic food container. Then, as he wrote out a check for four hundred thousand dollars, the bell sounded. He no longer kept a wife or full-time staff. He answered the bell and buzzed BB through the gate. The limo pulled up to the front door.

"Good morning, Peter. I've got that wonderful painting for you." BB stepped from the limo, and the drive went to the trunk to get the crate.

"I'm excited." Peter spread his arms affably, then stooped to pick up the paper. "Bring it in and let's have a look."

Minutes later in his cavernous off-white living room, Peter Axelrod stood nodding at the painting. BB stood next to him, arms folded. The art was on the floor, leaning against one of the coffee tables.

"Terrific. Absolutely terrific. I'm beginning to feel like a real collector, here. I think"—he turned

and pointed—"it'll go right over that couch. It'll get
reflected light from the skylight and . . ."

The buzzer sounded.

Peter puzzled a moment.

"I called the framer. But she wasn't going to come
until noon. Hmm."

The buzzer sounded again, and he answered it.
Then he turned back to his guest.

"BB, do you know anyone named Nicholas
Pahlinic?"

Barney fought the urge to retreat as he saw BB come
toward him down the drive. She looked ready to
give him a coco-knobby, or a bashie, of which he'd
had quite enough. But he didn't break character as
she intercepted him.

"I told you over the intercom to wait at the end of
the drive!"

He cocked an eyebrow at her, but sent his gaze up
toward where a confused Peter Axelrod stood in the
doorway to his home.

"I don't take orders from you, toots." Barney
sneered, adjusting the angle of his Greek fisherman's
cap. "Where's my painting? Does he have my painting?" Barney waved a hand shod in black leather and
breezed past her.

BB caught him by the arm.

"Who are you? What is it you want?" BB
growled. "You're going to ruin this deal!"

"Doesn't matter who I am. Deal's already on the

fritz, honey. Read this." Barney handed her a clipping, which read:

ROBBERY AT STRUNK GALLERY, February 27—The East Side gallery of Osman "Ozzy" Strunk was robbed last evening by a man described as a Chinese gentleman in a porkpie hat, carrying a carpetbag and brandishing a sawed-off pool cue. The owner of the gallery, Osman Strunk, who lives on the premises, was abducted when he returned to the gallery around nine PM. Mr. Strunk was forced to deactivate his alarms before being locked in a closet. An hour later he managed to force his way out of the closet and call the police. It was when the police arrived that the painting *Day After Day* by Herbert von Clarke was found missing.

"I...I don't understand." BB crumpled the clipping, a glassy look in her eye.

"Here's the deal. One: you've got to get..."

"BB, why don't we all go inside?" Peter called from the doorway, clearly becoming perturbed. "Bring your friend and..."

"I'm so sorry, Peter, really. Go inside, sorry for the interruption. I'll be right in." BB smiled mechanically in his direction, and Peter withdrew.

Barney continued.

"One: get the Moolman back. We know C. S. Rautford has it. It could get very embarrassing. If you need to, explain that it's stolen and that you can fix it for him."

"Are you mad? Rautford will never deal with me again! And I still don't understand about—"

"Two: go ahead and sell the von Clarke to Axelrod. But the proceeds all go to Osman Strunk."

"Wait a minute. I . . . I've been set up by you and Osman Strunk! That robbery was a charade—for the insurance, and you and Nicholas . . ."

"Very good. Yes, we know about how your Chinese goon took out Dr. Bagby, and we know he killed Nicholas. I'm offering you a way out of this without complete ruin."

"You can't substantiate . . ."

"Then again, maybe we can. Does Karen know about your fun and games, or maybe she just suspects? We can definitely tie you to the Chinese guy and the two paintings through her, which'll be enough to destroy your reputation at the very least. Ozzy's willing to go all the way and stick to the Chinese guy story if he has to. He's got nothing to lose. He's been looking to sell the von Clarke anyway."

"But what about this item in the paper? When Axelrod sees it . . ."

"Tell him that I came here from Strunk to explain that it was a mistake. Osman will be his flaky best and tell the cops that he forgot he sold it to you. Just as soon as he gets the money. How much?"

BB didn't miss a beat.

"Four hundred grand," she hissed through gritted

teeth. It looked like her jaw muscles might just jump out of her face. "I'll have Peter make the check out to Strunk."

Barney almost felt sorry for BB. Almost.

But as he walked back down the driveway, he fingered the bruise on his forehead, and figured she was probably just the type to give someone a coco-knobby.

He climbed into the Caprice, where Maureen, Nicholas, and H sat waiting.

"How'd it go?" Maureen asked, pulling the sedan away from the curb.

"She took the deal."

"I'll bet she was none too happy about it." H winced. "Nicholas, you had to come along and mess up my sweet courier arrangement. BB must know I got something to do with this."

"Sweet? She couldn't even pay you," Nicholas barked. "I saved your ass, pal. You were mixed up with stolen art. I got you out of it. Believe it or not, you have a reputation to protect."

H laughed bitterly. "What I didn't know sure wasn't hurtin' me."

Barney cleared his throat. "Maureen, can I borrow your phone?"

She handed it back to Barney, steering the sedan onto Route 9.

"Uh oh." Nicholas smiled. "You're not calling who I think you're calling, are you? This should be good."

Barney didn't answer, he just dialed. "Nicasia Grieg, please." There was a pause.

"Grieg here."

"I'll make it up to you, sugar lips, I swear."

There was a pause, a withering sigh, and a sniff.

"I didn't know they were going to tell you I was dead," he added quickly. "I was thinking about you the whole time, but I couldn't call. Once I realized they planned to kill me, I couldn't let them involve you. I didn't want them to maybe come after you."

"Barney, you ever do something like this again and *I'll* kill you," Nicasia quavered.

"All I want to do is come home. To you."

There was a pause, and for a second, Barney thought she'd hung up.

"When?"

"Two hours too soon?"

"Not soon enough." She hung up.

"Sugar lips?" Nicholas knit his brow.

"Men never say sweet things like that to me." Maureen batted her lashes at Nicholas. "Or maybe they would if they had a mind to take on a partner."

"Maureen, I told you, I don't have enough work for—"

"You smug bastard." Maureen chuckled, freckles aflame. "You may not have enough work for two people. But what makes you think I don't?"

"Well..." Nicholas faltered, waving a dismissive hand.

"Now you're in for it." H nodded. "Hey, Maureen, you need some help on something? I've suddenly found I can spare some of my time, thanks to Nicholas."

"Oh, yeah, you two..." Nicholas snorted.

"Olbeter, let's lunch." Maureen locked eyes with H through the rearview mirror.

"Yeah." H folded his arms. "Just you and me, two highly skilled investigators. What you got, lady?"

"It so happens," Maureen began, "that Newcastle Warranty contacted me the other day. They paid me to tell them what I was investigating, and to keep them informed of what I found out about Drummond. Now I think they want me to find out what happened to him, and if he's not dead, track him after he retires. I think they suspect he's skimmed and stashed some of their money."

"Oh, I see!" Nicholas slapped his knee, feigning indignance. "And here I thought you were working for me."

Maureen didn't favor him with a glance. Just a smirk at the road ahead.

"Oh, man. Way to go, lady." H laughed, patting her on the shoulder. "They give you a retainer?"

Maureen nodded. She kind of liked being called "lady," and her smirk dissolved into a smile. Her phone rang, and she flipped it open.

"Hey, Brady." Her smile only got bigger.

Nicholas scowled. "Not Moondoggie again?"

Chapter 26

B. Belarus's downtown gallery opened a week later, in what some considered a bit of a rush. But the place was packed with art, talent, scene-makers, swillers, buyers, and sellers. Some expressed mild astonishment over the domestic champagne, while others thought the Korbel more acceptable than the "finger sandwich" catering. But make no mistake, it was a feeding frenzy. Bargain prices were the blood in the water, and it was all BB's new assistant, Winnie, could do to keep up with the sales amid the gnashing teeth.

"Bea, you're looking thin, babe, you really are." Ozzy wagged a finger in her face. He took her hand and squeezed it. "Oh, Ozzy isn't such a monster—I won that round, and I'm sure you'll get me next time but good! Everything's going to work out fine, hon, really. You're a survivor!" He chortled, and buzzed away.

"Rat bastard," BB fumed. She waded through the sea of excited chatter to where Xavier Gliche was holding court with a gaggle of fresh sycophants.

"Xave, I was so sorry to read about the robbery at your studio."

He nodded, looking suitably outraged.

"What times we live in." BB tsked. "And just think of what it will do for the provenance of those pieces, hm?" She had to get her digs in too. BB had little doubt Gliche had orchestrated the robbery to give his product a boost.

He sighed, eyebrows up, as if the concept had only just occurred to him. Pompous fop didn't even register the sarcasm. No satisfaction in that, she thought, and moved on toward Winnie.

"We going to make it?" BB said through smiling teeth.

The blond Spanish girl looked up slyly, very much like she had the first time BB met her at the gym.

"Just topped a million five. All we gotta do is collect."

"Mind if I cut in?"

BB turned, and was confronted by a man in a teal-checked tweed suit.

There was some commotion as people called for water, then for air. Moments later, BB found herself on a balcony at the rear of the gallery, Winnie waving a docket in her face.

Behind Winnie stood Nicholas, looking concerned but very much alive.

BB recovered quickly.

"Winnie, get that out of my face and get back in there. I'll consult with...Mr. Palihnic...privately."

Winnie retreated without betraying any suspicions.

"What happened to Karen?" Nicholas stepped up to where BB stood at the railing, savoring that edgy twitch in her strained smile, the black malevolent eyes aflame like those of a cornered viper. "Split when she realized you were passing hot canvasses?"

"She has her life, I have mine, and apparently... you have yours."

"I know H was supposed to come get the Moolman, but I wanted to make sure it was the genuine item. I know how resourceful you can be."

"Go downstairs." BB popped open a compact, turning her back on him. "The guard at the cellar door will give it to you." She vainly tried powdering the flush from her cheeks. "And may I say, I hope you choke on it."

Nicholas had expected a more spirited response from BB, what with her being confronted by her victim's ghost. Something in the way of screaming, throwing ashtrays, or scorching invectives struck him as more appropriate. But he guessed his disappointment wasn't as great as hers.

"Lighten up, kiddo. You might actually need me sometime. *Ciao.*"

He exited, picked up the crate, and hailed a cab.

But a van cut off the cab before it got to him. It screeched to a halt, the side door slammed open, and two hockey-masked hoods latched their hands onto Nicholas's shoulders and hauled him inside.

Chapter 27

Mel was hard at work in her time machine. The Oklahoma DMV was open on one screen, the Federal Corrections database on another. The door buzzer broke her concentration. She glanced at the time on the screen. That would be the laundry delivery. She grabbed three dollars from atop a monitor. The gratuity.

Tiptoeing through a field of Legos spread across the living room floor, she buzzed open the downstairs door and stepped into the hallway. Looking down the stairwell, she expected to see the stocky Ecuadorian with her red laundry bag.

"Angie?"

"Hi!" Angie smiled from one flight down.

"What are you...well, I mean..."

"Oh, I'm sorry to barge in. I was just in the neighborhood, thought I'd stop by."

Angie came up the last flight, carrying a large box tied with string.

Mel crossed her arms, then put them in her pockets, then took them out. Angie was the last person she expected to see.

Angie reached the top step and smiled. "I'm lying, of course."

Mel's cordial smile wavered.

"Here." Angie handed her the box.

"What's this?"

"Well, Dottie loved the tookie tookie bird so much, Garth and I decided she should have it."

Mel looked at the floor, handing the box back. "Thanks, Angie, that's very nice of you, but really, we couldn't."

"We insist!" Angie studied Mel.

"I can't." Their eyes met.

"Oh." Angie blushed. "I'm sorry. I guess I...we assumed..."

"It's not your fault." Mel tried to laugh it off. "The other night was just one of Nicholas's little subterfuges. You know."

"Well, don't I feel like a jerk? Garth told me this wasn't a good idea."

"I appreciate it, though, Angie. It was a nice thought."

"Angie!" Dottie ran into the hallway. "How's the tookie tookie bird? Do you know the Tarzan song? Nicholas taught me the Tarzan song, and there's a tookie tookie bird in it that goes *AW! AW! EE! EE! TOOKIE TOOKIE!*"

"OK, Dottie, that's enough now." Mel tried to shoo her back into the apartment.

"Angie?" Dottie pointed. "What's in the box?"

Mel loosed a frustrated sigh at the ceiling, tucked her hair behind an ear, then looked at Angie. "You want some tea?"

Chapter 28

A week had passed since Barney had returned from the dead and reconciled with Nicasia. He'd been called on the carpet, make no mistake. The illegal nature of his romp with Drummond had caused quite a stir. But love can be a lenient master to contrition, and things were beginning to settle back to normal.

Barney had never much cared for life on Manhattan's Upper East Side where he and Nicasia lived. He had himself pegged as more of a West Village/Tribeca sort. Even though he was hard put to knock Nicasia's civilized door-manned digs, what with amenities like elevators and terraces, it was just a little too nice, a little too "just so." The dingy store where he bought coffee in the Village, for example, had sawdust on the floor, an ancient flame-fed roaster, two irritable Italian proprietors, and a clientele comprised mainly of whiskered matrons preoccupied with pinching loaves of semolina. Uptown, on the other hand, Barney found himself in a white-tiled shop queued with professional types cooing about mocha double-lattes.

"No Mocha Java? No straight Mocha Java beans?" Barney rubbed his jaw, handing the countergirl his plastic "Take One" number.

"But our Mocha Java Blend is rich and creamy and . . ."

"I don't want rich and creamy. How about Kona?"

"Yes! See, I have decaf and . . ."

"That's preground."

"And vacuum-packed in Hawaii!"

"And about twenty-seven bucks a pound." Barney sighed. "I'll take Sumatran beans, two pounds."

He tried to console himself with the idea that in a matter of days he and Nicasia would be winging their way to a Costa Rican vacation—an actual trip to Costa Rica—where native beans would be plentiful. With that in mind, he peeked inside his jacket to make sure the tickets were still there. The travel agent had been his first errand, coffee the second. The first was a gift for Nicasia, the second a gift for himself. She'd had a pretty tough go of it. Barney thought the prospect of a tropical getaway and vows of eternal legitimacy might just calm stormy seas. And it might have the bonus effect of calming Barney's nerves. It couldn't hurt to be out of town if Drummond came to call.

Saluting Roger the doorman, Barney sauntered through the apartment lobby hefting a duffel bag over one shoulder, shopping bag with coffee in the other. As he boarded the elevator, his thoughts focused on how Nicasia would welcome him, what he would say. His nerves were on edge. He had betrayed her trust. Could he win it back?

A hand jammed into the closing doors. "Mr. Swires?"

"I almost forgot," Roger the doorman drawled. "This here came for you." He handed Barney a shoe-box–sized package neatly wrapped in brown paper and string.

The doors closed and Barney inspected the parcel as the elevator whizzed him toward his lofty floor. He stabbed the fifth-floor button, changed elevators, and headed for the garage. If it was a bomb, it might have an anaerobic fuse meant to go bang with barometric change, like going from the first to the twentieth floor.

Barney knew the unmarked, forbidding package was from Drummond just by holding it. He'd been hoping that even if the Hell Gate gang had survived the ruckus, they'd left town thoroughly discombobulated. And perhaps with subsequent infighting, they would not pursue the matter further. Wishful thinking.

He sat on a curb in the parking garage and considered his parcel, finally deciding that until Drummond had the gold, he wouldn't be so foolish as to kill Barney. But just to be safe, he tossed the box across the garage a few times before popping the strings.

It was the pistol box, but it was too light to contain that big silver automatic. Instead it contained a note and Nicasia's wallet.

His heart slid up into his throat. "My God."

Barney hadn't been stupid enough to underestimate Drummond's resolve. Like any stage magician, he hadn't entirely pinned the success of his act on a flappable audience. Following the Hell Gate to-do, he'd spent a few days doing research for another illusion, a precaution that he now prayed would be the showstopper. And the duffel bag he'd retrieved from his storage locker contained the props for pulling the rabbit out of his hat. He'd just been hoping he wouldn't have to use it.

But if they killed Nicasia, he had no idea what he would do. To Drummond, or with the rest of his life.

Twenty minutes later, Barney shoved his way through a sliced chain-link fence and trudged quickly over broken macadam toward a vacant Sanitation Department barge depot. The float plane was parked at the pier next to the building. As instructed in the note, Barney tromped to the first-floor entrance.

He stopped at a filthy metal door atop the stairs and listened. He scanned his surroundings and gave his jaw an anxious rub. "Showtime."

He shoved the door open. The place looked empty.

"Greetings," Drummond's voice hailed gloomily from above. He stood on a railed gantry next to where the garbage trucks had once dumped refuse into the barges. The place still had the sickly smell of sour milk and oranges, the stink of garbage. He wore a black turtleneck under a blacker trench coat, a long red scarf, and the expression of a gambler with a stacked deck.

The Pazzos stood at Drummond's left wearing their dirty driller's coveralls, goalie masks flipped atop their heads, chewing gum for all it was worth. The white-bearded pilot del Solar stood sheepishly behind them, one eye blackened and a palm-sized bandage on his forehead. Silvi stood just to the right of Drummond, her face covered in small scrapes and badly wind-chapped. Beside her were Nicholas and Nicasia. They were both inverted, hanging by their feet from rope slung over the rafters.

"Nicasia!" Barney stepped before his jury and dropped the bag. A metallic crunch from the bag caused his inquisitors to stand a little taller with expectation.

"Barney!" Her cry was part desperation, part anguish.

Barney looked up at Drummond. His tranquil blue eyes were raging seas. "If you want to see any of that gold, you cut her down right now!"

"You miss the point, Mr. Swires." Drummond adjusted his scarf. "Silvi, cut the woman's ear off."

"OK, people, let's settle down," Nicholas piped up. "Barney will give you the gold, won't you, Barney?"

"Cut off his ear first." Drummond smiled.

"Hey!" Nicholas protested as Silvi turned toward him. "Hey!"

Barney's anger nestled back into the strategic certitude of measured but deliberate debate, his hands slipping down into his pockets. Showing panic would only reinforce Drummond's advantage. Barney's eyes were locked with Drummond's, and he didn't watch as Silvi clicked open a stiletto and knelt next to Nicholas.

"Barney!" Nicholas boomed.

"Barney!" Nicasia screamed.

Cocking his head at Drummond, Barney let slip his secret smile.

"You cut either of them and you'll never see a cent of that money." He spoke quietly, but the words seemed to echo around the depot like a yodel.

Silvi paused, Nicholas's ear in her grip, knife poised.

"In the first place"—Barney looked to the floor, pursing his lips—"the *Bunker Hill* never carried the sixty thousand ounces of gold."

"Smith, Barney's right. There's no gold," Nicholas grumbled.

Drummond stepped up next to Nicholas and gave him a short kick to the back of the head. "Silence, dear Nick. Didn't I always say that when you're in the hands of hostile forces and don't know what to say, it's always best to say nothing?"

Limping to the railing, Drummond leered down at Barney. "Sam, get that bag next to Swires." Drummond sneezed loudly into a hanky.

Sam broke rank with Joey and the pilot to descend the ladder.

"You're a poor liar, Mr. Swires," Drummond sneered. "After your little party, we went back to the borehole and found traces of the gold you took. We know there was gold in that ship! Now for the last time..."

"Newcastle didn't look close enough at the historical record." Barney began to pace before his jury. "Look at the documents in the bag, Drummond. The gold you found was part of what New Haven Steam Ship Line used to dupe Newcastle Warranty back in 1855."

Sam hustled the bag up to Drummond's feet and unzipped it. Drummond pushed him aside, found a folder of documents, and opened them on the railing.

"Le'go my ear!" Nicholas squirmed free of Silvi's grip, and she gave him a quick backhand slap to his face.

"Drummond, they just put gold in the top of some of the most accessible bags so that when they were inspected..." Barney rolled one hand in the air. Perry Mason had nothing on him.

Drummond flipped through the documents, squinting. "You're trying to tell me that you can prove an insurance fraud from 1855? If so, then why did you set up the elaborate double cross? With the boat, and the two sets of barrels full of gravel?"

"Because at the time I thought the gold really *was* at the bottom of the hole. But believe me, I wasn't trying to double-cross you. I was just attempting to buy myself a little life insurance."

"Bloody hogwash!" Drummond sputtered. "Silvi! Cut him."

She didn't move.

"C'mon, Drummond, I mean, it was pretty obvious once you told me to kill the Pazzos..."

"Whoa!" the Pazzos chorused.

"Fuck you, man!" Sam pulled off his mask, menacing Drummond like a rival hockey player.

"Shit yeah, Sam," Joey added. "Fuck him."

"Well, what was I to think, Drummond?" Barney looked hurt. "I couldn't help but guess you meant to double-cross all of us. I don't see where you hold any moral high ground."

"We want that gold, Swires!" Drummond fussed with his hanky.

"I knew that if their lives were that cheap to you, what was I? For that matter, what was Silvi? And that pilot?"

Stiletto at her side, Silvi rose and took a step closer to Drummond.

Del Solar took a step back, eyes on Drummond.

"The gold, Swires!" Drummond produced a .38, cocked it, and pointed it at Nicasia. Silvi eyed him cautiously.

"The 'gold' is right here in my hand." Barney pulled his hand from his pocket and held out a handful of green rocks. He tossed them up onto the gantry. "Brass. Oxidized brass pellets. You must have found some of those in the hole, too, didn't you?"

Drummond was about to answer, but he sneezed instead, nearly squeezing off a round into Nicasia.

"If there was gold, I'd give it to you in a second for my friends." Barney pulled another handful of green rocks from his pocket. "The sacks were filled with brass shot."

The Pazzos, del Solar, and Silvi each picked up a few green rocks for inspection.

Drummond put his gun on the railing, snatched up the folder, and began a renewed inspection of its contents. Barney continued.

"So I wondered what happened and did a little research at the New-York Historical Society. What I came up with were some court records showing that New Haven Steam Ship Line was near bankruptcy at the time the *Bunker Hill* went down. Seems it had been bilked by the owner, James D. Bird, and creditors were on his back. So in April of 1853 he filed for protection under the 1841 U.S. Bankruptcy Law. According to the records you have there, and an assessment by their lawyer, they wouldn't even have been able to honor the Bank of Boston courier contract if they got it. There's also a bill of sale..."

"A bill of sale from 1855?" Drummond blinked at

a photocopy of a handwritten invoice for "Muntz brass foundry shot."

"It was part of the continuing bankruptcy protection filing. Seems they didn't pay the bill for a few tons of rough brass shot they ordered from Redhook Foundries in Brooklyn. Same tonnage as the gold. Coincidence?"

"Surely you don't think I'm that stupid, Swires," Drummond spat. "LAD research shows that they obtained gold from the Bank of Boston for the shipment. What happened to that?"

Barney cocked his head. "I can only assume that James D. Bird swiped it, along with the insurance money. I included his obituary in the file. For someone who went bankrupt, he died a very rich man."

"Where did you get these files?"

"The New-York Historical Society, the Public Library, and New York Custom House records. Have your people check it out."

Drummond looked sour as Campari, and about as red.

"Fuck." Joey gave Sam a disconsolate shove.

"If you're through with us now . . ." Nicholas nodded in Nicasia's direction.

"Cut us down, dammit!" Nicasia blurted, spittle hitting the floor.

Silvi waved a hand at the files. "Big losers, eh, Drummond?"

"What the fuck . . ." Joey began, but then wheeled a finger down at Barney. "Hey, so, if, like there's no gold, what do you mean we'll never see a cent of that money? What money?"

The echo of Joey's voice was replaced by a moment of communal silence, all eyes on the duffel bag.

"However"—Barney smiled—"the venture was not a complete washout." He nodded at the duffel bag. "I approximate that there was somewhere in the neighborhood of two hundred pounds of gold that Bird used to top off the bags, some of which I used to top off the barrels you flew off with. The rest is in a storage locker in Brooklyn. Key is in the bag. In all, I managed to vacuum about seventy pounds of gold. I took the precaution of removing my seven percent share, as we originally agreed. Which leaves you all with about three hundred seventy thousand dollars' worth of gold. Split five ways, that's seventy-four thou apiece."

"Whoa," Sam erupted, "not too bad, man, after all . . ."

"Hold everything." Drummond thrust his paw in the air, lip atremble. "An even split? I think not. I planned this, I have the connection to sell the gold—" He was interrupted by another sneeze.

"No way!" Sam protested.

"Then there's the matter of the cheese," Barney added, looking at his nails.

Drummond finished blowing his nose. "Cheese?"

"Cheese. You may find this difficult to believe, but there are people who collect rare cheese."

"Hey!" Sam smacked himself in the head. "You

mean like the fuckin' shit we found in the first hole?"

"Few years back, a British collector paid fifteen hundred dollars for a one-ounce lump of two-hundred-year-old Tibetan cheese at a Sotheby's auction."

"Fifteen hundred bucks? For old cheese?" Silvi gaped contemptuously.

"Would we get fifteen hundred dollars an ounce for the fucking cheese in that hole?" Joey perked up.

"Not quite. However, the manifest for the *Bunker Hill* includes..."

"Five hundred two-inch waxed balls of New York State Gouda," Drummond said distantly, he being only too familiar with the original manifest.

"Yoo-hoo?" Nicholas shouted. "Remember the two hanging provolones over here?"

Drummond gestured testily to Silvi. She scowled and lowered the hostages. "What are you getting at?" Drummond pounded the railing.

"I vacuumed some of the cheese balls up, about two hundred eighty in all. I called around, and I think you might be able to get a thousand apiece for them. Gouda turns out to be the rarest of the Colonial cheeses, which were almost exclusively cheddars and..."

"Two hundred and eighty thousand dollars' worth of old cheese." Drummond blinked as if something more than indignation was in his eye.

"Better than nothing. Everybody's stake is upped another fifty-six thou."

"Slam!" Joey high-fived his brother.

Drummond's red-rimmed eyes blinked up at a shaft of sunlight. "Twenty-three million dollars," he whispered.

Barney clapped his hands, giving them a good rub. "The cheese is in the locker with the gold. I'm not taking a cut of that. It's all yours, just to make sure there's no hard feelings." Barney smiled, adding: "Though I don't know why I'm giving it to you. I don't doubt that you planned all along to kill me, kill us all. So take the cheese, give me my friends, and we part company without recriminations."

Barney helped Nicasia to a cab while Nicholas brought up the rear with his crated Moolman. As their cab pulled away, Barney looked back. The Pazzos, Silvi, and del Solar were in a heated debate onshore next to the seaplane.

"Guess that takes care of that." Barney tried to lighten the mood. "Tell you what. I'll make it up to you guys. How about I spring for dinner?"

"Stop this cab," Nicholas fumed, opening the door well before the taxi was at a full stop. A passing SUV practically obliterated *Trampoline Nude, 1972* when he stepped out. He slammed the door and limped off in the direction of Yucca Flats Bar & Grille.

His brow knit, Barney didn't say anything for a while. He just hugged Nicasia, kissing the top of her head periodically, relieved to have her safe. And she hugged him back, though she'd occasionally soft-punch him in the chest as her mood shifted between love and anger. Barney figured he'd better wait to spring the plane tickets lest he rock the boat in the wrong direction.

Drummond stood at the railing of the garbage slip for some time after Barney and company left, staring out at the sun rippling on the Hudson River, the file still in his hands. Silvi came back into the depot from the seaplane, slamming the door. He didn't turn to look at her as she sauntered up next to him, contempt on her lips.

"To me it is surprise Newcastle would trust a burnout like you with twenty-three million dollars in gold. Why we trusted you, that is more surprise. We have been talking, and have decided on a new way to split the money."

Drummond arched an eyebrow quizzically at the water, but said nothing, did nothing.

Perhaps in his younger days he would have been more deft, but having his plans unravel so completely, his retirement slip away, left him in a daze. It took the blade of the stiletto in the back of his neck to bring Silvi's point home. He fumbled mechanically for the revolver in his pocket. But by the time he had it out and had turned, he was already to his knees, watching the gun drop from his numb fingers. Doves of white paper from the file wafted through the air. He fell to his side, his entire body stinging with pain. The ants were finally eating more than his soul.

Silvi's blur stood over him with a mocking expression, a shaft of sunlight making long shadows of her features.

"Sorry, no gold watch."

Chapter 29

After a drink at Yucca Flats, Nicholas cabbed across town. Hobbling down Dover Street, he made a right on Water Street. His legs were still wobbly from hanging upside down for two hours, and the icy sidewalk and cumbersome crate weren't helping him navigate the way. But his course was set for his apartment and a tall Macallan, and he failed to notice the gray Crown Victoria that rolled slowly down the block, pulling to the curb behind him.

"Cheese," he muttered derisively, shaking his head as he entered his building. It was all his feet could do to ascend the stairs. The simple act of unlocking the door weighed heavily upon his legs. Stumbling into his apartment, he dropped the crate next to the wall, tossed his overcoat on the floor ...

and his knees gave unexpectedly. He turned sharply toward the kitchen counter to keep from falling.

A shadow passed over him, and the floor creaked. He shoved himself off the kitchen counter toward the wall as something buzzed past his ear.

Mr. Porkpie had his steel cue raised again, and this time it made a divot in the wall as Nicholas rolled back toward the front door, falling on his back to the floor. He latched on to his overcoat and grabbed his sap.

Porkpie lurched toward him, but the throw rug slipped under him and he nearly fell on top of Nicholas. The cue's blow glanced off Nicholas's shoulder and into the wall.

Nicholas swung the sap. Like a fist punching a side of beef, it connected with a solid *fwap* to Porkpie's temple. The assailant spun from the blow. In one motion Nicholas threw the coat over his head and rolled away from the front door toward the window.

Porkpie reeled, his back slamming the front door.

Just as Detectives Hatchet Face and Roly-Poly shouldered it open.

Nicholas saw Porkpie stumble forward, slip on the throw rug again, and catapult headlong toward him.

Nicholas covered his head with his arms.

Glass shattered, wood splintered: Nicholas peeked up through the crook of his arm just in time to see Porkpie's feet disappearing out the window.

A silence followed as Hatchet Face and Roly-Poly

shared an incredulous reverie. Finally, they said in unison: "Holy shit."

Nicholas carefully brushed the glass from his hair, groaning as he got to his feet. "Never thought I'd say this, but I'm glad to see you boys."

He turned to the broken window and looked down. Roly-Poly and Hatchet Face stepped up next to him.

"They're not gonna like this down at Hundred Centre, Billy." Hatchet Face wagged his head like he was gazing down upon the dearly departed.

"Not to mention at the precinct, Marty." Roly-Poly bit his lip. "That Ford was new."

Below, Porkpie's lower half protruded skyward from the windshield of the detectives' Crown Victoria. His tennis shoes had popped off and landed on the car's roof. His exposed white-stockinged feet were twitching.

Nicholas withdrew from the window and clapped the detectives on their shoulders. "Looks like you boys got your man."

Roly-Poly shoved Nicholas. "Five-pound salami, four-pound bag—it don't fit. We saw you come in with that crate. It's got the Mule Man in it, I'll bet."

"It sure does." Nicholas's brain sizzled with schemes, and one popped out. "I just now came from reclaiming the Moolman from Slugger down there."

He sauntered over to the bar cart and picked up a glass. "After reclaiming the painting, I dropped into a bar—Yucca Flats on the West Side, around noon.

Made a call, had a drink, and caught a cab. Driver's name was Ahmed. He dropped me at the corner. That sound like a guy trying to get away with a hot painting?"

Roly-Poly and Hatchet Face exchanged doubtful expressions. Nicholas continued, pouring himself a scotch with a trembling hand.

"Slugger obviously wasn't happy about losing the painting he stole from Bagby... You boys want some scotch?" Nicholas held up the bottle, realizing he'd have to work on exactly how he'd swiped it from Slugger.

Hatchet Face squinted. "How's that?"

"That guy sticking out of your windshield's the guy that killed Bagby. Look." Nicholas plucked the steel cue butt from the floor with a cocktail napkin. "See this little crown on Slugger's sawed-off pool cue? Remember the medical examiner's report? The mark on Bagby's neck was a little crown. Just like in the *B* of the Brunswick trademark here on the cue. He kept this baby in that big carpetbag, which he was carrying the night I saw him exit Dr. Bagby's." Nicholas shivered, stuffing a couch cushion into the obliterated window. "Slugger's also the guy that tried to hold up the Strunk Gallery last week."

Hatchet Face and Roly-Poly didn't so much dislike the story as Nicholas's smooth telling of it. They fingered their cuffs and attempted to stare Nicholas down.

"Hold it, Palihnic." Roly-Poly grinned. "Sounds

like you been obstructing justice. If you knew he killed Bagby..."

"Hey, don't you get it?" Nicholas was on a roll. "I only just today set up a meeting and swiped the Moolman back from him. As you can see by the shiner, it took a little doing." Drummond's kick to Nicholas's head at the barge depot had left its mark. He took another swig of Macallan. He could have fingered BB, but she was a potentially rich client worth protecting. Besides, he had a weakness for the dastardly ones. "Today's the first time I've seen Slugger since that night on Mott Street. But he tried to come take the painting back a little faster than I thought."

Roly-Poly snorted as he radioed EMS. Hatchet Face put his thumbs in his belt loops, scrutinizing Palihnic. "Is this for real, pal?"

Palihnic shrugged. His eyes twinkled knowingly.

"You got a dead guy sticking out of your windshield who *definitely* killed Dr. Bagby and is behind the art thefts of the Moolman and the Strunk Gallery. Who knows what else he's been up to? Probably has had his rap sheets bound. And let's face it. Porkpie isn't exactly in any position to contest any of it."

"Maybe that's what you're counting on." Hatchet Face folded his arms.

"We're not kids, am I right?" Nicholas collapsed onto the couch. "A closed case is a closed case. I got the painting, you got the murderer. What more do you want?"

Sirens sounded down the block, and Roly-Poly went downstairs to greet the troops. Nicholas could tell from Hatchet Face's sidelong look that he was tempted to respond: *I want the truth*.

But they both knew that "the truth" in police work was a conviction.

Or a closed case.

Or just good old-fashioned results.

Nicholas frowned, reflecting. But there was another kind of truth, outside of police and insurance work. The kind Mel wanted, and the kind Nicholas didn't have a handle on.

Hatchet Face went over to the bar cart, splashed some scotch into a glass, and drank it straight down. He shot Nicholas another sidelong glance.

"If it doesn't hold, you're in deep shit. Not just with the law. But with me. How's that grab you?"

Nicholas raised his glass and winked. "Just super."

Chapter 30

A few days later, Nicholas stalked past Garth's black 1966 Lincoln, the one that had been their father's, and up to the apartment door.

He brushed past his brother into the apartment, scanning the taxidermy as he always did: suspiciously. He was slouched and looked irritable, and he failed to notice the glass of scotch Garth tried to hand him.

"Yoo-hoo?" Garth tinkled the ice in the glass.

"Look, Garth"—Nicholas took the glass and drank half of it—"I wish you guys would just cut this Sunday dinner shit out."

"Oh?" By contrast, Garth was in a positively jolly mood, which further irked Nicholas.

"We are not a family." Nicholas looked Garth up and down, scrutinizing his brother's lack of style. Still with the college professor look. "These Sunday dinners are a sham and you know it. They're just some way of you two trying to make me something I'm not."

"Nikolai!" Otto burst into the room and fairly tackled Nicholas.

"Get the hell off me!" Nicholas tried to free himself from the gnomish Russian's embrace.

"Ve drink, yes? Eetz good! Where to be Mal? Dah-tay? Very pretty."

"Garth, I'm outta here, just as soon as I . . . would you get him offa me?"

"I think he likes you." Garth smiled blithely. "Oh, been meaning to tell you. I contacted those insurance people. They didn't have anything for me, but said they get stuff all the time. Said they only recently needed an appraisal of an ivory-billed woodpecker."

"God dammit! Would you get him . . ."

"Nikolai!" Otto suddenly released Nicholas, completely oblivious that the latter had been trying to escape his bear-trap hug. "Otto to make very special cheeken for you, my friend. You to make very heppy."

"That tears it." Nicholas downed the rest of his drink and handed Garth the glass. As he reached the door to leave, Angie opened it. "Hi, Nicholas!"

She held his face and gave him a kiss, patting his cheek.

Nicholas reddened. "Look, Angie, I was just telling Garth that I've had it with these—"

"Mai tai!" Dottie raced in from behind Angie, fist

in the air. She stopped in front of Nicholas, her dark eyes shining up at him.

"Mai tai!" She waved her fist at him, waiting.

The color drained from his face, and he scrunched his nose at Angie in anger. "Oh, this is low, Angie. Dirty pool."

She batted her eyes at him and smiled, taking off her coat.

"Mai tai!" Dottie insisted. *"AW! AW! EE! EE! TOOKIE-TOOKIE!"*

"Mai tai." Nicholas bumped her fist with his, then glared at Angie and Garth. "You two think you can play cupid, is that it? Mel is going to walk through that door, isn't she?"

"Nope." Angie breezed past him to the counter and poured herself some wine. "She doesn't want to see you. But Dottie did."

"Will you sing me the Tarzan song, Nicky?"

Garth raised his eyebrows. "You sang her the Tarzan song?" Their father used to sing them that song to put them to bed.

Nicholas scowled at Angie and Garth. "Well, isn't this just super."

He cut past Dottie and slammed the door as he left. A cab was pulled over down the block, discharging a passenger, and he trotted down to it.

This fiasco called for somehow getting in touch with his inner self, like going to Gravy's and working his magic on that bartender, Judy, his peanut in her capable hands.

But the back door to the cab opened, and Mel

stepped out. She was wrapped in a shawl, her short black hair blowing in the briny breeze from the Hudson River.

Her chin raised defiantly, she drew her shawl closer.

"Great." Nicholas flapped his arms at his side. "I suppose this was Angie's little trick too?"

Mel avoided his eyes and said softly, "It was my idea to come." As she stepped onto the sidewalk, Nicholas skirted around her and into the cab, thinking that he'd never really noticed how great she smelled, even just in passing. He slammed the door.

He connected with the driver's eyes in the rearview mirror, and heard him say, "Where to?"

"Where to?" Nicholas snorted.

"Yeah, where to?"

Mel was at Angie and Garth's door when a hand on her shoulder spun her around.

"Look." Nicholas's eyes were ablaze. With anger? She couldn't tell. "I'm going to say this one time. You listening? Good. I'm not in love with you. You can't make me be in love with you. The only person I love is me. Got it?"

Her eyes searched his.

"Even if I were in love with you," he continued, "which I'm not..."

"Nicholas?"

"What?"

Mel finally had him. She finally knew what his

problem was. Or so she thought. Nothing so pat as that he was afraid of commitment. And with this insight came the serenity of knowing.

"Why are you so upset?"

"Because I like who I am. I don't want to be controlled. By Angie, or by you or by Dottie and certainly not that Russian wrestler..."

"Controlled? Isn't that another way of saying loved?"

"Bingo!" He clapped his hands. "I don't want to be loved, and I don't want to love. My father loved me, and I loved him, and look what happened? He *trusted* me. I ruined him and our family's finances. I broke his heart, and he died. *I killed him.*"

Nicholas heard his shouts echo and vanish across the buildings like an escaped bat, down the block, and off into the cold night.

"Did I just...?" Nicholas began, wincing. "Did I just say that I'm emotionally stunted because of my relationship with my parents?"

The cold wind whistled off the building fronts around them.

Mel tucked a lock of dark hair behind one ear, a smile sneaking up one side of her face. Her eyes met his. "It wasn't me who said it. *For a change.*"

Nicholas groaned, looking for some avenue of escape. There was none, and he slumped back onto a parked car. "So what now, Doctor?"

She stepped up to him and latched her hands on to his lapels. "Fortunately, I think there's a cure for your condition."

"Yeah, what's that?"

"Jeeze, Nicholas. Is it so hard to open your heart to me, and let me open mine to you? It's really not that hard, you just have to trust me, trust yourself. And just because I want an emotionally available and committed man doesn't mean I don't want the charmer, too. I like him. A lot."

"Does that mean I have to kiss you now?" Nicholas wrapped his arms around her. "Is that the cure?"

"Kiss me *and* call me in the morning."

Chapter 31

It was an antebellum mansion backed by rain forests on a hill overlooking the expanse of the capital, and each room had a name. "The Rhett Butler." "The Five Oaks Suite." "The Aunt Pittypat." Barney and Nicasia's room had a balcony, French doors, flowing curtains, and a sweeping view. It was "The Scarlett O'Hara."

After a leisurely cocktail in the Jacuzzi, they repaired to the bedroom for an afternoon nap. It was evening by the time they arose, the lights of San José ablaze at the foot of their bed. Barney lit some candles and they dressed for dinner. By eight they were downstairs in the Atlanta Room at a table garnished with yellow bougainvillea, candles, and goblets of wine.

"Barney, did you notice what the placard said?"

Nicasia sipped her fumé blanc, her pumps falling from her squirming feet.

Barney tugged at his tie. "Placard?" He looked around the candlelit ballroom.

"Not in here, in the lobby." Nicasia tugged playfully at his outstretched hand.

He smiled. "I've been so fixated on you..."

"Yeah, right." She pulled her hand away in mock annoyance. "Whisking me off to Costa Rica. After all that time with me thinking you..."

"Now we weren't going to talk about that." Barney waved a finger at her. "Or about Palihnic, or any of that. We had a deal, OK?"

The waiter stood in the doorway to the lobby. He gave Barney a wave and held up one finger. Barney held his hand below the table and flashed one finger, followed by a fist, and then eight fingers. The waiter disappeared.

"So, did you see the placard?"

"Uh huh." The waiter was back in the doorway, showing him two fingers. Barney flashed two, made a fist, and then one.

"They're having an auction here tonight."

Barney nodded. "Across the way."

Barney peered at her over the rim of his wineglass as he flashed the waiter two oh two.

"Too pricey for us, though. You won't believe this, but they've got that book Nicholas recovered a few years back."

"Nicasia, about *Tamerlane*..."

"Yes, that's the book, *Tamerlane and Other Poems*,

by Poe." Nicasia raised an eyebrow at the waiter in the doorway, who suddenly took to straightening an end table.

"Listen, Nicasia, there's something I've been meaning to tell you and I just, well..." Barney flashed two, made a fist, and then three under the table. "It's like this, Nicasia. I love you, and I want to come clean about my past. The full truth."

Nicasia flushed slightly, put her wine down, and dabbed her lips with a napkin. Without looking up, she said, "You were a thief."

Barney rubbed his jaw, and the waiter ducked out of the room. "Uh, yeah, well, I didn't think you knew, is all."

"Oh, Barney." Nicasia looked up at him, eyes moist and chin crinkling. "You're such a dope. I'm an investigator, for Christ sake. You don't think I believe that crap Nicholas fed me about you being from a vault and safe company, do you?" She smiled warmly at him. "I've been waiting, though, to hear it from you. I'm glad you respect and love me enough..."

"Excuse me, *señor, señorita.*" The waiter stepped up to the table, handing Barney a receipt and a pen. He glanced sidelong at Nicasia.

"What's this, Barney?"

Barney signed the receipt and handed it back to the waiter. "I have thirteen million dollars in a bank in Montserrat."

Nicasia paled and took a gulp of wine.

"You mean in 1855, James D. Bird didn't switch

the *Bunker Hill* gold with brass shot?" she whispered, the corners of her mouth curling. "But the files..."

"Some of it is true. New Haven Steam Ship did go bankrupt. I just, well, twisted the facts. The files are real enough, only I altered them here and there. A little creative photocopying."

Nicasia put a hand to her forehead. "But you said...you told them to check your research. What happens when Drummond or Newcastle goes to the files at New York Custom House?"

"I managed to manufacture not only the evidence but the source, either by replacing an original photocopy with a doctored one or by inking entries into ledgers. They don't let you take the files out of the building, but they don't exactly frisk you when you leave. So I went, swiped, left, returned, and inserted. Or I used a quill pen when they weren't looking." Barney took a sip from his wine. "Brass shot, as it turns out, was a regular commodity bought in large quantities by most ship companies for the manufacture of nautical fittings and hardware, so those receipts were genuine. I seeded the boreholes with brass shot. Besides, Newcastle won't be looking into this again. They're the ones I sold the gold to. Drummond didn't hire me. Newcastle hired me to be hired by Drummond and get the gold out from under him. They knew he was likely to double-cross them, and they needed a thief to catch a thief."

"So, where was the gold, then?" Nicasia gasped, then whispered: "You left the gold in the ground until they flew away, until after Nicholas and Maureen left?"

Barney winked, beaming.

But Nicasia wasn't smiling. She put a hand on his. "Barney, why?"

"Why?"

"I know you were basically doing what you've been doing, ferreting out a thief. But there's more to all this. You stole again, and lied to me." Their eyes were locked. "I need to know why, and to know that you will never lie to me again."

Barney pursed his lips, eyes dropping to the table. "I needed to know that, too, and that's why I did it. It's complicated . . . there was a man once, when I was a kid. His name was, well, it doesn't matter. But he had a certain, I dunno, magic."

"Magic?"

Barney rubbed his jaw. "He taught me something I didn't learn until I was much older, if that makes sense. Until I met you. About a sense of my own destiny, and the value of truth. I have to be truthful to myself before I can stop living a life of lies and love you with all my heart."

Nicasia knit her brow. "I'm not sure I understand."

Barney glanced at her, smoothing the edge of the tablecloth.

"He once told me: *A man must have balance of mind between his accomplishments, that which he desires, and that which he must be.* I'm a thief, Nicasia. I was always meant to be a thief, down deep, and I know that. And while I can't go on stealing, I needed a connection back to that part of me. This making any sense?"

She looked down at her plate, then at the receipt on the table.

"So . . . you just bought *Tamerlane*, a book worth over two hundred thousand dollars, in the auction across the way?"

"Uh huh."

"Let me guess. You once stole it?"

"Uh huh. It was the first thing I ever stole."

"And this means you'll never lie to me again?"

Barney looked at her until her eyes rose to his. They were moist with tears, uncertain, and lit with candlelight. *My God*, he thought, *how I love this woman.*

His secret smile blossomed, and he squinted. "Pretty sure."

About the Author

BRIAN M. WIPRUD is a New York City author and outdoor writer for fly-fishing magazines. He won the 2002 Lefty Award for Most Humorous Novel, was a 2003 Barry Award Nominee, a 2004 Independent Mystery Booksellers' Association Bestseller, and a 2005 *Seattle Times* Bestseller. Information on his tours and appearances can be found at his website, www.wiprud.com.

Don't miss

Brian M. Wiprud's

SLEEP WITH THE FISHES

"*The Godfather* meets Carl Hiaasen in this darkly humorous meeting of the Mob and fishing. . . . A good, quick, amusing read."
—*Mystery Ink*

Available from Dell Books in October 2006

Read on for an exclusive sneak peek
and pick up your copy at your
favorite bookseller.

"If Carl Hiaasen wrote for *The Sopranos*,
it might be half as good as this....A page-turner
that's part wicked humor and part just
plain wicked."—Lee Child

SLEEP

with the

F SHES

BRIAN M. WIPRUD

Award-winning author of *Crooked*

SLEEP WITH THE FISHES
On sale in October 2006

Front wheels locked sideways, the Volkswagen Rabbit spun backward, sparks flaring as it snapped the cable guide rail and flipped over the embankment. After a few protracted somersaults, the puckered chassis slammed roof-first onto a collection of boulders. Shattered safety glass rained from the windows, and snakes of fire raced up rivulets of gas, igniting the engine. The dark ravine was suddenly dancing with light from the blaze.

Headlights flashed above, and a white Mercury Marquis pulled to a stop on the road. A man in a jogging suit and windbreaker emerged, walking casually to the edge of the embankment, the blaze below reflecting tiny campfires in his eyes. The whole underside of the Rabbit was afire now, and the man figured it would only be a minute before she blew.

"*Adios.*" He smirked, tugging on one ear absently, turning back toward his Mercury.

A cough sounded in the ravine, and the man froze. Looking both ways along the road, he pulled a small revolver from his waistband. He cocked it, then stepped back to the edge of the ravine and peered down the embankment.

"Oh, that's just friggin' beautiful," he moaned. A bearded man lay sprawled on the embankment below, steam rising from his coughs into the cold night air.

"Oh my God," drawled a woman's voice. "There's been an accident!" The man wheeled around and staggered with surprise.

"What the hell?" He quickly slipped the gun back in his waistband. "Angel! What the ... Jesus! What're you doin' in my backseat?" he sputtered.

Her painted face twisted into a scowl as she emerged from the blanket she'd been hiding under.

"Well, big shot, mind tellin' me what you always goin' out late at night for?" she shrieked. "Sure, you keep sayin' 'I got business, Angel.' Business my butt. I'm here to find out who she is."

"Who?" he yelled, throwing his arms wide. "So help me, Angel, I oughta kill you for this!"

"Sid, I heard you talkin' tuh Johnny. You said somethin' about how you got an appointment with Sandra." Angel opened the car door and stepped out onto the pavement in her panty-hosed feet. "And what, for this tramp Sandra, you come all the way up here to Connecticut?" She tugged at her angora sweater.

Another cough echoed up the ravine, and Sid looked anxiously down at the stirring figure below.

"Well, are you just gonna walk back and forth there, flappin' your arms like a pigeon, or are y'gonna help the poor guy? Jeez, go on, hurry, he could be dying or something!" Angel wailed, leaning on the car and squeezing scarlet pumps onto her feet.

Flabbergasted and red-faced, Sid ogled his girlfriend's scarlet shoes and shook his head, trying to wake himself from this nightmare. Then he scrambled down the embankment to the victim. Peering down at the flaming wreckage, he could see the arm of another victim protruding motionless from where the windshield used to be. He slipped the gun from his waist and put it to the bearded man's head.

"OK, Evel Knievel, just keep your eyes and your mouth shut, and I'll save your sorry ass, you got that?" It didn't look like the poor schnook could make out much anyway. Probably wouldn't live. So he tugged, heaved, huffed, and puffed the bearded guy by the collar up to the shoulder of the road, dropping him none too gently.

"Angel—into the car." Sid wheezed harshly, his white pants and arms smeared with dirt and leaves. "We gotta go get help for this guy." He grabbed Angel by the arm and thrust her into the backseat.

"Hey!" Angel bleated. "What about—"

"Shuddup, already. We gotta hurry, get to a phone, get this guy an ambulance or somethin'." He could hear a truck shifting gears, a possible witness, coming up the hill. The Mercury's engine revved, its tires squealed, and it sped quickly away.

There was a whoosh like a sudden drumroll as gasoline around the Rabbit caught fire. Shrieking flames burst the gas tank, the bearded man's crumpled form silhouetted by an ascending swirl of fire.

Cryptobranchus alleganiensis is a salamander of grand proportions. It has a record length of twenty-nine inches and almost exclusively haunts rocky-bottomed segments of the Susquehanna River. By all reports, this muddy, girthsome, and deeply wrinkled beast is like some aquatic English bulldog, and twice as handsome. They call them hellbenders, and their apocryphal appearances in the Delaware River are favored upon a dot on the map labeled "Hellbender Eddy, Pennsylvania." There hadn't been a sighting of one since 1888.

It was a frosty May dawn, and the counter at Chik's Five Star Diner was filled with locals. The joint was old, the walls painted a zillion coats of cream semigloss, its linoleum counter stalwart, long, and black. White and black tiles made a checkerboard of the floor, and deco wall sconces gave the place a dull warm glow. A giant urn brewed coffee by the gallon, residual steam making the hashery mighty humid indeed. Two potted palms in the back thought they'd died and gone to heaven.

On weekdays, most of the locals drifted through Chik's for a container of coffee and a sauna.

Big Bob Stillwell and Little Bob Cropsey made their usual appearance on the way to the construction site.

"G'morning, fellahs." Chik smiled, his pencil-thin mustache curling devilishly. "Usual?"

Little Bob poked around Big Bob's jump-suited girth with the camcorder he bought at a tag sale. "Yes, Chik, we will have the usual. Tell us what the usual is, Chik."

Chik looked into the lens, hesitating and smoothing his hair.

Big Bob lifted a meaty arm and looked down at Little Bob like something in his armpit stank.

"Must ya fool with that darn thing so early in the mornin'?" Big Bob let his arm drop and turned to Chik. "*Not* the usual. Just coffee and buttered rolls. Gotta cut out the fat." Big Bob punched himself in the gut.

"Chik, look into the camera. I want the usual. I don't got no weight problem." Chik smoothed his mustache and flashed a dirty smile at the camera. Then Little Bob saw Big Bob's un-shaven face fill the view screen.

"I ain't got a weight 'problem.' I'm not talkin' about fat, I'm talkin' about cholesterol. Eggs and bacon is cholesterol, Bob. Choles-terol is bad for you too. Don't ya even read the papers? Chik: coffee and rolls." Big Bob was a faithful reader of *Newstime Magazine,* and con-sidered himself quite the scholar of current events. As a heavy-equipment operator on ma-jor construction projects, there were plentiful lulls in the pile driving that could be spent memorizing the news.

"Hey, Doc." Little Bob squirreled over to Lloyd Conti, who was farther down the counter. "Tell me about cholesterol, Doc. Into the camera." Video Bob was also an equipment operator, but unlike Big Bob, he was kept busy switching between backhoes and front loaders.

Lloyd swiveled on his stool, mopping his lips and Vandyke with a paper napkin. A pack of plastic-tipped cheroots peeked from a top pocket.

"Bob, I am not a doctor. I keep telling ya that. Just 'cause I do electrolysis doesn't mean I'm a doctor. And do ya think that if I were a doctor I'd be doin' small-engine repair on the side? Don't ya think I'd be removing gallblad-ders or somethin'?" Lloyd turned back to his breakfast.

"Hey, Bob. Com'ere, I'll tell ya about choles-terol!" Jenny Baker was down at the last stool, a cracked leather jacket draped over her shoulders and her blond hair pinned to the top of her head with a cocktail stirrer. A bit of a looker past her prime, Jenny drove a ten-wheel tanker for Red Eft Trout Farms. Everyone knew the routine: Chik liked to toy with her, get a little fresh, make her take a swing at him. It had become a game of sorts. He kept tally with a pencil on the side of the coffee urn.

"OK, Jenny, tell us about cholesterol. Why is it bad for skinny people?" Little Bob stalked over to Jenny, zooming in and out on the beguiling smile she'd worked up for him.

"Lemme show ya. See this piece of toast? Ya focused your little camera on it?"

"Got it, Jenny. Now what?"

"Well, see how when I dip it in the egg yella? That there, stuck to the end of my toast? Come in real close now."

"Got it, Jenny. Now what?"

"That's cholesterol."

"But why is it bad for skinny people? It don't make us fat."

"No, it doesn't, Little Bob. But it ain't too good for their video cameras."

Bob's image of Jenny was suddenly smeared yolk yellow.

"Hey! Hey! You put egg yella on my lens!" Little Bob poked his camera around, looking for a napkin. Gentle early-morning chuckles filtered through the patrons. Little Bob felt a clamp on the back of his neck. It was Big Bob's meaty grasp.

"Must ya fool with that darn thing this early in the mornin'? C'mon, we got our stuff, now let's let these folks breakfast in peace." Big Bob led his stooped protégé out the door just as Russ Smonig slipped past them with a sleepy nod.

"Howyadoin', Russ?" Chik was freshening coffees along the counter. "Heard you got into the shad real good last week. How many does that make it now?"

"Yeah, they're comin' up. Small bunches, all bucks." Russ was sandy-haired, with a prominent jaw, squinty eyes, and an edgy manner that betrayed the hardships of rural life. But strictly speaking, Russ wasn't a local. That is, he hailed from Hartford, where he'd been an insurance executive. Pennsylvania became his roost about ten years before, after some domestic trouble, some said. Now he tried to make a go at being an outdoor writer while getting by tying flies and guiding. He lived in a two-tone sagging trailer on a quality slice of riverfront south of Hellbender Eddy. The land was his outright, his total net asset. He'd once had a five-year plan in which he became widely published, hosted a fishing show, and replaced his shack with a palatial log cabin. Now he didn't make plans beyond the next three weeks.

"But how many does that make it? What's your total?" Chik persisted. Huge numbers of shad entered the Delaware River each spring to spawn like salmon, and those who angled for them seriously kept score.

Russ looked a little uncomfortable, but divulged his tally.

"Seventy-five. Chik, just gimme a half-dozen sticky buns, two cups regular, and fill this thermos, OK?" Russ plunked his thermos on the linoleum and pushed back on his stained fedora, trying not to look at the patrons along the counter as they rustled with awe.

"Seventy-five already, huh? Sure took a quick lead. Got a client this mornin', do yah, Russ?" Chik queried from a cloud of steam at the urn.

"Yeah, I got a sport this morning." Russ let his gaze wander over the ceiling before snatching a glance down the counter. The whole lot was giving him the envious, expectant eye.

"Well?" Russ looked back at them, and they shifted, looking from one to the other. Jenny spoke up.

"C'mon, Russ. We want the shad report. Lot of us've been to all the usual spots—fish all day an' just pick up a handful. Where are ya taking 'em? An' don't give us that doo-doo about 'trade secrets.' We ain't your sports. Not one of us can afford your guiding services. But we are your neighbors, and, well, the neighborly thing to do is tell us where you're takin' 'em, that's all. It's not like there's a shad shortage or anything, is there, Russ?"

The group grunted, nodding agreement.

Russ worked up a fatigued smile, the only kind of which he seemed capable anymore. Living was hard and the rewards increasingly scarce. Either he was up at 4:00 AM and on the river with a sport jigging for walleye, burning the midnight oil tying up four hundred dry flies to fill an order, or he was huddled next to his kerosene heater laboring on yet another article that would be rejected by *Sports Astream* or *Bass Blaster*.

His transition from amateur to professional angler was complete: he caught a lot of fish and could land enough for three square meals at will. But it was all he could do to stay financially afloat, much less give away freebies to his neighbors.

"Tell you what, Jenny. Neighborly is as neighborly does. You throw some free trout into Ballard Pond, and I'll give you a river sweet spot. Lloyd, you give a tuneup on my Evinrude, and I'll point out where and how you just might get Mr. Musky you're always talking about. And, Chik, you..."

"No charge, Mr. Smonig." Chik winked at Russ and pushed forward the thermos and white bag crammed with sticky buns. Russ plucked the pen from behind Chik's ear, tore out a receipt from his pad, and started to draw a little map. Folks at the counter craned their necks to see. Russ kept lowering his shoulder to block their view.

"There you go, Chik. Walleye. See you use

that size Rapala in that color, and troll it right along through those holes just as early in the morning as you can." Russ collected his stuff and turned sharply to the audience. "Good day, neighbors." He backed out the door.

Reverend Jim was waiting for him on the porch with one foot on the railing, his sharp red tongue poised in anticipation, and an ocher eye angled up at Russ. Reverend Jim's affection for Russ was genuine, but the emotional tie did not keep him from robbing Russ blind. He had been banished from the Smonig abode for stealing coins, and would loot the truck's glove box at any opportunity. Russ walked past the Reverend, dipped his shoulder, and the crow hopped on, expressing joy with flicks of his tongue and fanning wings.

Reverend Jim was named for a popular TV evangelist. As Russ climbed into his truck, the Reverend took his place on the International Harvester's gearshift knob. He would hop down every time Russ shifted gears, then pop right back up. Turning the pickup's key for a while, Russ whispered curses at his reluctant ignition and eyed his black thieving friend.

Eating a piece of toast slathered in jam, Jenny sauntered out of the diner and over to the truck.

"Well, seeing as how you're at least willing to barter, might ya accept information? Hey, Reverend Jim—how's my baby?" Jenny waved at the bird, who uttered a low, curious rattle like dice in a cup.

Russ gave the key a rest. He dished up his fatigued smile for Jenny.

"OK, Russ, just to show that I for one know how to be neighborly, I'll give ya the information free and see if your conscience doesn't do the rest. Ya have a new next-door neighbor." She chomped her toast, licking grape jam from her lips.

"At the Ballard Place, I'll bet. I heard some cars over there. So?"

"Well, Russ honey, my brother Matt was over there turning on the water and gas and such. And do ya know what he saw?"

She arched an eyebrow. Russ's eyebrows remained the same.

"I'll tell ya what he saw. Your new next-door neighbor is not only from the city, but he is also loaded with fishing tackle. He's got rods sticking out all over the place. And in his pocket he keeps a wad of bills this thick. Tipped Matt ten bucks, just like that." Jenny shoved the rest of the toast in her mouth.

"Might not need any guiding if he has all that tackle." Russ's lips puckered in thought.

"Russ, don't be a dope," she said around the toast, swallowing hard. "It don't matter how many rods he got. He's not from around here! He doesn't know the hot spots like you do, now, does he?"

Russ's eyebrows arched. Reverend Jim began clucking impatiently.

"Let's put it this way, Smonig: If you do get this new neighbor as a sport, I want a little map like you gave Chik, but with an 'X' marks the secret shad spot." Jenny licked jam from her thumb.

Russ looked up at her sharply.

"It's a deal." He cranked the key and seemed to catch the ignition off guard. The truck started.